TEA AT THE MIDLAND

by
David Constantine

About the Author

David Constantine (born 1944 in Salford) was for thirty years a university teacher of German language and literature. He has published several volumes of poetry, most recently, *Nine Fathom Deep* (2009). He is a translator of Hölderlin, Brecht, Goethe, Kleist, Michaux and Jaccottet. In 2003 his translation of Hans Magnus Enzensberger's *Lighter than Air* (Bloodaxe) won the Corneliu M Popescu Prize for European Poetry Translation. His translation of Goethe's *Faust, Part I* was published by Penguin in 2005; *Part II* in April 2009. He is also the author of one novel, *Davies* (Bloodaxe) and *Fields of Fire: A Life of Sir William Hamilton* (Weidenfeld). His three short story collections are *Back at the Spike* (Ryburn), the highly acclaimed *Under the Dam* (Comma), selected by *The Guardian* and *Independent* as one of their Books of the Year, and *The Shieling* (Comma), which was shortlisted for the 2010 Frank O'Connor International Short Story Award. His story 'Tea at the Midland' won the 2010 BBC National Short Story Award. He lives in Oxford, where until 2012 he edited *Modern Poetry in Translation* with his wife Helen.

Contents

Tea at the Midland

THE WIND BLEW steadily hard with frequent surges of greater ferocity that shook the vast plate glass behind which a woman and a man were having tea. The waters of the bay, quite shallow, came in slant at great speed from the south-west. They were breaking white on a turbid ground far out, tide and wind driving them, line after line, nothing opposing or impeding them so they came on and on until they were expended. The afternoon winter sky was torn and holed by the wind and a troubled golden light flung down at all angles, abiding nowhere, flashing out and vanishing. And under that ceaselessly riven sky, riding the furrows and ridges of the sea, were a score or more of surfers towed on boards by kites. You might have said they were showing off but in truth it was a self-delighting among others doing likewise. The woman behind plate glass could not have been in their thoughts, they were not performing to impress and entertain her. Far out, they rode on the waves or sheer or at an angle through them and always only to try what they could do. In the din of waves and wind under that ripped-open sky they were enjoying themselves, they felt the life in them to be entirely theirs, to deploy how they liked best. To the woman watching they looked like grace itself, the heart and soul of which is freedom. It pleased her particularly that they were attached by invisible strings to colourful curves of rapidly moving air. How clean and clever that was! You throw up something like a handkerchief, you tether it and by its headlong wish to fly away, you are towed along. And not in the straight line of *its*

1

choosing, no: you tack and swerve as you please and swing out wide around at least a hemisphere of centrifugence. Beautiful, she thought. Such versatile autonomy among the strict determinants and all that co-ordination of mind and body, fitness, practice, confidence, skill and execution, all for fun!

The man had scarcely noticed the surf-riders. He was aware of the crazed light and the shocks of wind chiefly as irritations. All he saw was the woman, and that he had no presence in her thoughts. So he said again, A paedophile is a paedophile. That's all there is to it.

She suffered a jolt, hearing him. And that itself, her being startled, annoyed him more. She had been so intact and absent. Her eyes seemed to have to adjust to his different world. – That still, she said. I'm sorry. But can't you let it be? – He couldn't, he was thwarted and angered, knowing that he had not been able to force an adjustment in her thinking. – I thought you'd like the place, she said. I read up about it. I even thought we might come here one night, if you could manage it, and we'd have a room with a big curved window and in the morning look out over the bay. – He heard this as recrimination. She had left the particular argument and moved aside to his more general capacity for disappointing her. He, however, clung to the argument, but she knew, even if he didn't know or wouldn't admit it, that all he wanted was something which the antagonisms that swarmed in him could batten on for a while. Feeling very sure of that, she asked, malevolently, as though it were indeed only a question that any two rational people might debate, Would you have liked it if you hadn't known it was by Eric Gill? Or if you hadn't known Eric Gill was a paedophile? – That's not the point, he said. I know both those things so I can't like it. He had sex with his own daughters, for Christ's sake. – She answered, And with his sisters. And with the dog. Don't forget the dog. And quite possibly he thought it was for Christ's sake. Now suppose he'd done all that but also he

2

made peace in the Middle East. Would you want them to start the killing again when they found out about his private life? – That's not the same, he said. Making peace is useful at least. – I agree, she said. And making beauty isn't. 'Odysseus welcomed from the Sea' isn't at all useful, though it is worth quite a lot of money, I believe. – Frankly, he said, I don't even think it's beautiful. Knowing what I know, the thought of him carving naked men and women makes me queasy. – And if there was a dog or a little girl in there, you'd vomit?

She turned away, looking at the waves, the light and the surfers again, but not watching them keenly, for which loss she hated him. He sat in a rage. Whenever she turned away and sat in silence he desired very violently to force her to attend and continue further and further in the thing that was harming them. But they were sitting at a table over afternoon tea in a place that had pretensions to style and decorum. So he was baffled and thwarted, he could do nothing, only knot himself tighter in his anger and hate her more.

Then she said in a soft and level voice, not placatory, not in the least appealing to him, only sad and without taking her eyes off the sea, If I heeded you I couldn't watch the surfers with any pleasure until I knew for certain none was a rapist or a member of the BNP. And perhaps I should even have to learn to hate the sea because just out there, where that beautiful golden light is, those poor cockle-pickers drowned when the tide came in on them faster than they could run. I should have to keep thinking of them phoning China on their mobile phones and telling their loved ones they were about to drown. – You turn everything wrongly, he said. – No, she answered, I'm trying to think the way you seem to want me to think, joining everything up, so that I don't concentrate on one thing without bringing in everything else. When we make love and I cry out for the joy and the pleasure of it I have to bear in mind that some woman somewhere at exactly that time is being abominably tortured and she is screaming in unbearable pain. That's what it would

3

be like if all things were joined up.

She turned to him. What did you tell your wife this time, by the way? What lie did you tell her so we could have tea together? You should write it on your forehead so that I won't forget should you ever turn and look at me kindly. – I risk so much for you, he said. – And I risk nothing for you? I often think you think I've got nothing to lose. – I'm going, he said. You stay and look at the clouds. I'll pay on my way out. – Go if you like, she said. But please don't pay. This was my treat, remember. – She looked out to sea again. – Odysseus was a horrible man. He didn't deserve the courtesy he received from Nausikaa and her mother and father. I don't forget that when I see him coming out of hiding with the olive branch. I know what he has done already in the twenty years away. And I know the foul things he will do when he gets home. But at that moment, the one that Gill chose for his frieze, he is naked and helpless and the young woman is courteous to him and she knows for certain that her mother and father will welcome him at their hearth. Aren't we allowed to contemplate such moments? – I haven't read it, he said. – Well you could, she said. There's nothing to stop you. I even, I am such a fool, I even thought I would read the passages to you if we had one of those rooms with a view of the sea and of the mountains across the bay that would have snow on them.

She had tears in her eyes. He attended more closely. He felt she might be near to appealing to him, helping him out of it, so that they could get back to somewhere earlier and go a different way, leaving this latest stumbling block aside. There's another thing, she said. – What is it? he asked, softening, letting her see that he would be kind again, if she would let him. – On Scheria, she said, it was their custom to look after shipwrecked sailors and to row them home, however far away. That was their law and they were proud of it. – The tears in her eyes overflowed, her cheeks were wet with them. He waited, unsure, becoming suspicious. – So their best rowers, fifty-two young men, rowed Odysseus back to Ithaca overnight and lifted him ashore asleep and laid him gently down and piled all the gifts he had been given by Scheria around him on the sand. Isn't that beautiful? He wakes among their gifts and he is home. But on the way back, do you know, in sight of their own island, out of pique, to punish them for helping Odysseus, whom he hates, Poseidon turns them and their ship to stone. So Alcinous, the king, to placate Poseidon, a swine, a bully, a thug of a god, decrees they will never help shipwrecked sailors home again. Odysseus, who didn't deserve it, was the last.

He stood up. I don't know why you tell me that, he said. – She wiped her tears on the good linen serviette that had come with their tea and scones. – You never cry, he said. I don't think I've ever seen you cry. And here you are crying about this thing and these people in a book. What about me? I never see you crying about me and you. – And you won't, she said. I promise you, you won't.

He left. She turned again to watch the surfers. The sun was near to setting and golden light came through in floods from under the ragged cover of weltering cloud. The wind shook furiously at the glass. And the surfers skied like angels enjoying the feel of the waters of the earth, they skimmed, at times they lifted off and flew, they landed with a dash of spray. She watched till the light began to fail and one by one the strange black figures paddled ashore with their boards and sails packed small and weighing next to nothing.

She paid. At the frieze a tall man had knelt and, with an arm around her shoulders, was explaining to a little girl what was going on. It's about welcome, he said. Every stranger was sacred to the people of that island. They clothed him and fed him without even asking his name. It's a very good picture to have on a rough coast. The lady admitted she would have liked to marry him but he already had a wife at home. So they rowed him home.

Asylum

PRISON MORE LIKE, said Madeleine.

    Come now, said Mr Kramer.

    If I run away they bring me back, said Madeleine.

    Yes but, said Mr Kramer.

Mr Kramer often said, Yes but to Madeleine. Something to concede, something to contradict. Now he said again how kind everyone in the Unit was, all his visits never once had he seen any unkindness and couldn't remember ever hearing a voice raised in anger against any girl or boy. So: not really like a prison.

Then why's she sitting there? said Madeleine, nodding toward a nurse in the doorway. The nurse did her best to seem oblivious. She was reading a women's magazine.

    You know very well, said Mr Kramer.

    So I won't suddenly scratch your face and say you tried to rape me, said Madeleine. So I won't suddenly throw myself out of the window.

    That sort of thing, said Mr Kramer.

The window was open, but only the regulation few inches, as far as the locks allowed. Mr Kramer and Madeleine looked at it. She'd get through there, he thought, if she tried. Not that

7

I'd ever get through there, said Madeleine, however hard I tried.

The walls of the room were decorated with images, in paintings and collages, of the themes and infinite variations of body and soul in their distress. A face shattering like a window. A range of mountains, stacked like the hoods of the Klan, blocking most of the sky, but from the foreground, in a red zig-zag, into them went a path, climbing, and disappeared. Mr Kramer liked the room. Waiting for Madeleine, or whoever it might be, he stood at the window looking down at a grassy bank that in its seasons, year after year, with very little nurture or encouragement, brought forth out of itself an abundance of ordinary beautiful flowers. At this point in his acquaintance with Madeleine it was the turn of primroses. The air coming in was mild. Behind the bank ran the wall of the ancient enclosure.

Asylum, said Mr Kramer. What is an asylum?

A place they lock nutters up, said Madeleine.

Well yes, said Mr Kramer, but why call it an asylum?

Because they're liars, said Madeleine.

All right, said Mr Kramer. Forget the nutters, as you call them, and the place they get looked after or locked up in, and tell me what you think an asylum-seeker is.

Someone from somewhere bad.

And when they come to the United Kingdom, say, or to France, Germany or Italy, what are they looking for?

Somewhere better than where they've come from.

What are they seeking?

Asylum.

And what is asylum?

Sanctuary.

Sanctuary, said Mr Kramer. That's a very good word. Those poor people come here seeking sanctuary in a land of prisons. An asylum, he said, is a refuge, a shelter, a safe haven.

8

Lunatic asylums, as they used to be called, are places where people disordered in their souls can be housed safely and looked after.

Locked up, said Madeleine. Ward 16, they took Sam there last week.

So he'd be safer, said Mr Kramer. I'm sure of that.

Madeleine shrugged.

OK, said Mr Kramer. A bit like a prison, I grant you. Sometimes it has to be a bit like a prison, but always for the best. Not like detention, internment, real prison, nothing like that.

Madeleine shrugged.

Mr Kramer's spirits lapsed. He forgot where he was and why. His spirits lapsed or the sadness in him rose. Either way he began to be occluded. An absence. When he returned he saw that Madeleine was looking at him. Being looked at by Madeleine was like being looked at by the moon. The light seemed to come off her face as though reflected from some far-away source. Her look was fearful, but rather as though she feared she had harmed Mr Kramer. Rema says Hi, she said. Rema said say Hi from me to Mr Kramer.

They both brightened.

Thank you, Madeleine, said Mr Kramer. Please give her my best regards next time you speak to her. How is she?

Can't tell with her, said Madeleine. She's such a liar. She says she's down to four and a half stone. Her hair's falling out, she says, from the starvation. She says she eats a few beansprouts a day and that is all. And drinks half a glass of water. But she's a liar. It's only so I'll look fat. She phones and phones. She wants to get back in here. But Dr Khan says she won't get back in here by starving herself. That's blackmail, he says. She might, however, if she puts on weight. Show willing, he says, show you want to get better. Then we'll see. She says if they won't let her back she'll kill herself. Thing is, if she gets well enough to come back here, she thinks they'll send her home. Soon as she's sixteen they'll send her home, her aunty says. But Rema says she'll kill herself twenty times before she'll go back home.

Home's not a war-zone, if I remember rightly, said Mr Kramer.

Her family is, said Madeleine. They are why she is the way she is. So quite understandably she'll end it all before she'll go back there.

Rema told me a lovely story once, said Mr Kramer.

Did she write it?

No, she never wrote it. She promised she would but she never did.

Typical, said Madeleine.

Yes, said Mr Kramer. But really it wasn't so much a story as a place for one. She remembered a house near her village. The house was all shuttered up, it had a paved courtyard with a sort of shrine in the middle and white jasmine growing wild over the balconies and the wooden stairs.

Oh that, said Madeleine. It was an old woman's and she wanted to do the Hajj and her neighbours lent her the money and the deal was they could keep her house if she didn't come back and she never came back. That story.

Yes, said Mr Kramer, that story. I thought it very beautiful, the deserted house, I mean, the courtyard and the shrine.

Probably she made it up, said Madeleine. Probably there never was such a house. And anyway she never wrote it.

Mr Kramer felt he was losing the encounter. He glanced at the clock. I thought Rema was your friend, he said.

She is, said Madeleine. I don't love anyone as much as I love her. But all the same she's a terrible liar. And mostly to get at me. Four and a half stone! What kind of a stupid lie is that? Did she tell you she wanted to do the Hajj?

She did, said Mr Kramer. Her owl eyes widening and taking in more light, passionately she had told him she longed to do the Hajj.

So why is she starving herself? It doesn't make sense.

I told her, said Mr Kramer. I said you have to be very strong for a thing like that. However you travel, a pilgrimage is a hard experience. You have to be fit.

Such a liar, said Madeleine.

Anyway, said Mr Kramer. You'll write your story for next time. About an asylum-seeker, a boy, you said, a boy half your age.

I will, said Madeleine. Where's the worst place in the world? Apart from here of course.

Hard to say, said Mr Kramer. There'd be quite a competition. But Somalia would take some beating.

I read there are pirates in Somalia.

Off the coast there are. They steal the food the rich people send and the people who need it starve.

Good, said Madeleine. I'll have pirates in my story.

Madeleine and Mr Kramer faced each other in silence across the table. The nurse had closed her magazine and was watching them. Mr Kramer was thinking that from many points of view the project was a bad one. Madeleine had wanted to write about being Madeleine. Fine, he said, but displace it. Find an image like one of those on the wall. I have, she said. My image is a war-zone. My story is about a child in a war-zone, a boy half my age, who wants to get out to somewhere safe. Asylum, said Mr Kramer. He seeks asylum.

Tell me, Madeleine, said Mr Kramer. Tell me in a word before I go what feeling you know most about and what feeling the little boy will inhabit in your story.

The sleeves of Madeleine's top had ridden up so that the cuts across her wrists were visible. Seeing them looked at

11

sorrowfully by Mr Kramer she pulled the sleeves down and gripped the end of each very tightly into either palm.

Fear, she said.

Mr Kramer might have taken the bus home. There was a stop not far from Bartlemas where that extraordinary enclosure, its orchard, its gardens, the grassy humps of the ancient hospital, touched modernity on the east-west road. He could have ridden to his house from there, almost door to door, in twenty minutes. Instead, if the weather was at all decent and some days even if it wasn't he walked home through the parks and allotments, a good long march, an hour and a half or more. That way it was late afternoon before he got in, almost time to be thinking about the cooking of his supper. Then came the evening, for which he always had a plan: a serious television programme, some serious reading, his notes, early to bed.

On his walk that mild spring afternoon Mr Kramer thought about Madeleine and Rema. It distressed him that Madeleine was so scathing about Rema's story. How cruel they were to one another in their lethal competition! For him the abandoned house had a peculiar power. Rema said it was very quiet there, as soon as you pushed open the wooden gates, no shouting, no dogs, no noise of any traffic. The courtyard was paved with coloured tiles in a complicated pattern whose many intersecting arcs and loops she had puzzled over and tried to follow. The shrine was surely left over from before Partition, it must be a Hindu shrine, the Muslim woman had no use for it. But there it stood in the centre of the courtyard, a carved figure on a pedestal and a place for flowers, candles and offerings, and around it on all four sides the shuttered windows, the balcony, the superabundance of white jasmine. The old woman never came back, said Rema. It was not even known whether she ever reached Mecca, the place of her heart's desire. So the neighbours kept the house but none had any real use for it. Sometimes their cattle strayed into the courtyard. And there also, when she dared, climbing the wooden stairs and viewing the shrine from the cool and scented balconies, went the child Rema, for sanctuary from the war-zone of her home.

Mr Kramer was watching a programme about the bombings, when the phone rang. Such a programme, after the cooking and the eating and the allowance of three glasses of wine, was a station on his way to bed. But the phone rang. It was Maria, his daughter, from the Ukraine, already midnight, phoning to tell him she had found the very *shtetl*, the names, the place itself. He caught her tone of voice, the one of all still in the world he was least proof against. He hardly heard the words, only the voice, its peculiar quality. Forest, memorial, the names, he knew what she was saying, but sharper than the words, nearer, flesh of his flesh, he felt the voice that was having to say these things, in a hotel room, three hours ahead, on a savage pilgrimage. The forest, the past, the small voice from so far away, he felt her to be in mortal danger, he felt he must pull her back from where she stood, leaning over the abyss of history, the pit, the extinction of all personal relations. Sweetheart, said Mr Kramer, my darling girl, go to sleep now if you can. And I've been thinking. Once you're back I'll come and stay with you. After all I cannot bear it on my own. But sleep now if you can.

Mr Kramer had not intended to say any such thing. He had set himself the year at least. One year. Surely a man could watch alone in grief that long.

The Unit phoned. Madeleine had taken an overdose, she was in hospital, back in a day or so. Mr Kramer, about to set off, did the walk anyway, it was a fine spring day, the beech trees leafing softly. He walked right to the gates of Bartlemas, turned and set off home again, making a detour to employ the time he would have spent with Madeleine.

In the evening, last thing, Mr Kramer read his old notes,

a weakness he always tried to make up for by at once writing something new. He read for ten minutes, till he hit the words: Rema, her desire to be an owl. Then he leafed forward quickly to the day's blank page and wrote: I haven't thought nearly enough about Rema's desire to be an owl. She said, Do you think I already look like one? I went to the office and asked did we have a mirror. We do, under lock and key. It is a lovely thing, face-shaped and just the size of a face, without a frame, the bare reflecting glass. I held it up for Rema. Describe your face, I said. Describe it exactly. I was a mite ashamed of the licence this exercise gave me to contemplate a girl's face whilst she, looking at herself, never glancing at me, studied it as a thing to be described. Yes, her nose, quite a thin bony line, might become a beak. Pity to lose the lips. But if you joined the arcs of the brows with the arcs of shadow below the eyes, so accentuating the sockets, yes you might make the widening stare of an owl. The longing for metamorphosis. To become something else, a quite different creature, winged, feathered, intent. Like Madeleine's, Rema's face shows the bones. The softness of feathers would perhaps be a comfort. I wonder did she tell Madeleine about the mirror. Shards, the harming.

The Unit phoned, Madeleine was well enough, just about. Mr Kramer stood at the window. The primroses were already finishing. But there would be something else, on and on till the autumn cyclamens. It was a marvellous bank. Then Madeleine and the overweight nurse stood in the doorway, the nurse holding her women's magazine. Madeleine wore loose trousers and a collarless shirt whose sleeves were far too long. She stood; and towards Mr Kramer, fearfully and defiantly, she presented her face and neck, which she had cut. Oh Maddy, said Mr Kramer, can't you ever be merciful? Will you never show yourself any mercy?

The nurse sat in the open doorway and read her magazine. Madeleine and Mr Kramer faced each other across the small table. All the same, said Madeleine through her lattice of black cuts, I've made a start. Shall I read it? Yes, said Mr Kramer. Madeleine read:

Samuel lived with his mother. The soldiers had killed his father. Some of the soldiers were only little boys. Samuel and his mother hid in the forest. Every day she had to leave him for several hours to go and look for food and water. He waited in fear that she would not come back. There was nothing to do. He curled up in the little shelter, waiting. One day Samuel's mother did not come back. He waited all night and all the next day and all the next night. Then he decided he must go and look for her or for some food and water at least because the emergency supplies she had left him were all gone. He followed the trail his mother had made day after day. It came to a road. She had told him that the road was very dangerous. But beyond the road were fields and in them, if you were lucky, you might find some things to eat that the farmers had planted before the soldiers came and burned their village. Samuel halted at the road. It was long and straight in both directions and very dusty. A little way off he saw a truck burning and another truck upside down in the ditch. But there were no soldiers. Samuel hurried across. Quite soon, just as his mother had said, he saw women and girls in blue and white clothes moving slowly over the land looking for food. Perhaps his mother would be among them after all? At the very least, somebody would surely give him food and water.

Madeleine lifted her face. That's as far as I got, she said. It's crap, isn't it? No, said Mr Kramer, it is very good. Crap, said Madeleine. Tell me, Madeleine, said Mr Kramer, did you write this before or after you did that to your face? After, said Madeleine. I wrote it this morning. I did my face two nights ago, after they brought me back here from the hospital. Good, said Mr Kramer. That's a very good thing. It means you can sympathise with other people's lives even when your own distresses you so much you cut your face. I know the rest, said

15

Madeleine with a sudden eagerness. I know how it goes on and how it ends. Shall I tell you? – Will you still be able to write it if you tell? – Yes, yes. – You promise? – Yes, I promise. – Tell then.

She laid her sleeves, in which her hands were hiding, flat on the table and began to speak, rapidly, staring into his eyes, transfixing him with the eagerness of her fiction.

In among the people looking for food he meets a girl. She's my age. Her name is Ruth. The soldiers have killed her father too. Ruth's mother hid with her and when the soldiers came looking she made Ruth stay in hiding and gave herself up to them. That was the end of her. But Ruth was taken by the other women and hid with them and went looking for food when it was safe. When Samuel came into the fields Ruth decided to look after him. She was like a sister to Samuel, a good big sister, or a mother, a good and loving mother. When it was safe to light a fire she cooked for him, the best meal she could. After a while the soldiers came back again, the fields were too dangerous, all the women hid in the forest but Ruth had heard that if you could only get to the coast you could maybe find someone with a boat who would carry you across the sea to Italy and the European Union, where it was really safe. So that's what she did, with Samuel, she set off for the coast, only travelling at night, on foot, by moonlight and starlight, steering clear of the villages in flames.

Sounds good, said Mr Kramer. Sounds very exciting. All you have to do now is write it. You've looked at a map, I suppose? The nearest coast is no use at all. That's where the pirates are. You need the north coast really, through the desert. And crossing the desert is said to be a terrible thing. You have to pay truckers to take you, I believe. Yes, said Madeleine, I thought she'd do better on the east coast, with the pirates. A pirate chief says he'll take her and Samuel all the way to Libya but it will cost her a lot of money. When she says she has no money he says she can marry him, for payment that is, until they get to Libya, then he'll sell her to a friend of his, who will take her and Samuel into the European Union, which is like the Promised Land, he says, and there she will be safe, but she'll have to marry his friend as well, for the voyage from Libya into Italy. I asked Rema would she do it and she said she wouldn't, she couldn't, because of the things at home, but she said I could, Ruth in my story should, it would save the two of them, they would have a new life in the European Union and God would mercifully forgive her the sin. She says Hi, by the way. She asked me to ask you are you all right. She said it seemed to her you were a bit lonely sometimes. Thank you, said Mr Kramer, I'm fine. And guess what, said Madeleine, she doesn't want to do the Hajj any more, not till she's an old woman, and she doesn't want to make Dr Khan have her back here either. No, she's decided she'll be a primary school teacher. Plus she's down to four stone. So it's all lies as usual.

A primary school teacher is a very good idea, said Mr Kramer. But of course you have to be strong for that. As strong as for a pilgrimage.

I told her that, said Madeleine. So she's still a liar. Anyway, another thing about Ruth is that when she's with the first pirate, as his prostitute, all the way up the Red Sea he sends her ashore to the markets – Samuel he keeps on board as a hostage – and she has to go and buy all the ingredients for his favourite meals, I've researched it, baby okra and lamb in tomato stew, for example, onion pancakes, fish and peppers, shoe-lace pastry, spicy creamy cheeses, all delicious, up the coast to Suez. So she makes her Lord and Master happy and Samuel gets strong.

Will they stay in Italy, Mr Kramer asked, if the second pirate keeps his word and carries her across the Mediterranean? No, said Madeleine, breathless on her story, they're heading for Swansea. There's quite an old Somali community in Swansea. I've researched it. They've been there a hundred years. At first she'll live in a hostel, doing the cooking for

17

everybody so that everybody likes her. Samuel goes to school and as soon as he's settled Ruth will go to the CFE and get some qualifications.

Madeleine, said Mr Kramer, it's very hard to enter the United Kingdom. Ruth and Samuel will need passports. I've thought of that, said Madeleine. The first pirate chief has a locker full of passports from people who died on his boat and because Ruth is such a good cook he gives her a couple and swears they'll get her and Samuel through Immigration, no problem.

Rema should go to the CFE, said Mr Kramer. I believe the Home Office would extend her visa if she was in full-time education. And if she trained as a primary school teacher, who knows what might happen?

She's a liar, said Madeleine, very white, almost translucent her face through the savage ornamentation of her cuts. She's supposed to be my friend. If she was really my friend she'd come back here. Then we'd both be all right like we were before she left me.

You want to stay here?

Yes, said Madeleine. It's safer here.

Why overdose? Why cut yourself?

The nurse was watching and listening.

Because I'm frightened.

My daughter was frightened, said Mr Kramer, and she's twice your age. All the time her mother was ill, four and a half years, she got more and more frightened. And now she's gone to the Ukraine, would you believe it, all on her own and not speaking the language, to research our family history. She phoned me the other night from the place itself, a terrible place, I never want to go there, all on her own, at midnight, in a hotel. Write your story, won't you? You promised me. Somalia is very likely the worst place in the world and

18

Swansea is a very good place, by all accounts. What an achievement it will be if you can get Ruth and Samuel safely there!

Madeleine's white hands with their bitten nails still hid in her sleeves. All the animation had gone out of her. I'll never get to Swansea from Somalia, she said. Never, never, never. I can't even want to get out of here.

First the story, Madeleine, said Mr Kramer. First comes the fiction. Get Ruth and Samuel out of the killing fields, get them by the cruelty and kindness of pirates into a holding camp on the heel of Italy, get them north among strangers, not speaking a word of the language – devise it, work out the necessary means. You promised. Who knows what might happen if you get that lucky pair to Swansea?

Ayery Thinnesse

AND HOW WAS your Christmas?

OK. The usual. How was yours?

OK. Well, sort of. My sister left home and came to stay with us. For a few days, she said, while she thought what to do next. In the end she stayed a month. Then Russell more or less asked her to leave. He said she was putting a strain on our marriage. So she left.

She went home?

No. She says she's not going back home. That's it now. Finished.

The owner of the place brought their coffees. They leaned away from the small table so that he could set the blue-china cups on the white cloth between them. He looked from face to face, the woman's, the man's, with a candid and friendly interest and they looked up at him and smiled.

I like it here, said Leila.

Funny about Christmas, said Jackson. I suppose because it lasts so long and the weather's awful, it never gets light, and there's family, too much or too little family, and when you meet people again, when it's finally over, and ask the usual questions, any number have died, just given up, it seems to me, or have done things like your sister which may be the very opposite of giving up, for all I know.

I wouldn't say Jo had given up, said Leila. She's had enough, but that's not the same as giving up.

Yes, said Jackson. Often it's at Christmas. Suddenly someone has had enough.

In Jo's case it was the turkey, said Leila. They had a lot of family, mostly his, Pete's, her husband's, but she managed to get rid of them for three or four hours while she cooked the dinner and when they came back they'd had a drink or two so it should have been all right and it would have been, she said, but for the turkey.

We don't have a turkey, said Jackson. Haven't for years.

No, said Leila, and when Jo told me about hers I wished we didn't but when I mentioned it to Russell he said that's your sister talking, Christmas wouldn't be Christmas without a turkey.

Revolting creatures, said Jackson. Not their fault, of course. I had a friend once worked on a turkey farm, they get too fat to copulate and it was his job to – Well, you can imagine.

Yes, said Leila, yes, thank you, I can. Jo could hardly lift it out of the oven and even after four hours in there it wasn't done. Pete said it had to be that big for the number of family he'd invited.

Jackson saw the horrors coming into Leila, a sort of tensing, almost a freezing, of her features, a widening of her eyes, truly, as he always thought, the onset of possession, so he took her hands, which were cold, and said, That's Jo, then, it was the turkey and she left.

Yes, said Leila. And came to our house quite early on Boxing Day, I was still washing up and she came past the kitchen window and in at the side door with a suitcase and said she'd left home and wasn't going back again and could she stay with us till she'd thought what to do. She helped me with the dishes.

Another thing I've been thinking lately, said Jackson, not exactly changing the subject but moving it on so that Leila would at least get the turkey out of her head, is that since you and I don't live anywhere, so to speak, don't belong anywhere together, there's nowhere for us to leave, nowhere to walk out of, and whenever I hear of someone leaving house and home and never coming back, and I often do and now your sister, for example, I think well that can't happen to Leila and me.

Leila considered him. Often his ideas, as she called them, made no real sense to her. She wondered at them; or at the fact that he had them.

I mean, he continued, we don't have a locality. Nobody in a shop would ever say to you, Haven't seen Jackson for a while – not left, has he? And nobody would ever stop me on the street and say, Where's Leila? It's a while since I saw Leila.

Leila freed her hands, leaned back from the table and looked at the day's menu written up on the wall above the counter behind Jackson's back. For a main meal you could have cawl, lamb kofta, the All Day Breakfast, souvlakia (chicken or pork), stuffed aubergines. On display were cheese pies, spinach pies, Welsh cakes, baklava and bara brith. I like it here, she said again. I feel quite hungry looking at his menu. Perhaps he's from Cyprus. I like the way he says good morning to people when they come in. The door sticks and he looks a bit embarrassed that they have to push. There's a little movement of his hands as though he's helping them. And when they're in he's all smiles and says good morning as though he means it. And he knows everybody. I think we're the only ones he doesn't know. But wasn't he just as nice to us?

Leila could see the door. Jackson was watching her face.

Listen, she said. The old couple come in now are speaking Welsh to him. All three of them think it's a great joke that they have a little chat in Welsh.

Jackson smiled. She attends, he thought. And it makes me more attentive. She is really here. She could tell me a life story for everyone in the room and I'd believe it. I could give her the map reference for this little place, eastings and northings, six figures. But she is really here. If you're hungry we can eat now, he said. No reason why not.

Leila leaned forward, took his hands again, turned her attention away from the comings and goings at the door and the counter, to him. She said, I don't know whether you think it good or bad that we don't have a neighbourhood and that you can't leave me and I can't leave you because we have nowhere to leave.

Jackson shrugged. Good sometimes, when I'm anxious. If you're nowhere it's a bit like being everywhere. The connections stretch. What will your sister do now? Where has she gone?

She's on her own in a bedsit in Hackney. For the time being, she says. While she sorts herself out.

'For the time being' is a funny phrase, said Jackson. I wonder has anyone sat in a room and stared at himself so long in the mirror he could see the aging actually taking place.

I shouldn't think so, said Leila. But you see me again in a place where we don't belong, you see my face again after the passing of quite some time, and you must think, she has aged.

Ayery thinnesse.

What did you say?

Like gold… Ayery thinnesse.

Yes, I thought that's what you said. Jackson, I know about ayery thinnesse and I doubt if he did and I'm very sure you don't. No one can live on ayery thinnesse, I've tried it, I had no appetite till I met you, please don't make me go back to having none again.

Leila's face was white. Especially around the lips she looked stricken.

Or perhaps I should? Perhaps it would be better if I did, of my own volition, before it is forced on me? Jo told me that was her twenty-first turkey and the first one of them all that didn't cook. It was probably the biggest. Probably it got bigger and bigger every Christmas as the family he invited grew. Jo said that for Christmas Day it was just about cooked enough. There was enough of it done on its horrible great breast and thighs and Pete didn't notice anything was wrong. But for Boxing Day he invited some other bits of family round, for turkey and chips. He likes that almost better than turkey on the day itself: cold turkey and stuffing and perhaps a few extra pickles and heaps of chips. Jo got up early and had a good look at it. She said it was the most revolting thing she's ever seen. The uncooked blood had seeped through overnight. The remains of the white flesh had turned pink. The pits of the thighs were liquid red. It lay on its back in a jelly like wallpaper paste mixed with a red distemper. Big and heavy as an obese toddler. Jo went upstairs and woke Pete and told him to go down and have a look at it and while he was doing that she packed her case.

Did he throw a fit?

On the contrary, he was very magnanimous. Jo said she was leaving anyway but if she hadn't been, his magnanimity would have made her. He let her see he was very upset, his day and the whole Christmas were utterly ruined, but it was the first time she had let him down like that and he forgave her, he was sure it wouldn't happen again, they would go to the pub with his family and watch the mummers and have a bite to eat there and say no more about it. And at once, to show he meant it, he slid the thing off the plate into a big plastic bag – with a wet slithering noise and he had to put his hand on the parson's nose and shove – and said he'd just pop out the back and put it in the bin. Before you do, Jo said, I'm leaving and I want you to know it's not really you, or not just you, it's the turkey. Then he smiled his smile, she said, no doubt supposing her to be too distraught to know what she was saying, and went out by the back door and she left by the front.

Leila stood up and went to the toilet. Jackson looked out of the window at the crossroads and the clocktower war memorial in the middle of it. Local traffic and people. He counted forty-five names on one face of the memorial, from Alban to Lewis. So that would be half of them, all very local. Soon be spring. Such a lot to look at through that window. But then Jackson forgot his whereabouts and started on a train of thought.

When Leila came back she said, I like it that the *patron* doesn't know our names and will never see us again. I shall always think of his café with love. And I'll be glad when we leave here and go on our way wherever it is we're going. I think we should buy a spinach pie and a cheese pie each to take with us. If I was local here and saw two strangers like us come in and enjoy the place for a while and leave, they would seem to me as free as birds and I should envy them, I know I should. Think of the scores of places we have left like that. They amount to something, don't they?

Jackson said, I was thinking about that place we found, the first time, when with all my map-reading I got us lost.

Not really lost, only on the map lost, but it was getting dark and it began to rain. That house on the hill, miles and miles from anywhere. Its one big sycamore and the row of bent hawthorns, the sheep smell under them, that smell and the blossom. The door wasn't locked.

The shepherds used the house. There were empty bottles of the stuff they need for sheep.

There was a coat hanging behind the door, one big chair by the hearth, the floor was black slates, big flags of slate.

Two or three candle ends in the hearth, two or three Guinness bottles, fire-irons.

You said you'd check upstairs. You came down and said there was a little fireplace upstairs too, and a brass and iron bed frame, and wallpaper still on the walls and the floorboards pretty well intact.

The smell of soot.

You were worried about the ceiling in their bedroom. You said some plaster had fallen in one corner and the wet come through. You said we'd be better off downstairs. You cleaned out the grate. I sat in the big chair watching you. You said they'd had fires not long ago and why shouldn't we?

Though I was worried there might be nests in the chimney. I didn't want the chimney catching fire.

You went to get some wood.

Any amount of wood in the outhouses. And some old newspapers stuffed into the walls, quite dry. And the wrapping paper from off our cheese.

When the flames started you kept looking up the wide chimney. Then little by little you stopped worrying and built the fire. You fetched in water to make our tea.

There was a spring with dressed stones around it. I shone my torch. The water was crystal clear, in a blackness.

We ate our food. We drank our tea. I sat in the big chair. You fetched the coat from off the door and laid it over me. I pulled it up to my chin. It was hardly damp at all and the fire warmed it. I liked the smell of it, of a man having worn it in the weather and come home. You sat on our things on the slate floor and leaned back against my legs. I slept.

The rain.

How it rained!

And the fire.

Let's go now, said Leila. Let's quickly pay for the coffee and buy our pies and leave.

Alphonse

LEG IT WHILE you can, said Alf. And with that he spun on his wheels and sped from the room. Norman – as he called himself then – nodded. Alf had a broad back and powerful arms. The chair Norman sat in was an easy chair, but very low, hard to get up out of; and from it, through the window on his left, he could not see much, only sky. Late summer. Norman gazed at a snow scene on the floral wall – not really a scene: no mountains, fir trees, frozen lakes, skaters, only snow and a snowman, and he had no face, no carrot nose, no coal buttons, only a bare round head on a stout trunk, and no scarf, no red hat.

Alf wheeled back in, fast, and halted close to Norman, bearing over him. A powerful head he has too, Norman observed. Hair like a flue brush, but dirty white. Don't leave it too late, Alf said. Once the assessment's done, your window's a week, max. After that, you're lost. And this particular room, he added, does not have a happy tradition. Natural causes here: three months at most. The spirit leaks away. You'll have seen the black bags? Norman nodded. That was Graham. Eleven days he lasted, four days beyond assessment. I reckon she leaves the bags out there on purpose. This afternoon you'll hear her shouting at the nurses, but if you ask me, she has the binbags lined up on the landing to discourage the next man. It's my belief she makes more on through-put than on the long-term. But suit yourself, said Alf. Croak if you want. What's the family want? The family is a major player in the end game. It's my belief she gets a cut if you pop off

29

soonish, and that's why through-put is her preferred option.

Alf wheeled himself to the window. There's a nice horse down there, he said. One thing Graham said to me was how much he liked that horse. It's a white horse, and very patient. Graham told me he'd seen it standing there in the pouring rain not moving a muscle, just standing still getting pelted on. He believed it stood there all night. Graham was an early riser, but no matter how early he rose the horse was already there on that bit of grass, standing stock still, whatever the weather. I'm not sure what the family wants, said Norman. Pop off soonish, I'd say, said Alf. That's the general wish. Which is why I say to you leg it while you can. His mobile pinged. He read the message. Damnation, he said and again wheeled swiftly from the room, only pausing on the threshold to cry, over his left shoulder, Beware the Power of Attorney!

Norman told me all this and much else and not just me but anyone who sat next to him on his particular park bench in a rather dirty town in the south of France. By then he was telling people to call him Alphonse. Immediately after his escape from Avalon he had changed his name to Alf, as a mark of respect for his saviour, as he called him, and in hopes of transmitting to himself, with the name, some of that strong man's strength. Then in France – in Paris, on the Pont des Arts, to be precise – a young woman who, perhaps thinking he was about to drown himself, had got into conversation with him, said, in English, that henceforth he must surely call himself Alphonse. At that very moment, he said, my mobile phone went off. I took it from my pocket and flung it, ringing, into the black waters of the Seine. Whereupon the young woman kissed him on both cheeks, wished him *bonne route* and swore that their meeting would live in her for ever.

Alphonse (as I don't mind calling him) told me in a matter-of-fact voice that since his escape from Avalon he had done very well with women. He was strongly built – in his youth, so he said, he had played prop forward for a local club

– with a broad and candid face. He wore pillarbox-red trousers, a dark blue jacket, a shirt of a lighter blue, a scarlet neckerchief and espadrilles. But more attractive than all that was surely his being a stranger passing through with – as he freely told you – at most six months to live. I can't, for the moment, think of anything more seductive than that.

It is true, Alphonse was not in good health. He had some sort of heart trouble, for which reason and for what they called the onset of dementia, his family had confined him in Cookham, in the home whose name was Avalon. He had been on the road for several months when I met him in Montpellier, his face was brown but with a sickly cast over it. And a more obvious marker of illness was his suddenly falling asleep. Like a driven cloud, an immense fatigue would sweep over his features and in mid-sentence he halted, slumped and slept. The story of his life was continually interrupted in this way and even if you sat by him and thought your own thoughts till he woke again, he might very well not resume where he had left off. And if he went back to the beginning, very likely he would change even quite significant details in the retelling. Most often, of course, his listener moved away and a new one was sitting by him when he opened his eyes, shuddered, fetched a great breath like a man coming up from nine fathom deep, and spoke. Feeling rather abject myself – my own *évasion* had ended badly and I was crawling home – I did sit by him longer and heard more of his story than perhaps anyone else in Montpellier that early summer.

I went to Cookham once, for the sake of Stanley Spencer. Though not much interested in painting, I did, at that time, have quite a keen interest in resurrection – resurrection now, I mean, not at the Last Trump – and the barmy Sir Stanley had for a while strengthened my hope and faith. But half an hour in Cookham flattened me. Like most such places – places of vision and pilgrimage – it would be better to have gone there fifty or five hundred years ago. As soon as I got off the train I knew there was no more

31

likelihood of resurrection in Cookham than in my home town of Bootle. I persevered, of course, but it did more harm than good. I visited the small gallery, I sat in the churchyard itself, I walked by the river, had a pub lunch, looked a hundred people full in the face, and the end of it all was the complete annihilation of even the wish for, let alone the hope of, resurrection. But years later – nothing is wasted – in the rather sordid park in Montpellier I was glad of my day-trip to Cookham. I could locate Alphonse's Avalon pretty exactly. I remembered Lob Lane, I remembered the shrivelling of my spirit as I walked down it. And I saw yet again, listening to his account, that what you think can't possibly get worse always can and very likely will.

When it came to choosing a home for their father, it was Milly, the youngest of his three daughters, who trawled the web until she lit upon Cookham and Avalon. She had a lively interest in painting, she was of a romantic bent, and Spencer's rapturous town combined very propitiously in her mind with the name of the home, alluding as it did to her father's West Country origins. Furthermore, Avalon was advertised as being 'in the very heart of a vibrant community'. So there'll be plenty for him to look at, said Milly. He won't be bored. Milly's husband and the rest of the family noted chiefly that he would be within easy striking distance, they could nip over in no time and cut out any trouble before it spread. For by then their father, like so many fathers nowadays, with his heart, his brain and the police, had indeed become a trouble.

The two elder sisters delivered Norman, as he then was, into care in Avalon and reported that all looked good. Of course, there's still the assessment, they said. But, fingers crossed, that will be fine as well.

On the park bench in Montpellier, facing a cracked concrete depression that had once been and in the future perhaps would again be a lake, Alphonse told me Alf had warned him that the psychiatrist who did the assessing at

Avalon was barking mad. Avalon was one of several homes in his portfolio. He dedicated his Thursdays to this work, and for the rest of the week, including Sundays, in a nice room on the ground floor of the local psychiatric hospital, he pursued his research into dementia, leaving his wife and two children to their own devices. But, said Alf, lately the good lady had begun to rebel, and at any hour of the long working day she might appear with Aaron in the push-chair and Francesca in the sling and parade to and fro on the lawn under his window; which was very distracting, as he said, and, if a colleague happened to be present, also very humiliating. So Doctor Mountjoy, always nervous, looked forward to his Thursdays and his secret itinerary round the county's homes.

Alf's warning, as he freely conceded, was of little practical use. Sane men like Alf, Norman or Graham, confined in a place like Avalon, could never hope to answer the questions of a powerful madman like Doctor Mountjoy in any way that would persuade him they were sane. Whatever you say, said Alf, he'll mark you down as an imbecile or a psychopath. Everyone aims for the imbecile. You stay here at least. The regime's a bit easier than Broadmoor. But in my case, so I've heard, it was touch and go. When he asked me who I most admired, Mother Teresa or Adolf Hitler, I reasoned that the psychopath, being naturally very devious, would say Mother Teresa, so I said Adolf, with a silly smile. I heard on the grapevine that nearly did for me. Eddie upstairs, he continued, tells me, though I can hardly believe it, that this Doctor Mountjoy has a right to everyone's brains in here and in all the other homes he assesses in, for his experiments, when we pass away. And he feeds these brains to his favourite patients, in their porridge, to see if he can halt or at least slow down their degeneration. And what do you think about that? says Eddie. Then the fatigue overwhelmed Norman-become-Alphonse. He pillowed his great head on the saddle of his bicycle, which was propped against the end of the bench, and fell asleep.

Waking ten minutes or an hour later (I was still there, I had lost all sense of time), Alphonse gave a shuddering sigh, heaved up the necessary breath and said: For thirty years I was a quarryman. I quarried the honey-coloured stone to restore the old town houses. But when they closed the quarry and made me redundant I discovered a gift for woodcarving, and fashioning horses for carousels became my trade. I had noticed his hands. The fingers were all clutched in, almost clenched, so that when I extended my own hand to greet him, what he offered me in return was a large soft hollow fist. As a quarryman I was never a trouble-maker, he continued. Even when they sacked me, I shrugged and took the cash. It was only last year, witnessing the occupation of a locked garden in one of the spa's wealthiest squares, that I saw the light. By God! I cried, Where have I been all my life? Next morning, a Monday, I drove through a barrier in my white van and set up seven of my best horses among the young people on the lawn they had annexed for the public good. How beautiful my horses looked that morning in the sun! How proud I was of them! Small children sat astride them dumbstruck with the wonder of it. Three days and three nights I was there in that happy company, laughing and singing. Then on the fourth day, before dawn, Security moved in and slung us out. One big fat bastard whacked my favourite horse with an iron railing, whacked and whacked at him till he'd broken his neck and all his legs. If he'd done it to me, I'd not have felt worse pain. And all seven they flung on the concrete like so much junk. It was then, fighting back and blacking out, I discovered I had heart trouble. And that morning, in court, came other trouble too.

I had no desire to doubt Alphonse's stories. Candidly he showed me the hands that less than a year ago, he said, had been carving the prancing horses and painting them white, brown, black and piebald, every one different, and all their straps and saddles, the bits, bridles, ribbons and reins, in blue, vermilion, silver, jade and gold. Attached to his bicycle was an open trolley in which, so he said, were all his worldly goods, and strapped uppermost upon them a guitar. You play? I asked, glancing again at his softly clenching fingers. Not much, he answered, not well, a few chords. It's my voice they like. I know every song Ella Fitzgerald every recorded. That's what the young people like to hear. You should come, he added. You'll find us by the fountain under the stars.

I didn't see Alphonse then for three or four days. I found a public library they would let me sit in, and there I sat, doing nothing much. The fountain, between the park and the main square, was itself the centre of an act of occupation. All day the occupiers sat around it, drinking, singing and shouting at passers-by. When they got too hot, they sat in the water. The tramps pissed in it at nights, so Alphonse told me. But under the stars and by moonlight and lamplight the upsurge and fall of the water looked passably beautiful and the falling and overflowing of water, listened to, is always persuasive. All that, with the music and the singing, was doubtless a fine thing. But then the municipality shut off the supply and the basin drained to concrete. The police said enough was enough, the young women and men were an eyesore, a public nuisance and a health hazard, and would they kindly clear off. I was in the library, but I learned from Alphonse, by now beloved and honoured among them as an old *soixante-huitard*, that the occupiers, having symbolically restored one form of elemental life (water) to public enjoyment, at once moved to take another. Led by him pedalling slowly on his bicycle, and behind him a small brass band, they quitted the dead fountain, marched back into the park and there, very suddenly, outwitting the police, three groups of three of them broke from the procession, slung grapnels and ropes into three stately plane trees and in no time at all were lodged out of reach in forks already reconnoitred. Their comrades encircled the trees, and the makings of homes – planks, sheeting, cooking pots, wine, bread and water – were swiftly hoisted aloft. The police shrugged and withdrew, the band played louder.

Before his escape from Avalon, Norman, as he then was, had never been much of a traveller. As a young man he had toured with his club to the frontiers of Rugby Union in Great Britain – by coach, everything organized, never more than one night away. In his late fifties then, at a fairground, a foreigner admiring his horses asked him would he be attending the annual Congress of Carvers of Carousel Horses, to be held that year in Rietberg, a small town in Westphalia; and suddenly stirred by the possibility of an enlarging life, he answered that he knew nothing about any such congress and, blushing and mumbling, asked the foreigner for details. In a wonder at himself he applied for and was sent a passport; he booked a ticket on the night boat fom Harwich to the Hook; drove across Holland to Rietberg; and in the Congress Field arranged seven of his best horses in a welcoming semi-circle before the open doors of his white van. And though he never attended another Congress, not even the one held in Lewes three years later, this was not out of disappointment at his trip to Rietberg, nor out of fear that he might be disappointed if he tried the experience again. Quite simply, Rietberg was enough. He hoarded the few days there, the company, the common passion, the beautiful horses assembled from as far away as Siberia and the Ukraine, that gathering of craftsmen and their work, the goodwill, the free exchange of admiration and advice through the barriers of many languages – all that and more that had come to him in Rietberg, Norman took with him through his transformation into Alphonse as a strength thoughout his remaining life.

Nor before the night of 13 September 2011, when the young woman on the Pont des Arts had kissed him and christened him Alphonse, had the former Norman ever slept rough. But that night he did, not far from where he had become Alphonse, on the *quai*, in a dank place, traffic passing close above his head, the great black river muscling by, lights dancing on it and on the streets beyond, so many lights. Thereafter, until he began to be taken in by strangers who wanted his company, Alphonse always slept rough, shaved in public toilets, kept himself as clean as he could. He learned barely a word of French, genially addressed the world in broad West Country English, but never wanted for food or wine or friendly tips on survival.

Idling on the *quais* in a late summer warmth, his keenest pleasure was watching the great barges passing upstream or down; and he soon noticed that many, under the washing lines and alongside the pots of bright geraniums, carried bicycles. And after the first night too cold to sleep, he plodded with his small bag to the Gare de Lyon, two things in mind: the river and a bicycle. Yes, he said, having only, at most, six months to live, I decided I must go south. And again he showed me his hands: how well a bike's handlebars would fit into his clenching fingers.

Luckily for Norman, his family delivered him into care in Avalon late on a Thursday afternoon. He had a week's grace before his assessment by Doctor Mountjoy. Warned and advised by Alf, he took stock of his situation. What to do for the best? His room was at the back of the house and he, like Graham, often stood at the window and admired the patience of the white horse. But, he said to himself, if I stay here my prospects are a good deal worse than his. No barking mad doctor will declare him to be an imbecile or a psychopath. And as a lover of horses and having some elementary knowledge of their physiology, in the matter of natural causes I'd give him a damn sight longer than three months. And when he passes away, surely he will be set in the heavens as a new constellation, which, unless I bestir myself, won't happen to me.

From day one, after his first meeting with Alf, Norman accustomed the staff to seeing him seated in the window seat at the far end of the binbag landing outside his room. From there he gazed down on Lob Lane (Death Row, Alf called it) with every appearance of feeble-minded contentment. Well, that's very nice, Norman, said Matron. We do like to see our people enjoying the community.

The community was a road linking the town's main thoroughfare with the riverbank. It was gated at both ends. The houses, all large and detached and with their high fences, gates, security lights, CCTV cameras and magnolias, much resembled Avalon; and in time, one by one, as the market dictated, they would morph that lucrative way. If Doctor Mountjoy lives a few more years, Lob Lane of itself will be fieldwork and goldmine enough, and he may pursue his researches into the fog and desolation of dementia a richer and richer man. Norman meanwhile, from his window seat, beamed pleasantly on the life of Death Row and strengthened his spirit for the escape. The best, he said to me on another park bench in Montpellier, music drifting down to us from the three jolly tree houses, the thing that did most for my resolution, was the sight that Friday afternoon of a fat man in a convertible remotely opening the portals of his mock-Tudor castle, sitting there then as they closed behind him, the car roof slid over him and the double-doors of his garage swung wide to welcome him home. Risky, I said. That sight, anyone inclining to despair might be finished off by it. Nonsense, said Alphonse. A fat man in his shirt sleeves, a shaven-headed adult male of the human species, eases his BMW on to the crunching gravel, the lid slides soundlessly over him, he passes into the cavernous garage like a coffin through the curtains, the doors close upon him, a fat magnolia petal falls like an elephant turd on the empty forecourt – at the very thought of it poor stinking Lazarus himself would leap forth with a yell.

Norman shared his experience with Alf. Very good, said Alf. You're coming along nicely. A glance at the river now, and Alcatraz couldn't hold you.

Sunday is the day to see the river at Cookham, a hot Sunday if possible, and Norman, luck running his way, got that. He asked Matron would she mind if he went and sat in the churchyard for half an hour. He felt the need, he said, it being Sunday. And he smiled his foolish smile. Why not? said Matron. We do like our people to enjoy the community. And you do still have the use of your legs. Go along the riverbank. That's much the prettiest way. Lenka will go with you. We can't have you wandering off and drowning, can we?

Late morning, Lob Lane is already fugged with barbecues. Music, shouts and splashings from the pools, rise on the smoke through blooms and leafiness in a medley of ringtones towards the implacable sky. Shuffling along, Norman began to teach Lenka English. Big house, he said. Big white car. Stopping and pointing. So that when, having passed The Grove, Mews Cottage, Homeland, The Holt etc, they reached the gates and from the back of an envelope she read out the code to herself in Serbo-Croat, mischievously peering over her shoulder Norman said each digit in English: one, seven, seven, oh! and got her to repeat them. Very good, he said. We are coming on nicely.

Snout to bum, not a sausage-gap between them, the cabin cruisers park along the bank. The Sweet Louise, the Hiawatha, Blue Moon… On deck, prone, lie the browning women, upright the red-swart menfolk, turning the sizzling meat, their midriffs melting over the trunk-tops, their bare domes, angry as boils, dripping into the grill. Flesh, so much flesh, cooking or being cooked, oozing a living sweat or the juices that still moisten the dead meat. Boat, said Norman. Flag. Big dog, big lady and gentleman. They are having a nice time.

After two hundred yards a lane leads into the churchyard and there Norman sat for fifteen minutes with Lenka, occasionally teaching her another word. Then he pressed three pound coins into her small palm. Thank you, he said. Now we'll go home.

Along the barricade of boats it is nearer to feeding time, the glasses raising, slopping, the jovialities loudly multiply, they travel from grill to grill, on rosé, lager, Pimm's, perhaps a mile and back again, the line has its own long atmosphere, curving with the riverbank, roughly sausage-shaped, but bluish. Say after me, said Norman: One, seven, seven, oh!

Good, said Alf. Now for the funds. Leave it till Tuesday.

Listening to Alphonse, I began to feel that on my day-trip I had perhaps seen Cookham at its best. There were fewer boats, larger gaps between them, I saw swans, a skiff, a canoe, and though Lob Lane appalled me there were no gates then, you had free access either to the river or to the main road, both of which, with a peck of faith, could be thought of as escape.

Tuesday, Norman asked for and got permission to go into town with Lenka, to Nancy's Pantry, for a cup of coffee and perhaps a biscuit. Again Matron recommended the river walk. Once in the churchyard you are nearly there, she said. And she added, On Thursday Doctor Mountjoy will see you. Our normal little meeting. Nothing to worry about. And he may mention Power of Attorney. Again, nothing to worry about. Norman smiled his smile.

At the gate Lenka said the code aloud, in English: one, seven, seven, oh! Very good, said Norman. We really are making progress. In Nancy's Pantry, slipping her a five pound note, he indicated by pointing to the street, then to their table, and unfolding all his fingers as far as they would go, that he would be away for ten minutes. In the bank he withdrew £500 from his current account and arranged for the entire contents of his deposit account to be tipped into that hole as soon as possible.

Tomorrow, said Alf. He sat, Norman stood, at the window contemplating the stoical white horse. Alf's mobile pinged. Good, he said, reading it. She'll be waiting. She? Betty, said Alf. I'm coming with you, you wheel me, just to the other side of the weir. Then you leg it to the railway station. You want a single to Dover, catch the 12.21, change Maidenhead, get off at Paddington, Circle Line to King's Cross, catch the 14.05 from St Pancras, you're in Dover 15.20, the ferries are every hour. Pack a very small bag, I'll hide it under my blanket. Betty says her ex (deceased) left things that will do for me. Matron goes to London on Wednesdays. Her lover lives in Bermondsey. They are both very partial to eel pie. She catches the 11.21. Leave a note for Milly. Tell her you can't stand it here. Say you've gone home, back to the West Country, and there you'll stay, until the Lord decides. And tell them in the office you'll push me up and down Lob Lane for half an hour, show me the boats through the railings. You know the code? Norman nodded.

Worked like a dream, said Alphonse. I made a mistake in Calais, caught the slow train, not the fast one, didn't reach Paris till gone 11. But I learned a bit more about my weakness on the way, about sleeping, how I must just let it take me when it comes. A girl in one of the tree houses was hauling up a basket of fruit to her bare knees. Who was Betty? I asked. She had a narrow boat, said Alphonse, the Esperanza. Sick to death of the Home Counties, she was pining for Cumberland. Alf worked out the canals for her on the office computer. And the wheelchair? She assured him that would not be a problem. She would lash him safely to a stanchion by the tiller. He would steer. Besides, said Alphonse, Alf gave me to understand that once out of Avalon he was hopeful of a miracle cure. Betty, he said, had raised sicker than him.

The last time I saw Alphonse he was sitting in the square on the white folding seat he carried around with him for when he felt he must take a nap. His guitar stood beside him, leaning against the bike. A small jazz band was playing – clarinet, trumpet, double bass – and Alphonse sat no more than three yards away from them, plumb in front. Really, he was the only audience. Others strolled by, paused, moved on, but he sat there. He had told me that next day he intended to leave for Salamanca, a town he had always longed to see. And he added: time is running out. I began to cross the square, to say goodbye, but soon knew him, by the whole set of his body, to be sound asleep. I walked away, but very irresolutely, and soon halted again, behind him, at a distance.

The musicians played fast and loud, their eyes addressing one another, passing their discoveries to and fro, try this, take a risk, the unending possibilities. As I think of it now, my memory clears the place of everything else: there was a centre, in it Alphonse and the three musicians, on its circumference myself, watching and listening. Clarinet and trumpet, differently piercing, lifted to the blue sky, the bass bowed between them, fingering very fast, cocking an ear, listening the sounds out, his instrument touched into the life of the earth and drew it forth. Three young men, they stood, the music swayed and jigged them, but they stood, their feet were on the ground, the music shook them, and lifted. I was drawn closer, as in a dream, to within a few yards of Alphonse. He looked to be fast asleep. I committed him to memory: his slumped head, the straw hat oddly tilted, the red kerchief, blue collar, broad shoulders. Then I turned and left the square quickly. I wanted to be gone before the music stopped.

There is more, much more. Not one tenth enough have I thought about Alf, his flue brush of dirty-white hair, the look he had of a creature being backed into a corner who at the last minute, scared and canny, will escape. And was he useful at the lock gates? Did he steer well? How did Betty get him below deck? Skulking in Calais, I found a public library in which they would let me sit. On one of their computers I worked out how you might get by narrowboat from Cookham to Cumberland, the whole complicated leisurely itinerary, the Thames, the Oxford Canal, the Coventry and Ashley, Trent and Mersey... I got nearly to Kendal, I wrote it all out. And as for Alphonse... Cycling from Lyon along the left bank of the ice-green, prodigious Rhône, his fatigue overwhelmed him almost every hour. Then he halted, lay down if he could, slumped otherwise, and slept some strength back into his frame. On a large curve, where the river threw off its flotsam and jetsam, he found a folding white plastic chair, and carried that with him thereafter. But more wonderful still, he said, best of all, on a stretch miles from anywhere, late afternoon, not a soul in sight, he fell asleep in the saddle, slid to the ground, slept there by the bike which the trolley kept standing, slept and slept, and the next he knew a vast barge carrying great cubes of limestone had moored within six feet of him, and a nut-brown man and wife were kneeling over him, and how they chortled, he said, when he opened his eyes. They took him aboard, him and all his worldly goods, gave him food and wine, sat him in the bows on a sort of throne, he said, and like that, royally, he sailed into the south, under the endless white rapids of the stars.

An Island

20 October

THERE WEREN'T MANY on the boat – mostly birders coming over to observe the departures and for sightings of any rare vagrants. I eavesdropped a bit, on deck and in the bar they talked about nothing else. Before we left, one of them got texted that a red-eyed vireo had just been seen on Halangy dump and when he told the others they were taken up in a sort of rapture, big grown men with their beards, bad-weather wear and all the equipment. They made sounds that were scarcely words any more, little shouts and squeals, a hilarity, in the enchantment of their passion. I loitered on the fringes.

After a while, when we were clear of the harbour and coasting quietly along and had passed the first lighthouse, I went downstairs, right down to the lower saloon, below the water line, and lay on a bunk under a blanket. There was nobody else down there. I felt OK on my own in the big throbbing of the engines, I felt them to be in my chest, like a heart, but I was OK, I kept seeing the faces of the birders when they received the news about the red-eyed vireo, I heard their voices, the transformation wrought in them by their enthusiasm, and it seemed to me that I knew what it was like to be in a company of friends in a common passion that would do no harm. Then I must have slept, but not deeply, near the surface, in the rapids of sleep, not restful, and in the white-water hurry of the images the clearest, flitting not abiding but as clear as the blade of the moon when it cuts

45

through the clouds, was you. And I believed you wouldn't mind if I wrote to you now and then. Everyone needs a fellow-mortal to address. You won't mind?

When I went up on deck the islands were coming into view. I watched them materialise in their own domain of light. It seemed to me a quite peculiar blessing that a place so manifestly different, far away, out on the borders, could be approached by me.

At Halangy I went down the gangway among the birders in single file and soon found the boat to Enys.

So here I am, camped snugly in the angle of two walls for shelter against the expected weather, the site to myself, the season ending and the small birds resting up here in the tamarisk hedges before they launch themselves across the ocean.

Sunday 25 October

The island is barely half a mile wide at its widest. There's a channel of the sea on the east and open sea on the west and my home (for now) is mid-way between, just under the winds that mostly come from the west. My first evening there was a pause, a complete silence. My second, and all through the night, the weather came over me like nothing I have ever been out in or lain under before, so thorough in its strength, loud in its howling, the wind, the rain, the waves after hundreds of leagues without impediment making their landfall here. Weather knows itself at last when it finds some terra firma to hit against, and best, most thoroughly, knows itself when there are some habitations too and creatures in them who can feel what it is like. Soon after daybreak the rain ceased and I went out in the wind, crouching and gasping for my own small breath in it. The scraps of abandoned fields were strewn with stones, wreck, seaweed, dead things that had lived in salt water. The waves slid up the sheer face of the northern headland and spilled back milk-white off the crown. Nowhere are we higher than a hundred feet above the sea. I crawled along the chine in a blizzard of spindrift through the tumuli home to this tiny lair with every stitch of dress and pore of exposed flesh sticky and proofed with salt. My little stove was a wonder to me, its hoarse flame, the can of drinkable water, the inhalation of the steam of coffee.

Since then, though the wind has dropped, I can always hear the sea, like a vast engine working just over the hill. It's as though I've been taught something, had my ears and my heart opened to a fact of sound I was ignorant of and now I shall always be able to hear it, even in the city where you live, there on the pavement in the din of traffic if I paused and bowed my head I would hear this sea.

Tomorrow night I'll be closer still, but more secure. The woman who runs the campsite has offered me accommodation in a shed. I can fit it out as I like, she says, there's a table and chair and a camp bed in it already and she'll lend me a bigger stove. In return, I'll paint the wash-house here, do a few repairs, clear up, make myself useful. If she thinks me odd, she didn't say so. Generally someone blows in, she said, about this time and quite often over the years they've been about your age. You'll pick up more work if you want it, she said. If you're handy, if you want to stay. And it suddenly seemed to me that I *am* quite handy, that I do want to stay, that I'll be glad to be an odd-job man for a while and possess my own soul in patience in a shed within a stone's throw of the sea.

It's dark an hour earlier from today. I know you don't like that day of the year.

If you did want to write, c/o the campsite would find me. In fact, c/o Enys would, enough people have seen me by now on my walks or at the post office.

26 October
I went in the church today. It's down by the quay. Every now and then I remember – I mean, feel again – why I was ever

with the monks. Four solid walls containing stillness, the light through the windows. Really it's only that, the possibility of being quiet and of receiving some illumination. I don't think that's too much to ask once in a while. Afterwards I mooched among the graves. There aren't many different names, half a dozen families seem to own the place. Newcomers get cremated and are remembered on tablets by the gate. The sea is so close, who wouldn't want to be buried or at least remembered here?

I like my shed. It smells of the sea. It's roomier than I expected and with electricity too because there's a workshop on the same plot, not used now but still connected. Mary lent me a heater as well as a stove, I trundled them down in a wheelbarrow with the rest of my gear and now I'm nicely at home. I cleaned the place out, mended the roof where the felt had blown off, shaved the window so it closes tight … Things like that. A few other jobs want doing and there are all manner of tools lying idle in the workshop. Help yourself, Mary said. Tomorrow I'll start on the wash-house. That's the deal.

I've put my notebook, my writing paper and my couple of books on planks from the sea laid over two packing-cases. That's what Mary meant by a table. It's to write on, read at, eat off – under the window that faces out towards the sea. The chair's a real one, decently made. It came in off a wreck many years ago. The bed I shall call a truckle bed because I like that word. I took your photo out and did think of standing it on the planks to glance at while I write to you – but I shan't. I keep my eyes on the page, the nib, the black ink, the making of the letters and the words. If I stare out of the window towards the dune that hides the sea, if I let the vagueness come over, if I don't keep my eyes by force on the here and now, I see you at once, it's my gift and my affliction.

31 October

The last boat of the season arrives and leaves today. That's not as final as it sounds, there's a helicopter from Halangy once a week and I daresay I could scrape together enough for the fare if I panicked and had to get out. But the way things are now I don't think I shall panic. I'm as well off here as anywhere. Wherever I was, there'd still be the want of you.

Yesterday, if you'd been watching, I think you would have laughed out loud. (Your laughter is like nobody else's, it always made me feel there were deeper, freer, more abundant sources of mirth than I would ever have access to.) The birders arrived. I looked up from writing and there they were, about thirty of them, all men, in army camouflage, with their heavy tripods, cameras and telescopes, they must have come over the hill to this west side and they lined up barely twenty yards away, with their backs to me, in silence, in the mild early-morning light. After a while I went out and stood behind them. None paid me any attention. And when I asked I got two words in reply: rosy starling. I could see where they were looking – through the opening of the hedges, slantwise about three hundred yards down the length of the dune – but I couldn't see any bird. Then they all gasped and made the sounds of communal glee I had heard on the boat, then a great shout and they gathered up their equipment and began to run heavily away. The one I was standing next to, a fat man even more laden than his comrades, set off last. The others were almost out of sight and hadn't waited for him and nobody turned round to see was he following or not. His cumbersomeness troubled me for the rest of the day.

Sunday 1 November

I couldn't sleep for some hours last night. I thought very *brokenly* of you. Or, to be more exact, very *breakingly* – you were breaking, or my power to remember or imagine you was impaired, like sight or hearing, and back came the worry that everything I ever held true will crumble, perish and turn to dust from within, from within me, the power to uphold any faith and hope and love will erode, perhaps very quickly the way a cliff might collapse that was riddled through and through and nobody had known. I got up, to be less at the mercy of all this, and went out to the dune, the tide was high, close, but the washing, sliding, unfurling and withdrawal of it was very muted under cloud and in a light fog. That bay is a horseshoe, its headlands and an island behind and some reefs in part barricade it, so that in a storm the ocean breaks through very violently, being fretted, slewed and rifled by these hindrances, but last night it made a lingering and gentle entrance, at leisure, dispensing itself, its immensity, easefully and as though mercifully. Having seen this and after my fashion understood it in a light without moon or stars, a light embodied in drifts of vapour, silvery, I went back into my shed in the embrace of the tamarisks and behind closed eyes I insisted on that gentle incoming and could still hear the sounds of it, the breathing of water over shingle, and this morning I felt something had been added to my stock of resources against disintegration: an ocean entering quietly and giving bearably.

Sunday 8 November
There was a bonfire last night, on the beach that twins with mine, over the hill. They built it well below high water on the fine shingle and the weed. I haven't stared into the heart of such a fire for years. It was mostly old pallets and wood-wormed timbers, but loppings from the pittosporum hedges too and their leaves flared and vanished with an almost liquid sizzle. I noticed that flames can live for a second or two quite detached from the substance they were burning – in the air, just above, they dance and vanish. There was hardly any wind so that the fire extending in sparks reached very high.

I met a few people. Several came up and said hello and I got a couple of offers of labour, cash-in-hand, which I need since what I do on the campsite I'm paid for with my shed. The hotel manager offered me some painting and decorating.

He has closed for the winter. He kept open last year but this year trade is worse. Amiable chap, a bit nervous. Then a young man who farms at the south end asked had I ever cut hedges and I said yes, I had, years ago. He said there'd be plenty to do for him, if I liked. When I was with the monks I simplified the whole business into the two words: work and pray. The work was all with my hands, and by prayer I meant concentrating on whatever good I could imagine or remember, so as not to go to bits.

The women had made soup and hotdogs and there was a trestle table with beer and wine on and things for the kids. You helped yourself. I put my last ten pound note in the kitty. I felt very blithe. And when after that I got my offers of work I wondered at my ever losing faith.

Much later, I came back. I wanted to watch the sea overwhelm the fire, and I did so, very closely. The hissing and the conversion of flame to steam were remarkable but best I liked the ability of fire to survive quite a while on blackened beams that floated. The sea swamped the *ground* of the fire but strewed its upper elements for a briefly continuing life on the surface left and right. True, the waves were soft. Breakers would finish it quickly.

20 November

The island is used to people passing through – or people trying to settle and failing. There are the few families who rule the graveyard, that stock won't leave and it will be many years before they die out or get diluted and lose their identity among the incomers who take root. A family from Wolverhampton, another from Bristol, another from Halifax are powerful and one of them may dominate in the end. But if they want to be buried they'll have to go elsewhere, here they'll have to make do with a tablet on the wall by the way in. So some do settle, they blow in and root tenaciously. But the chief impression you get is of instability. Whether it's sex or panic, I can't tell, but every year there's some break-up, re-arrangement and departure.

I think they quite like the people who are passing through. The island economy, such as it is, depends on them. Of course, they're a risk as well, any one of them might become the solvent of a marriage and perhaps of a small business too. There was a baker here till a few years ago, then a girl came to help in the café and he left with her for London when the season ended. I guess some wives and husbands watch very anxiously who will land when the season starts again; others will watch hopefully. And it is certain that several in houses on their own have watched year after year, have gone down to the quay when the launch came in and have idled there and were never looked at by a stranger who might have stayed. They watch long after the likely time has passed. One such, a very lonely man, against all the odds and beyond all rational hope was chosen, as you might say, by a visitor not half his age. She stayed three years, then left him and the islands without warning.

I've got more than enough work now. In fact the manager offered me a room in the hotel but I like my shed too much. I'd pay Mary some rent but she won't have it, so I've begun tidying her workshop. Well, more than tidying it. I'll clear all the junk out, repair outside and in, see to the tools. She says that's a job long wanted doing and who would do it but somebody blown in? She's a Jackson, one of the old families, widowed, her two sons fish for crabs and lobsters, she has a couple of holiday-lets. The workshop was her father's, that's his boat there in the nettles. He was in his workshop or out in his boat most of the time. There was something wrong when he came back from the war. He more or less gave up talking, she said.

The hotel manager, Brian, is on his own. His wife left him at the start of the summer holidays, went to the mainland. It's not even that she fell in love. Suddenly she'd just had enough and she left him, taking the children. He dresses well and is altogether particular about his appearance and his environment. He's a rather fussy employer, which I don't mind. I see through his eyes, at heart he is terrified. He talks a lot to me and I don't mind that either. I guess he's ten years my junior. This is the first year he's had to close and it worries him. Not that he owns the place. A very rich man does. You don't have to stay here, I tell him. If it fails. No, of course not, he says. With my qualifications I can go where I like.

He's taken three other people on, all young. A boy from Melbourne on his way round the world, called Chris. A girl from Manchester, Elaine, who used to come here as a child and should be at university but couldn't face it and is having another year off. And Sarah, from Nottingham, who has finished university and is wondering what to do. I could have had a warm room on a back corridor with this attractive trio. I don't think they would have objected to me.

The hotel is shut till the end of March but Brian opens the bar a couple of nights a week and the regulars arrive. I make an appearance when I feel up to it. If asked, I tell the makings of a tale about myself. Nobody probes. Either it's tact or they're not very curious. My kind come and go, every year there's at least one of us. Mostly they talk and I listen. I'm a good listener. From the hotel back to my shed is no great distance. I go past the Pool, quite an extent of water with only a bar of sand between it and the sea. The Pool is very softly-spoken, even when there's a wind, at most you hear a steady lapping. The sea on my left, unless it's very low tide, makes an insistent noise. At high tide walking between the two waters it feels peculiar being a drylander who needs air to breathe. Some nights the dark is intense, the pale sand, the pale dead grass and rushes either side, are all the light there is. There's a lighthouse far out to the south-west, the wink of its beam comes round, and another, closer, to the north, but all you'll see of that one is the ghost of the passage of light on the underside of the cloud. I use my torch as little as possible. I like to feel my way, in at the opening of the tamarisks to my wooden home.

27 November

The work in the hotel is easy enough. We paint and decorate and we clear things out. Some days I drive the quad and trailer and take old fridges and televisions to the tip. Yesterday I fed fifteen hundred of last year's brochures into the incinerator, a rusty iron contraption with a tall chimney, we call it Puffing Billy. Children are mesmerised by it, Brian says.

Brian misses his family. They are living in the house they kept in Guildford just in case the venture here failed, which it has. He is not from Guildford nor is his wife. They moved there from the north, following the opportunities of his work. Brian detests Guildford and so does his wife. It distresses him that she would rather be there than here. And that she has nobody else, that she didn't fall in love and move to a new place with a new man so as to start again, that also distresses him. He has not even lost out to somebody more desirable. It is simply that she doesn't want to be with him. So she leaves, and takes her children with her, as of right. He hasn't the heart to contest it. Really, he agrees with her. In this beautiful place, a paradise some would say, she can't be happy with him, she can't even make do with him. Instead she takes herself and the children off to a place she detests, just so as not to be with him, and in his heart of hearts he can't blame her. It is not even passionate, she does not passionately hate him, wish to kill him, avenge herself on him for her wasted years. She just wants to be away from him. He tells me this in the bar when everyone else has gone. But he is quite sober, he is not a drunkard, nor is he a gambler, nor in a million years would he raise his hand against her, he scarcely ever raises his voice, he has never hit the children nor even frightened them by throwing things and swearing. It is not rational that she should leave him. It is not in her material interest. Still, she has. He hopes at least the children will come and visit him next Easter when the season has begun again and there are boat trips to the other islands. He will take a day off and perhaps they would like to go fishing. He tells me all this in the empty bar, quite late, still cleanly dressed in his suit and tie, and his watery eyes over his trim moustache appeal to me not for pity but for an explanation. And yet he knows it needs no explanation. I am in my work clothes, which are not much different from any other clothes I've got, my nails are broken and there's paint on my fingers. I know that he confides in me because he assumes I am passing through. Also that I leave his warm hotel and go back in the dark to a place of my own barely half a mile away but out on the rim, as far as he is concerned, eccentric, and when he looks me in the eyes and shakes me by the hand next morning, altogether affable, he knows or thinks he knows that he has nothing to fear from me. I think he assumes I am at least as unhappy as he is. And he is certain that before very long I will go away and he will never see me again.

Does Brian interest you? I am trying to interest you in him.

30 November
I learned this from a lone birder, itself a rare creature, who wandered, fully accoutred, into my precinct early yesterday: that in the winter, and especially about now, first thing they do on their computers every morning is check out the weather over the western Atlantic. They pray for winds, colossal storm winds, blowing our way, because on winds like that the nearctic vagrants get blown in. The worse the storms, the longer-lasting, the better for us, he said. Birds making laborious headway from, it might be, Alaska to, say, Nicaragua, for all their struggling get blown off course – three thousand miles off course – and land up here. Mostly singletons, my birder said, rare things, first-time sightings, and mostly, so far as anyone can tell, they don't, except in a thousand photographs, survive. The star last year was a great blue heron, a juvenile. The winds blew steadily for a week or more and the birders waited – not for a great blue heron in particular:

a varied thrush or a laughing gull or a Wilson's snipe would have made them happy enough. The GBH, as he kept calling it, was beyond their wildest dreams. The creature landed exhausted on Halangy, in the reeds of Lower Moors, around mid-day on 7 December and was observed and photographed by scores of enthusiasts, summoned from here, there and everywhere, all afternoon, feeding, until the weather worsened, torrential rain came horizontally in, the light declined and the juvenile vanished, 'never to be seen again'. My birder liked that phrase and repeated it, in tones of wonderment: 'never to be seen again'.

6 December

You mustn't think I live too monkishly. I'm never very cold and I eat pretty well. I found an old army greatcoat in the workshop and I put that round my shoulders when I sit and read or write. I can get most things it occurs to me to want at the post office near the quay and, besides, there's a shopping boat to Halangy once a week, though if the weather's very rough the supply ship from the mainland can't sail. I went to Halangy last week and spent a good bit on books. The one bookseller is giving up and he wanted rid of his stock. I bought a couple of things I know you'd like and now they and the rest sit on a shelf I made of a plank of driftwood.

Altogether my shed is quite well appointed. When I take junk from the hotel or from Mary's workshop to the tip I always look through what other people have thrown out. I got the brackets for my shelf from there, and an Italian coffee-maker, a Bialetti, one like yours, that works OK, and two nice cups. Two wine glasses and a beer mug also. There was a mirror I might have had but I didn't want it in the shed. I've the wash-house to myself just up the hill. Mary gave me a dinner plate. I'm OK. I don't think you would like the long hours of darkness but I don't mind so much. There's work in the evenings at the hotel if I want, and there's the bar some nights. But often I prefer it here. I do a bit more at the workshop. It's coming on nicely. And Mary gave me a little radio so I lie on my truckle bed and listen to that sometimes. You might think the news would be easier to bear being so remote but in fact it's worse. I suppose I'm not distracted. The little box in the dark is very close, the voices say the bad things direct into your ear. When I've had enough or if I don't feel up to listening to the radio I lie there and listen to the sea instead. And I think – though it's not exactly thinking, more like being a shade already in the underworld among the whispering of other shades in chance encounters out of time. You are among them some nights, though always as a visitor, you always make it clear you don't belong there. I've wondered lately when it was I stopped expecting or even hoping to be happy. I push the date back further and further, into my youth, into my childhood, vengefully, as though to wipe out my life, I cast my shadow back, longer and longer, to chill all the life I ever had in darkness though I know it is a terrible untruth I am perpetrating.

Here's OK. I do like the people and they interest me. And I like the work, especially in the fields southward. I cut the hedges. Nathan has given me a field to start with that hasn't been cut since he took over, the tops have shot up six or eight feet higher than they should be. He said the trimmer, fixed on the tractor, would hardly work and could I manage with loppers, a bow saw and the ladder? It would be slow work, he knew. I answered that suited me perfectly. I'll tash it with the pitchfork and come round after with a buckrake on the tractor. Fine, he said. So when the weather's kind I skip the painting and decorating and cut fence all day, on my own, content. I find the old slant cuts from years ago, where the height should be, and work along level with them. It's mostly pittosporum, a silver grey, they remind me of the olive branches, perhaps it was on Ithaca. They make a whoosh when they fall over my shoulder through the air. You cut an opening in no time and there's the sea, running some mornings a hard blue, then suddenly black, jade green, turquoise and you see stilts of sun far out probing over pools of light, and shafts of rainbow almost perpendicular, just beginning their curve, then they break off. If I stay I'll have cut the hedges of all of Nathan's fields. That will be something done. And why shouldn't I stay?

Nathan and his wife are making a go of it. She's local, he arrived. There's no future in bulbs and flowers any more so they're growing potatoes, broccoli, carrots, spinach, stawberries, all manner of things in abundance. The hotel buys from them and so do the self-catering visitors. His wife works as hard as he does. They'll make out all right, you can see it in their faces, the way they look at you, candid and appraising. They're settled, they'll make their way, their children will grow up here and have a good inheritance.

9 December

I had a shock this morning. I was at my table writing, concentrating hard, trying to be exact, vaguely conscious of the daylight strengthening, the sparrows and starlings in the hedges, the sea risen up under the dune, and I raised my eyes, for the right word, to get nearer the truth, and saw through the glass a face so close I had for an instant, long enough for a lifetime, the conviction that I looked into a mirror and the face I saw was mine: a big lopsided grinning face, bald-headed but for some white remnants, the eyebrows albino-pale, the teeth all angles, the blurting tongue very red, the eyes of a blue so weak it looked dissolved almost to nothing in an overwhelming blankness… Twelve hours later, writing this letter − I call it a letter − to you, I don't conjure up the face by force of memory to let you see it too, I can see it on the window pane, this side not outside, on the black glass which when there is no light in the tamarisk grove does indeed more or less distinctly reflect my own. The worst is its mix of senility and childishness − that raised the hairs on my neck, not for nearly a year have I felt such convincing proof that the heart of life is horror. He raised a hand and tapped on the window, his big head wobbled and wagged from side to side, then his hand went to his mouth, to cover his chortling, as though he remembered it is rude to laugh however ridiculous the stranger you are looking at may be. When he did that – made the gesture of consideration for my feelings – I knew there was no harm in him and tears came to my eyes, my face was wet with tears, I wiped them away, I smeared the salt of them across my lips, and seeing this he uncovered his mouth, showed me the palms of both his empty hands, made little grunts and mutters of pity for me, his features worked, sorrow possessed them, and I stood up, opened the door, to welcome him in. That was too much, too suddenly, he backed away, but as though he didn't wish to, as though he'd stay if he could be sure there was no harm in me. I put out my hand, as you might to a bird or an animal that – you supposed – had come to your door because it needed food or care, and he paused at that, near the useless boat, about fifteen yards between us. Then he shook his head, as though tired of it, as though dispirited, as though not wanting my company after all, and slouched away, out at the horseshoe opening towards the dune and the sea.

A minute later, while I still stood there in my borrowed army greatcoat, I heard a woman's voice calling from behind my shed, from in among the old bulb fields, calling his name, Eddie! Eddie! in a tone which sounded familiar with the tribulation but still not able to bear it. I turned, she appeared, she was bare-headed, wearing a big coat, which she huddled around her unbuttoned, over a long floral dress, and her feet in wellington boots. Her hair was as white as the sea when it slides back off the headland down the sheer cliff into the making of the next assault. Everything in the child-man who had lumbered off towards the shore was written in the lines and in the aura, in the whole spirit and bearing of her face. My son, she said. He's gone towards the shore, I said. She made a little cry, called out again, Eddie! Oh Eddie, don't go hurting yourself! and hurried away. I followed and saw her find him, scold him, wrap him in her arms, lead him by the hand down the sand path between the Pool and the sea.

17 December

I witnessed a thing last week you might have liked. There's a spit of pebbles at the south end covered at high water but running out to a lichened castle of rocks that stinks of birds, grows a rank verdure and is never covered. I came over the hill, one of the pocked-and-blistered-with-burials small hills, and saw a man out there on that low-water rope of stone and he was busy building. I got off the skyline quick, to watch. I was in the dead bracken, blotted out of view, like a hunter, watching him. About mid-way, where it would be covered a fathom deep, he was building an arch. I watched two hours, wrapped in Mary's father's army greatcoat, while the man exposed and utterly intent worked at his arch. I saw that to get the thing to stand he must build inside it also as it grew, supporting it all the way and especially, of course, where the curves, the desire of either side to meet in a keystone on thin air, began. He, by his cleverness, aided those pillars in their wish to curve, become the makings of an arch and meet. How he worked! – with tact, with care, with nous and cognizance of what any stone of a certain size and weight and shape could do and couldn't do. And when it was made and the arch was fitted around and relying on the merely *serving* wall of stones, I prayed a prayer such as I hardly ever prayed in all my time with the monks, that his keystone would hold and the two half-arches, so needing one another, so incapable of any life without, would by their meeting and their obedience to gravity (their suicidal wish to fall) over the void would hold when one by one he took his servant necessary stones away. It held: stone rainbow on its own two heavy feet, because the halves of its bodily curve had met and all desire to fall became the will to last miraculously for ever. The man, the builder-man, stood back and contemplated it and nodded. Walked all round it, pausing, viewing it from every angle, nodded again, glanced at his watch (acknowledging he would die) then set off fast from the spit of pebbles to the path, I suppose to catch a boat. And I crept down from hiding to have a close look at his work.

The tide, far out, had turned. I came back later and watched by starlight till the waves, washing in from either side, had entered under the arch and it stood in them. Any big sea would have toppled it but that was a quiet night, the ripples worked as the man had, little by little, very gradually and as it were considerately turning air to water. I watched his work disappear. Back in my bed I thought of the two curves meeting, the keystone weighing them secure, the water flowing and swirling through and over and all around. And I got up early, before it was light, and found my way down there again, past the Pool with its lapping and its queer aquatic voices, past the hotel with its anxious manager, to see the stranger's arch, whether it still stood. And it did! It had withstood the reflux and stood there draggled with green weed under the flickering beginnings of an almost lightless day.

The arch survived two more tides, then the sea got rough and when I went next there was a heap of stones and only its maker or a witness of its making would believe that such a thing had ever been.

Sunday 20 December

Some foul weather, I've been confined, for work, in the hotel. Chris is trying to persuade Elaine not to bother with university – waste of time – but to continue round the world with him. At the end of March he will resume his plane ticket. He thinks he will skip the rest of Europe and head straight for Goa. She should come with him, he says. Elaine isn't sure. She might stay on here, she says, if Brian offered her work for the season or if there was anything going in the café or at the post office. Chris says she should think bigger than that. Europe's finished, he says. She should come along with him, he'll show her a different life. Sarah is furious with Chris. She has short black hair, very bright eyes. He tells me she's probably a lesbian. She tells me she knows for certain he's made the same offer – what exactly is he offering? – to a Polish girl who works in a bar on Halangy, a Lithuanian girl helping at the school on St Nicholas, and doubtless a few more. She tells Elaine she should go to university, get a degree, and consider his 'offer' after that, if she must. Elaine points out that Sarah, with her degree, is painting the hotel kitchen, same as her. That's for now, says Sarah. I've got better ideas than trailing round the world after a beach-bum. Chris denies he's a beach-bum. He's got a diploma in hotel management. Any woman coming along with him might do very well for herself, in Australia.

They have these discussions while we work or around the table at coffee-time. I like all three of them. Sarah is very forthright, Chris is a bit afraid of her. He must be ten years older than Elaine but when Sarah is speaking neither he nor Elaine looks very self-confident. Chris tells me his mother came from Essex – Chelmsford, he thinks. She was in a home with her little brother and the home sent her, without her brother, to Australia, to another home, somewhere in the outback. She had a bad time, Chris says. She died when he was ten. He doesn't know who his father is. The Christian Brothers looked after him. He says in his opinion he did pretty well to survive all that and get to college and come out with a diploma in hotel management. I agree. All I say is Elaine needs some qualifications too, for her self-defence. Really I meant self-realisation but I couldn't think how to put it. Anyway, self-defence isn't far wrong. Chris shrugs. Elaine tells me the holidays she had on Enys were the best times of her life. The family was happy then and she values the holidays even more now that it isn't. When she has an afternoon off she visits the old places again. They stayed in a house by the beach where the bonfire was. I asked her did she remember Eddie at all. Yes, she said, poor Eddie and his poor mother. The first time she saw him she screamed and ran away but after a while she got used to him. He was only a child, she said, although a grown man. Once he gave her a wedding-cake shell, the way a little boy might. I've still got it, she said.

Christmas Eve

Brian's passion is family history. One good thing about being closed, he says, is it gives him time to work at that. He spends hours online. Even when he opens the bar for an evening he'll go to his room after they've all gone home, switch on, and at once he's back in 1911 or 1901. Those censuses, he says, are a lifeline to him. He shakes his head over the superabundance they open up. Last a lifetime, he says. He is very anxious to get things right, but, of course, having worked at it for some years now, in fact since the children were born, he's well aware that absolute certainty is impossible. Before the censuses and all the other resources came online, when he and his wife were still living in Guildford, he'd go down to the National Archive and root around for hours, whenever he could. And he wrote to surviving relatives in Britain, Ireland, Australia, New Zealand, Canada and the USA, to get their stories. He has an impressive collection, still being added to, of wills, deeds, private correspondence and certificates of births, marriages and deaths. Mostly he researches his wife's side of the family, it is more interesting than his, he has got much further back on her side than on his own, to 1685, to be exact, and he expects in the end he'll be able to prove they came over with the Conquest. Herself, she wasn't a bit interested in her family's history and whenever he told her something he'd found that he found very interesting – for example, that her maternal great-grandfather, a carter in Lower Broughton, was illegitimate and very likely the son of a priest – she looked at him in a way he remembers vividly now she has gone. Still he carries on with her side of the family more than with his, he still wants to know where she came from, so to speak. Of course, when the censuses were put online and you could spend all the time you liked in your own bedroom studying them, you pretty soon had to face the fact that an awful lot of things just didn't tally. Family stories handed down as gospel were quite often flatly contradicted by those lists of people resident or visiting at a certain address on 31 March 1901 or 2 April 1911. A Thomas Huntley, for example, dealer in calico, on Brian's side, always said to have abandoned his wife, a Gracey, daughter of a clerk in a tram company, and to have fled to Ireland on the day of Queen Victoria's diamond jubilee, is recorded in 1901 at 14 Goole Road, Tadcaster as head of the household with his wife and four children, among them Brian's great-grandmother through whom, presumably, the story that he was the black sheep had come down. On the other hand, you couldn't always assume the official record was right and the family story wrong. Surely not everyone told the truth on census day (many told nothing at all) and as a hotel manager Brian knew perfectly well that what people said about themselves wasn't always the truth. It only started to look like the truth if you wrote it down. And of course, if it ever got on to an official record card or on to a police computer then it looked very true indeed, until somebody proved it false.

Now Brian thinks I'm interested in family history, and perhaps I am. He thinks I'm as interested in his family history and his wife's as he is himself. So he might say, for example, without any preliminary, By the way, their first house wasn't where I thought it was – 11 Littleton Road, near the river, in that very insalubrious area – it was 311, one of the newest, out near the race course, almost in open country, so they must have been better off than I've been supposing – they being his wife's great-grandparents.

He is trying to forget it's Christmas. Well, that's not true. He's going to open the bar tomorrow and give everyone a drink and a mince pie who cares to come. That's typical of him, he does what he thinks he ought to. But for himself he's trying to forget it's Christmas.

I've been wondering would I have been quite useless as a father.

I counted thirteen swans on the Pool today. The water was very turbid, the wind blowing strongly. I saw them through the hotel window, I was painting the frames inside. It moved me to tears, how white they were on the turbid water and how they held steady against the wind, or tacked and steered into it, or let it drift them when they chose.

Elaine tells me that Sarah isn't in the least a lesbian, not that it would matter if she were. Men, especially men like Chris, always call women lesbians if they answer back. Sarah's degree is in marine biology. If *she* stayed, Elaine says, it would be to do some good.

A hedge of pittosporum when you've trimmed not just the tops but also the face of it there in a bright sun if the wind comes across, it shivers as though the shorn condition were hard to bear.

I've noticed that for some days after rough weather the sea may continue to be very troubled. The wind has lessened almost to nothing, but great rollers ride in from somewhere far far out. There might be no wind at all but a sea arrives that looks worked up by a tempest. I had taken to calling it the phenomenon of insufficient cause but that's not quite accurate. It's more a want of explanation. Such a sea and not a breath of wind. No apparent reason. That's closer. Of course there's an explanation, but far out, far deeper out, beyond my wits and senses.

Some nights you are as clear as the brightest and most definite among the many constellations. Other nights you look threadbare, the winds of space blow through you, your shape is still just about discernible but only by me and only because, even breaking up, it reminds me of something.

Mary tells me that before the war her father made the children's toys. She told me this when I told her I'd found an old treadle fretsaw and thought I could get it working again. He made a big dolls' house for the first two girls, all just right, very exact, with the proper furniture in every room, everything neatly and brightly painted. He made a monkey dangling on a wire between scissor sticks and when you pressed the bottom ends together the wire tightened and the monkey did acrobatics. And he made a yacht for the first boy, Joseph, with all the rigging perfect. He called her Star of the Sea. Mary remembers a day when Joseph – he's dead now – sailed that yacht on the Pool and the wind blew her right out among the swans and how upset Joseph was to see her out there in the middle among those big creatures. And Father said not to worry, and fetched the little punt up from the beach and launched it on the shallow Pool. That was the first time he gave Joseph an oar and said they should row back from the middle together, once they'd rescued the yacht. At first they went round and round like a leaf, not advancing at all, but then Joseph got the hang of it and they came in and was Joseph proud of himself! I said there were a couple of hulls I'd found in the workshop and also some rigging but that had perished. Mary said, You'll find all sorts in there. I found his marquetry knives, I said, and two or three packs of the veneers you need for marquetry. He made my mother some beautiful things, Mary said. One was his own boat heading out down the channel at dawn for the pots out near the lighthouse. We've still got that one. What became of the others I don't know. I don't suppose many do marquetry nowadays. He was often down here in his shed after the war, but he didn't make much, less and less in fact. Or he would go out in his boat but not really for the fishing.

I feel on edge, the least thing would do it. But also I feel something you'd hardly credit in me, an insouciance. Really I don't much care what happens next.

31 December

Quite a few came to Brian's Christmas party, thirty I should say. The men put on suits and ties and since I'd only ever seen them in work clothes before, they were very strange to me. I don't mean they looked in the least ridiculous or uncomfortable. On the contrary, it felt like manners: this is an occasion, this is how you look. But their hands and faces, especially the boatmen's, bare in their Sunday best, it brought the outdoors, the weather, the sea into the room, which Brian had gone to the trouble of decorating. The women had dressed up even more. They wore a good deal of make-up and jewellery. And the children, especially the girls, more children than I knew existed, they were also dressed for the occasion. I had no decent clothes to change into.

The first glass and the mince pies were on the house. Then Brian went behind the bar and Chris joined him.

I had a conversation with one of the boatmen – Matthew, I think his name was, he has a ginger beard – about the way things drift. I told him I'd found bits of charred wood here on the west side, bits of blue pallet, that I was pretty sure had come from the bonfire on the east side. He shrugged and said quite likely but I shouldn't make a rule of it, you never could tell. Tide, current, wind, you never know. People go in the water here and are never seen again. Perhaps they land up somewhere, perhaps they don't. Take Alf Lewis last summer, he went in the channel, drunk, so you can understand him drowning, but he's never come up again so far as anyone knows. I don't know about Alf Lewis, I said. Matthew shrugged. He blew in. Now he's gone. Good riddance, some say. I waited but he wouldn't say more. So instead I nodded towards the bar and said it was nice of Brian to give everyone a drink and a mince pie. Matthew nodded, but as though he'd have disagreed if I'd been somebody worth disagreeing with. Then I made a mistake. I asked did Lucy ever come to things like this. Matthew looked me in the eyes and slowly shook his head, which I took to mean, It's none of your business, and not, No, Lucy never comes to things like this. He's a big man, a big beard, with very small eyes. I asked would he like another drink. He said, No thanks, so I left him and went to the bar myself.

Later – I was already thinking of making my surreptitious exit – Sarah and Elaine came over to me in the window. I had noticed their transformation, among the other women, but close up it shocked me, they seemed sent in their beauty and gaiety to remind me of what I had never striven hard enough to possess and now never would and did not deserve. Their arms were bare, Elaine wore a necklace of pale jade, Sarah a bracelet of lapis-lazuli, her dress was a dark blue and that colour and the colour of Elaine's dress, a blue-green, I had often watched travelling over the sea from the top of my ladder in Nathan's fields in the wind and the swishing to earth of the olive-grey loppings of pittosporum. They were tipsy and full of mirth, knowing their own attractiveness, knowing how their dresses and the occasion, the decorations, the light of the sky and the sea through the window, the wine, how it all worked to increase their youthfulness and beauty, the life in them, beyond what I could bear to contemplate. They were close together, I think of them now as having each an arm around the other's waist, and a glass in the outer hand, and like that they came up close and kissed me, one on each cheek, so that I was for a moment fully in their aura, the scent in their hair, the wine on their breath, all the gaiety. Then they stood back, close together, childish. Elaine said, We came to say Happy Christmas, and nudged Sarah with her shoulder. Sarah said, We don't know anything about you. You're our workmate and we don't know anything about you. We know everything about Chris and quite a bit about Brian, and Elaine and I are best mates but we don't know a thing about you. Is it true you were a monk? Chris says he's sure you were a monk. He says he can always tell a monk, because of his early life.

Eyes and smiles, dresses and stones of the sea, they were cajoling me and I felt what it would be like (would have been like) to be a person with companions, alive in an easy exchange with a dear friend or two, and if I'd been able to speak I should have tried to say so, perhaps as a preamble, on the threshold of candour: that their youth and gaiety and delight in themselves had opened me, a little at least, so that for a moment, for the duration of their waiting to hear what I might answer, I saw into a world so spacious and cheerful my own felt like the cramped cast-off shell some naked crab had squatted in and years later still peered out of and dared not leave. I was, I said. Chris is right. But it was years ago, I was his age – younger even – I was about your age. They didn't want to be serious. Had there been the least music they would have danced. They didn't want to be polite, considerate, sympathetic. They wanted everything to be funny for an hour or so. And in their careless good nature they wanted me to be like that too. I should have taken each by the hand, there and then, and summoned up a syrtaki from Ithaca or Samothrace and danced the lumbering graceless dance of my leaden soul, right there among the dressed-up islanders, between two girls, danced, and they would have harkened either side of me and heard the tune in my head and taken it up, lifted and lightened it, and led me and I'd have followed, dancing, dancing, ugly bear of a soul, dancing, until I was changed. Were you chaste? Sarah asked. Was it hard, our age, being chaste? Were you obedient? Did you do as you were told? Will you obey Elaine and me if we ask you to do a thing? I can see you wouldn't mind being poor, I agree it is disgusting to be rich. But was it not hard, our age, being chaste? They wanted me to increase the laughter in them, they gave me the chance, but I could feel the shadow of me, of my seriousness, the stain, the leaden atmosphere of me, beginning to creep over them, like bad after-thoughts, like regret, like the sad obligation to apologise, and I knew I would defeat them and the whole occasion, the light dancing at the window, the sparkle and the fumes of wine, the will to gaiety, I would defeat it in them, so I said what I always say, Forgive me, and left.

I tell you this so that you will know, again, that you were right.

Leaving the hotel, I went to the church. There was a service Christmas Eve and another Christmas Morning. I didn't attend either. The first was the children's nativity play which they'd been rehearsing for weeks. The props – a crib in a stable made of blue pallets, the doll, the toy animals – were still there and the costumes (those of the Kings so scarlet, black, silver, gold and sparkling) were folded and laid to one side. All the church was decorated with greenery and the earliest narcissi and butcher's broom for holly. Six oil lamps hang from the ceiling on long chains, six beautiful brass bowls and the glass funnels of flame. Six windows: the two north illustrate the verses concerning the lily of the fields; the two east are without script or image, only light; the two south read, Let the waters bring forth abundantly the moving creature that hath life. And they show that life. The lights and colours of all six windows put me in mind of the dresses, the necklace and the bracelet of Sarah and Elaine.

Being with the monks soon killed even my desire to believe in God. But I love such houses as this one on Enys, so well built, so close to the quay where every day there is a busyness of boats and goods and people and the sea embraces equally the living worshippers and the dead. And the beautiful work in the house, the fitness of it, and the flowers and greenery of the island for decoration, the singing, the children's yearly acting out the old story, the light and the silence when everyone has left, how I love all that.

It was too early to go back to my shed. My nervousness and sadness were acute and I didn't think I'd be able to combat them well enough by any reading or by cleaning and sharpening the tools in Mary's workshop. Most days towards dusk it is like that. How will I secure the oblivion of sleep? I've often thought no sane and happy person could bear my life for even an hour if suddenly translated into it. Only because my life has *grown* to be like this, because it has habituated me to it, is it bearable. If it is bearable.

I climbed the hill that forms the southern headland of my little bay. All the six hills have their tumuli but here, nearest my shed, the remains are especially apparent. Many events of late have assumed a peculiar definiteness, like finality. They present themselves to me as though prepared – as though they are ready and they lie in wait. So on this hill I found that the best preserved of the tombs, which I last visited a couple of weeks ago, has been, so to speak, further clarified, made more compelling, by somebody outlining the shape of it with large clean ovoid pebbles through the gorse and heather. I supposed at once that the builder of the arch had returned and done this too. First because it was a labour. I counted two hundred and seven pebbles and they must have been carried, and surely not more than three or four at a time, up from the one beach under the headland where in all sizes the pebbles are smooth and egg-shaped. At his way into the zone of the tumulus he had placed two larger stones, each as much as you could carry from sea-level. And the kist, where the corpse had huddled up small and which I had always seen empty, he had floored quite deeply with clean limpet shells. The pebbles lay around the sinuous circumference the way you might lay out a necklace on a surface, to see what shapes it was capable of when not determined by a woman's neck and throat. The pebbles are smoothed more or less finely according to the coarseness of the granite's crystals – which decide the colours also, the shades of grey, white, pink, almost black, to which, as he strung his chosen stones to enclose the grave, he had paid close attention. The kist at the heart, floored with limpet cones, was bone-white and bone-yellow.

I stood there until the sky became as bleached as bone and the light far out as sheer and pitiless and uninhabitable as a work of gold, silver and steel. I let myself get cold. I was thinking of the builder's exertions, how he must have sweated, the faster beating of his heart as he climbed with the weight of stones, how warm his hands were, handling them, the brief lingering of his warmth on their egg-shaped surfaces, their resumption of their natural cold. And remembering how he had appraised his arch that he intended to go underwater, how he had nodded in approval and farewell, I felt sure he had done the same when he had made apparent the skeletal shape of the tomb on the windy hill and tipped a dry libation of limpet shells into the small space where the human had gone into the earth.

I think these letters may still be a sort of courtship. Not pleading that you will love me, only hoping you will remember me. And then I think even that is asking too much.

Sunday 3 January
I was on Flagstaff Hill when the year turned. Halangy had fireworks. From my distance the rockets did not seem to reach very high. Orion, on the other hand, seemed to walk quite low. The moon was lessening. Mostly what you are aware of is the water, the large lagoon of it, the ocean all around, in varying degrees of restlessness but always everywhere restless. Lights on the water, the four or five boats, the beacons winking where there are rocks and shallows. Odd lights of a habitation, near and far. Very faint haze of the mainland. The red lights of the wireless mast on Halangy, so many conversations pass through there. The blue-green watery earth spinning and circling till it stops. Lights, the man-made, amount to nothing, the constellations are shapes only to us and not one moon or star or sun or planet acknowledges the beginning we celebrate with fireworks, song and drink.

This morning I had a visit from Mary. I was in the workshop, the light pouring through, the sea behind the dune sounding very near. I was cleaning and sharpening her father's chisels. Steel has a smell when you get the rust off it and shape the blade razor-sharp on an oiled whetstone. I touch the edge and sniff it. I've made a rack above the workbench and as each chisel is done I slot it where it belongs in the order of diminishing width of blade. I've oiled the wooden handles, they have a dull glow now and a good smell. The saws, all of them, all shapes and sizes for various kinds of wood, for logs, planks, plywood, dowling, balsa, also for metal, are restored and they hang in place. Likewise his hammers, planes, pliers, screwdrivers, bradawls... The wood he never used is stacked or laid down so you could easily distinguish the piece you want. In a dozen or more very beautiful old pale green jam jars I've sorted nails and screws into various sizes. I've rigged up better lighting, planed and proofed the two windows and the door. With the heater from my shed you could work all night in any weather if you wished. Yesterday, still clearing a far corner, I opened a sack and found the mallets, chisels, gouges, knives you need for wood carving and a thick log of apple wood that he had begun to shape into a woman's head and shoulders, the rough tress of her hair coming over on the left side. Mary was surprised by that and surveying the whole place and how far I'd got with it, she said, in a tone I felt to be benevolent, You look set to carry on where he left off. I shrugged and asked her about Alf Lewis.

He came from the mainland, as they mostly do, and beached his leaky boat in Merrick Bay. It was late October. People said he was lucky he hadn't sunk. At the Post Office he bought a bottle of brandy and a frozen chicken. He asked might there be any work over the winter but nobody much liked the look of him and they were non-committal. For a week he lived on his boat and waded ashore at low water for provisions and to ask again was there any work. Then came a gale and a high tide, he smashed up under the tamarisks, on the rocks, and that was the end of his boat. But a woman looking after her grandchildren, Betty Daniel, who lived down there took pity on him and said he could live in her boathouse and do odd jobs for rent. And that was more or less the way of it, for fifteen years. He never did many jobs but Mrs Daniel never seemed to mind. The grandchildren loved him. He got down on his hands and knees and one rode on his back while the other led him by a rope around his neck. They called him Horsey, never anything else, even when they were too big to ride on him. He lived off social security and Mrs Daniel's charity. She lent him an old punt and he rowed across the channel, bought a Racing Post, sat in the Dorrien Arms and bet more than he could afford on the horses. When the tides were big he liked to walk across at low water. He'd time it so he'd get there only paddling and after a few pints he'd wade back, holding his paper and any other bits of shopping above his head. He did that, summer and winter, for fifteen years. Then last August when he stood up to leave the pub a fog had come in, thick as a bag, everybody said, and they said he should wait a couple of hours, there was a boat going back, he could take the boat for once. But he wouldn't be told, he left the pub and vanished. Nobody missed him for a day or two, then the bookmaker phoned Mrs Daniel and said to tell Alf his horse had won at 10 to 1 and was he coming over to collect his winnings. Afterwards that made people laugh, since he was never lucky with his bets. Mrs Daniel and the grown-up grandchildren were very upset but nobody else was. Still, said Mary, it gave her a chill around the heart to think of anyone vanishing in the sea like that, in a fog.

6 January
An orange wellington boot (the right foot), cuttlefish, a double sachet of emergency fresh water made by a firm in Bergen, a net tangled with its rope and plastic floats, a doll's head, the plastic handle of a knife, a packet of rusks from

Belgium, an orange starfish (dead and stiff), ribs and vertebrae of, I think, a dolphin, plastic bottles (milk, bleach, shampoo, anti-freeze, marmite), one trainer (left foot), one green rubber glove (left), cotton buds, a gin bottle, a very soft grapefruit, chunk of polystyrene, bamboo pole, 12-foot length of 4x4, dog-fish egg, cube of wood off a pallet, plastic fish-crate from Coruna and another (a yard away) from Goedereede, plastic clasp for a down spout, biro, oiled-up guillemot, plastic tulip, lid off a funerary urn, a cork, a condom, three cartidges, a black plastic bag, claws.

I had another visit from Eddie, earlier than last time, I was at my table, breathing in the steam of my coffee, watching the light becoming strong enough for a winter's day, and suddenly there was his face again, in the glass, as though mirrored, and again it shocked me to the heart and in a bad state some moments passed until I understood that what he wanted was my friendship. He tapped at the window, pointed to his face, then at me, smiled – the smile of a clown – showed me his palms, nodded his head, pressed his right hand on his heart, again with the pointing finger indicated me, and raised all the features of his face in a question. I let him in, and between glee at that and wonder at the place he had been let into, he got into a sort of ecstasy beyond the power of his hands and face to express. I sat him down on my chair, gave him coffee in my other cup, and cut him a slice of the cake that Mary had given me the day before. He can't really speak. At least, he can't make recognisable words. Instead he makes a great variety of sounds such as infants do when they are used to the babble of adult language all around them but can't or don't wish to imitate it yet – gurglings, pipings, chuckles, little runs of chirrups, squeals and cries, all in the timbre of a grown man's voice, wonderfully expressive. In a deep sense I at once knew what he meant. I've never been in the presence of such good nature and simple happiness before. Nothing in all his noises, gestures, bearing qualified in the least his joy and his goodwill. For that time he was absolutely good and joyful, unconditionally, without any safeguard, wholly open and delivered up in it. Everything about my shed delighted him. He gripped and stroked the plain chair, knelt at the bed (where I was sitting) and laid his hands flat on the rough blanket and on the cold white sheet folded back in a band across it. Fleetingly he laid his cheek on the pillow. Then he resumed his seat, crammed the cake into his mouth and gulped the coffee. His very pale eyes have the sags of idiocy under them, he drools, his hands are big, a stray white tress of hair falls over his eyes and he wipes it away. After a while he became quiet and fell to studying the objects in the room with a grave seriousness. My finds along the one shelf, arranged in a line next to the few books, attracted him, he rose, lifted up each in turn with extraordinary care, examined each, looked from it to me and back again to it, as though to understand the connection. So I watched myself being appraised in my finding, taking up, bringing home, setting down to live with: the long delicate skull of a gannet, the skull of a seal, three of its vertebrae, the severed and entirely desiccated wing of a tern, a fragment of wood honeycombed by shipworm… I could hear the wrens, the sparrows, the thrushes, the starlings, the blackbirds that with their various noises begin my every day. And the breeze in the tamarisks and the surf up under the dune. The light became strong and bright. Eddie stood at the shelf, his big hands were so considerate they could have cradled the skeleton of a shrew, and he looked at me and at the object in question and made the noises of his wondering and pondering.

He was there an hour, then Lucy came, anxious as ever, found him, scolded him and said she was sorry I had been intruded upon. I said he should visit whenever he liked, I'd be glad of his company and if he didn't find me in he should make himself at home and stay as long as he wished. And you'll know where to look for him, I said to her.

16 January

New moon. Brian has gone to the mainland to see his wife and children. He made an appointment. He is staying in a B&B just around the corner from the family home, though his wife said there was no need to go to such lengths, he could have slept in the spare bedroom. He says she wasn't unfriendly when he spoke to her, but quite definite that she doesn't want to live with him, not here, not over there, not anywhere. But she agrees it is only fair he should see the children now and then. She has emailed him some recent photographs of them (not of her) and promises to do that at regular intervals.

It is not just because he misses her and Amy and Zoë that he has arranged this interview (as he calls it). He also wants to ask her some questions for his family history, about her childhood in a village on the Lancashire coast. He spent his own childhood scarcely ten miles away, but inland, in a small town, and of course their experiences were very different. He admits her origins and her local habitation always did have, in his eyes, a romance quite lacking in his. The coast there is very flat. It is a queer zone of brackish water, salt grass, little channels, thousands of peewits, and the sheep graze, as it seems, far out on a terrain that belongs by rights to the Irish Sea. He and his wife went back there sometimes when they were courting and it has haunted him ever since. So now he has drawn up a list of questions – seventeen in all – which he hopes she will answer for him, before it is too late. He showed me the list. Among his questions are: What was her mother's Co-op number? What was the name of her Gran's farm where she used to look for eggs and where the pig burst out of its sty and scared her half to death? Which uncle was it who got stranded in his car – a Ford Popular? – on the dyke road during the 1953 flood? Were the toilets in her primary school outside in the yard? What was the name of the woman who walked seven miles to the nearest railway station and took the train to her mother's each time – nine times in all – she felt her baby was about to come?

I could remember the rest of Brian's questions if I lay on the bed under my army coat and thought. And not seventeen but seven times seventeen are the questions I could think of to put to you.

The tides are big. Brian left early, while there was still water for the launch, and we, his workforce, took the day off. Chris sat down at the office computer to plan the next few months of his life. He still tries for Elaine, but rather half-heartedly. Not that he's doing any better with anyone else. Sarah, Elaine and I went out on the Merrick Bay flats.

The islands make a broken rim around a sunken plain which floods on the incoming tide and empties on the ebb. At low water the walls of the lost fields continue downwards and out of sight under the sand. The maps still show the vanished causeways. There are obliterated hearths and wells. The tombs are on the surviving hills. And rammed up into the roots of the tamarisks, quite close to the boathouse that was his home for fifteen years, are the few remaining bits of Alf's boat, held down by the stones that smashed it.

Going out on the flats is like trespassing. You know you mustn't be found there when the owner returns. I've been out on my own, at Merrick Bay and elsewhere, several times, and always with that feeling of brief licence. In the two young women it excited a hilarity rather as the wine and the dressing up had done at Brian's party on Christmas Day. Poor Brian was away, they had the day off, they were pleased with themselves, they said I shouldn't go working in the fields for Nathan but should come out with them, on the flats. The day was cold and very bright with a breeze that gave the look of hurry to the ebbing water and an edge to their elation. In fact I had already decided I wouldn't work for Nathan. I was intending to go out, but alone, to get some idea of where Alf had vanished, and I kept to that purpose, but kept it to myself, and in a way I should perhaps be ashamed of I cherished it all the more in the company of Sarah and Elaine.

Sarah, at least to begin with, had her own serious purpose for which she carried a chart, a notebook, an indelible pen, a dozen small plastic jars, a lens and a sharp knife in a hard leather satchel slung across her shoulder so that it rested on her hip. Her idea was to collect some specimen periwinkles, of the four species, from different tide zones, and also fronds of serrated wrack to study what grew on them. Elaine helped her for a while. The tide was still falling. I watched the birds – two spoonbills, a rare arrival; the more and more common egrets; the local heron and swans; the countless waders I don't have the knowledge to distinguish; all in their characteristic fashions going about the endless business of probing, uncovering, stabbing, scooping, an intense almost leisurely concentration on getting enough to eat, the sea having withdrawn its protection from millions of edible fellow-creatures. Such grace and menace. The birds moved away from us only as far as they judged necessary. They kept to their purpose, warily.

I watched, walked on, halted, watched. But really I was drifting towards the diminishing channel that still made two islands of Enys and St Nicholas, I felt pulled as the waters were, so easy has it become to lapse out of human company. Then the girls called out, not my name, just a crying, not gull or tern or curlew or oyster-catcher, but of that order of cry, not-human, fit for the bubbling and coursing of salt water and the stink of weed. I waited, they came over. Like me, they were barefoot, their boots on the laces around their necks, trousers rolled up. Sarah said, We've done enough work. Elaine said, We've had an idea. Her tone was like Sarah's when at the party she asked was I obedient, would I do what they asked, was I chaste? I nodded. Yes, a drink. There's time if we're quick.

The channel was a wide river, shallow and flowing fast. Odd, an ocean quaffing a lagoon. The girls let go of me – they had me by either arm – and paddled through at once, wetted no higher than the knees. From the other side they called across. But for an interlude I was going into myself, into the room in my imagination where Alf stumbled, went under, surfaced, struggled and the cold tide like a shark took hold of him and dragged him off, never to be seen again. The girls hallooed, they were as strange to me as selkies. I splashed through and gathered them against me. I was high on the thought of Alf as he began his afterlife. Drinks, I said. We've got an hour.

The Dorrien Arms is no distance. We went there barefoot with our boots around our necks. A brandy each, quickly. Then wine, with bread and smoked mackerel. Monk, said Sarah, we like you when you get us tipsy. Their faces burned, from the flats. I never knew such proximity of life. The two young women, they might decide anything for the good of their lives, they might turn their gaze in a sweet and predatory way on anything, and take it. And there I sat, close and opposite, in pure admiration. You and you, I said. I drink to you. And Alf, already dead, turned in the current and set with it out towards nowhere, towards never being apparent to anyone ever again, he turned with the acquiescence of the dead and headed away and in the solemnity of our bread and fish and wine I took their hands, felt their warmth, kissed their fingers, relinquished them. Monk, said Elaine, you're nice when you've had a drink or two. The hour passed. There was no fog but it was winter and the afternoon did not have long to live. Another half hour. Come on, I said. Drink up. Your mothers would not forgive me.

And so we left, barefoot, the light of outdoors, brilliant, chased with breeze, leapt at everything, jaunty and careless, and all the phenomena were flung into keen appearance and the light that did it to them shouted triumphantly. And we walked out through the coils and spurtings of lives that live under the sand, over popping wrack and the harsh debris of shells to the channel we had to wade. The tamarisks of Merrick Bay were clearly visible but at a distance that looked too great ever to traverse. The tide had turned, the current had reversed, but if you slipped it would not deposit you safe on an islet within the inhabited ring. The ring is broken, the gaps are large and many, the suction of deep water will take you out. I thought we were not where we had crossed. Almost certainly we were not at the shallowest fording place. Wait, I said. But the girls stepped in and went knee-deep at once. Sarah took off her satchel, held it high and proceeded, Elaine following. The water split in a briefly cresting wave around each in turn, rose to their breasts, then lapsed. They stood on the far side shrieking with laughter. I took off my coat, held it in a bundle above my head. I could not have imagined the cold and the force of the water, the two together as one embodiment, and now I can, it went into my stomach, so now I shall remember it and in the imagination feel it again. An army coat, if you let it get sodden through, would take you under at once. I've told nobody – till you – anything at all of what I learned.

We hurried. Elaine, who could hardly speak for shivering, said Sarah said I should come back with them and be warmed up. But I parted company when we were near the beach. In my shed among my papers on my table top there was a gift for me: a vase, I guessed from Eddie and from the tip. My coat was dry, I went to bed in it. The vase was more than a bit chipped around the rim, but none the less beautiful – like a gourd in shape, with red poppies on a black glaze. For some time I shook with cold and my mind ran as fast as the water in a delirium. I wanted to hold the vase, have its roundness between my hands, offer its darkness and its poppies to a beloved person. And in my fever of cold that seemed to me an entirely reasonable wish and I felt sure it would be granted. Then I must have slept and when I woke it was dark and I was warm, glad, hungry.

19 January

Brian has returned from the mainland disappointed. He did

not advance at all in his dealings with his wife. On the contrary, she put him further off. She agrees that Amy and Zoë should visit him at Easter, if they want to, but he will have to fetch them and bring them back. She thinks if she came over herself it would put her in a false position, by which she means she doesn't want anybody here supposing their marriage might be on the mend. When he got nowhere 'in that department' Brian thought he could perhaps approach her through his seventeen questions. But there he was sorely mistaken. She refused point blank to answer a single one of them. And when – very gently, in his opinion – he suggested she owed him that at least, the questions being so important to him, she became quite hostile and told him straight her childhood was none of his business, which he found very hurtful because when they were courting he had believed she shared it with him. In the end she said, You don't own me, Brian, and after that all he could do was go back to his B&B. The girls were already in bed by then and he didn't dare call next morning and say goodbye to them as they left for school.

Now Brian hardly knows how he'll find the courage to start the new season and be cheerful with the guests. At the thought of it he feels very low indeed. He knows the rich man who owns the place will want to see a big improvement on last year, though money for most people, even the kind who stay in his hotel, is still quite tight. Brian panics when he thinks of the effort he will have to make. And he won't find much recreation in his family history. He feels almost prohibited from doing it by his wife's hurtful words.

Eddie came again. He brought me a fistful of white narcissi and nodded his heavy head in great delight and satisfaction towards the vase. They scent my room. But the best was that, having presented them to me and when I'd filled the vase with water from my can and set the flowers in and we had both admired them, then he sat down on my bed in complete stillness, all his usual small chunnering noises ceased, he became entirely quiet and calm. So much so that after a while I smiled at him and resumed the writing he had interrupted with his visit. And that is how his mother found us when after an hour or more she came looking for him. We were quiet. Eddie likes coming here, she said. He'll miss you when you leave.

Nests from last year, or from several years ago, held in the clasp of the new branches that sprout around the place where the tall upright was lopped. Once or twice I've found the skeletons of fledglings in them, delicate remains in the well-made and deeply protected home. Brambles that climb from the earth through twenty feet of dense euonymus or pittosporum, wriggling through and finally attaining what they were born always to seek: the light. My silver ladder stands in the grey-green fall of branches, twigs and leaves. The leaves quiver like a haul of fishes dying brightly in the sunlight on the net. And the wind, almost every day the wind, bustling through the unkempt crest that I will lop. I rob the wind of a resistance by which it makes the passage of itself felt.

21 January

I set the female bust on the workbench under the lamp and looked at it. A few more hours of work and she would have been there, manifest, come out of the wood, become real out of the idea of her. Even thus far emerged, with her roughed-out face and plait of hair and the swelling that would become her breasts, she has some force. I have sharpened all his cutting and gouging tools and wrapped them in an oily cloth that will keep then ready instantly for use. I sat to one side on a packing case and looked. I examined my hands. Really, I might have some chance of bringing her further out. She would never be wholly there, I don't have the gift for that. But some way, nonetheless, towards being there. And I'm not forbidden. Mary has said as much. Still I can't or shan't.

22 January

Most nights I sleep at once, then wake and see that hardly two hours have passed. Waking so soon, the night still to be got through, I fill up with disappointment and anxiety. I've slept worse and worse since I went away from you. In the night, lying awake, the night impossibly long, I undo all the good I did or that was done to me during the day. Every elation, I deflate. Every kindness, I convert to dust. Every insight, joy in a thing, hope of more such things, I worry soon to death. Truly, I can summon up a face that smiles at me and in whose eyes I see myself a welcome friend and I can turn that face and smile to deceit and mockery at once. Then I assemble all the arguments against me. I accumulate the proof that I'm not fit to live. Some nights the fear is such it drives me out of bed, out of the little warmth and comfort and homeliness I have assembled around me under a wooden roof and between four wooden walls, and I walk out through the lovely opening of my blessed horseshoe of tamarisks and climb the dune and huddle in a dead man's army greatcoat and stare at the sea and harken to its noise. And after some time, under the pulsing stars, the lighthouse winking mechanically every fifteen seconds, it all feels like a foolishness, the despair itself not worth the candle, the thought of killing myself seems laughably self-important, and all I want is my bit of warmth and shelter under the blankets and some sleep.

23 January

An enlivening tempest, the winds rode in on the risen backs of the Atlantic and I went out among the tumuli and showed my face and opened my arms to them and tried to breathe their force into my lungs. Just north of here, in a cavernous hole, enough timber has lodged to build a log cabin with and live alone in, in a bee-loud glade. When will you ever, Peace, wild wooddove, shy wings shut…? When I came home, caked in brine, from discovering that cache and wondering was it worth my while to wait for low water and go and lug it in, there was Eddie with more narcissi in his massive fist and again once they were breathing in his gift, the vase, we sat in silence and quietness, he and I, utterly companionable, I did not turn my back on him and write, but there we sat, listening to the gale, till Lucy came through it looking for him.

24 January
Mary looked in at the workshop door. There's a cake for you on your table, she said. I was standing by the bench, contemplating the unfinished carving. I'll miss seeing you in Father's coat, she said. In fact, I'd rather you took it with you when you leave.

I'll send these last four days together. Even so, they're hardly worth a stamp.

28 January
I'll leave a note on my table under the black vase asking that this pen, my notebooks, your photograph and a necklace that was my mother's should be sent to you. And I'll leave the postage. I'll take back to the tip the things I took from the tip and the things I got from beachcombing I'll take back to the beach. Elaine and Sarah can share the books and Lucy should have the vase itself. I'll add that to my note. And my rags and my camping stuff they can do what they like with. The tip. Mary will collect the things she lent me.

I always wanted to give you the necklace and never quite dared. The beads are of cherry amber. I've often imagined how they would look on you.

My notebooks will be worse reading than these letters. At least in the letters I was going out to somebody. If I say these letters are my better self you will realise what a poor thing I have been. And in my notebooks I say so, again and again. I fought against my impoverishment and lost. I had an eye for abundance, I could see it all around me, life for the living, a proper joy, proper sorrows, deeply among other people. I could see it but I couldn't do it. At least believe me when I say I loved. But I could never have and hold what I loved. Somehow I never had the knack. Or I never had the courage. So I have lived in poverty knowing all the while that life is rich, rich. And I have lived in obedience. I obeyed the orders that would harm me. Early on it was God and the monks and when I was shot of them I devised in myself even crueller, yet more nonsensical and in the end even madder dictators. So I lived in obedience to temptations and commands whose one purpose was to kill the life in me. Now and again I was disobedient, I answered back, I said no, joyously I transgressed. For a while I was a passable imitation of a man claiming his right to live. But I always came to heel in the end, knuckled under, took the punishment for my revolt. In my notebooks I wrote all this – the mechanics of it. I did once think that if I could describe it very precisely I could fight it better. That was a mistake. I never understood *why* I was like I was, but I did see very clearly *how* I was, how it worked in me, the mechanism that sided with death against my life. I knew I didn't understand why but I hoped that if I saw how it worked, I might escape. Must one know why? Should it not be enough to see how? Well, it wasn't enough. The best I ever got from writing it all down was the bleak satisfaction of making clear sentences. I could analyse and differentiate and split fine hairs and set it all out clearly but it didn't help. Nothing helped. I saw that I did not have it in me to save myself. I wrote these letters, which have been – grant me that much – more about other people and about the earth's lovely phenomena than about myself, to keep myself in dealings with somebody else.

Full moon this weekend. The weather is very still. In the abandoned bulbfields the daffodils and the narcissi are in flower. They find their way up into the sunshine through dead bracken, gorse and brambles. In the fields most recently let go they appear in their regimented straight lines, in a continuing discipline though the forces of law and order have departed. But in the oldest ruins the flowers have split and spread and they come up where they like through all the dead stuff gloriously. The tides will be very big again this weekend.

Saturday 30 January
Forgive me, I changed my mind. I've thrown my mother's necklace into the sea and fed my notebooks and your photograph into the hotel's incinerator that we call Puffing Billy. So nobody from here will post you anything after this. I was ashamed of my notebooks and didn't want them lodging in your mind. And again I didn't quite dare give you the necklace of a woman you heard me talk about but never met.

Sometimes I have imagined you burning these letters as they arrive, burning them all unopened and unread. Only very rarely have I had the sudden conviction that you do read them and keep them. Lately I've told myself you don't open them but you lay them down in a safe place in order of arrival so that the last would be first to hand. And now I am hoping that when, after a few weeks, nothing further arrives, you'll take up this last one first, for an explanation. There is no explanation – but only this request. *Please* burn the rest unread. They were my effort and it failed. There's no reason now why you should read them.

When I posted Thursday's letter Mrs Goddard said, You keep us in business, Mr Smith. I don't know how we'll manage when you leave. She is very happy these last days because her daughter is coming home from New Zealand with a husband and a baby boy she has never seen. They plan to stay three months and, who knows, they might stay longer.

I'll take this letter to Mrs Goddard and she'll say what she has always said when I've posted a letter to you on a Saturday: You know it won't go out till Monday now? I've always liked her for her tact. She has never said, You don't get answers, do you? I shan't tell her this letter will be the last.

Mary's workshop looks all shipshape. I'll walk through Nathan's fields. The hedges look very trim. I'll take my books to the community centre, except one each for Elaine and Sarah which I'll leave here. The rest, but for the vase which I want Eddie to give to his mother, is for the beach or the tip. I'll keep this heavy coat on. I'll keep this pen in its deep inside pocket.

Goat

THAT CHRISTMAS, THE coldest in living memory and his last, Goat skippered in the old Bluecoats School. Long before winter the lads had ripped out all the lead and copper they could reach and when Goat moved in the place ran nearly everywhere with water. The main staircase was a cascade. But he set up home in the headmaster's study and even when the freeze came, since he had a fire in there, he thought himself well off.

The Canon never forgot his one and only meeting with Goat. During the dismal endgame of his life, in the home his family chose for him near the M25, he would talk of Goat and that famous Christmas Eve to anybody who would listen or indeed to nobody. Yes, he said, I was crossing the market place on my way to the midnight service, when close by the equestrian statue of Lord Londonderry, under the Christmas tree, I met a young woman called Fay. Where are you going? she asked. To the cathedral, I answered. She wore hiking boots, jeans, a navy-blue peajacket, red mittens, red scarf, red Phrygian cap. Then just as well come with me, she said. I'm doing my soup-run and my next and last is Goat. So the Canon accompanied Fay back up the hill he had just come down. A few people who knew him, hurrying to divine service through the cold, raised their frosty eyebrows as they passed.

I'm sure you've seen me around, said Fay. I've seen *you* around. I've often wondered what you think about when you're shaving. I mean that face of yours in the mirror must surely make you think.

Half way up the hill, which the Canon had climbed and descended several thousand times during his long residence in that northern town, Fay halted between a cobbler's and an auction room at a pair of iron gates whose existence he had overlooked and which she pushed open now and tugged him through under a ruinous apartment straddling the gap. Here we are, she said. Having quitted the street, their light was starlight, glittering frost and the dull gleams of broken glass and broken ice. Iron, concrete and the smashings of bricks and wood were furred in a delicate culture of bright grey frost. This was their yard, she said. Those are the old toilets. Little Harry gets in there some nights but it's too cold at present. Goat won't let him share the warm. The school with its scores of shattered panes, its dangling gutters, keeling drainpipes and desquamated roof, bulked up enormously before them. From one of her deep pockets Fay took out a torch. Careful, she said. The ice. I needed wellies when I first came here. Now we need crampons.

Far south, till the end, the Canon would speak of the ice as a sort of Xanadu. He recalled the mouth of the old Bluecoats School, a charitable foundation awaiting demolition, as the gob of a hellish paradise, fangs either side and a long hard undulation tempting him up like the best, most forbidden, entertainment at a fair. The seven steps were perilous, he said. We clung to the stumps of what had been a wrought-iron hand-rail and reached the great doors which were busted open.

In the large vestibule Fay and the Canon stood together for a moment's silence. She played the beam of her torch over the high ceiling through which – through shattered laths and clinging plaster – hung swords of ice. The parquet floor below them, unevenly glazed with ice, was nubbed and bumped with the beginnings of stalagmites. Here and there lay the corpses of rats and pigeons, more or less gnawed or decomposed, in the fixative of ice. And bottles, cans, syringes, magazines and condoms, set fast in the glistering cold. The

Canon, remembering his own schooldays, was most moved by the rolls of honour high on the walls: the captains, sportsmen and the dead in wars, their names in letters of gold under a patina of frost. Stillness, not a whisper of the water whose present form was ice. You would have loved the water, Fay said. This main stairs was like a stream you'd climb in Wales to a cwm and a lake, springs bubbled up wherever you trod and your head was wetted with sprinklers. Present in the ice, the Canon felt himself rapt by Fay's words into visions of the waters of life unleashed, in spate, unstoppable. I thought you'd look like that if I brought you here, she said. Goat's upstairs. Be careful. Why do you call him Goat? the Canon asked. That's his name, said Fay. Just right. He's got two bumps on his forehead that look as though they might be horns. Also he's very randy. He suffers from priapism. Suffers? said the Canon. But Fay had begun the climb.

Of the banister here only the brackets had survived, and by these, step by step, very slowly Fay and the Canon climbed the glacier stairs. Often she turned round to him, shone the lamp, urged extreme caution. Perhaps I'll fit up a rope next time, she said. The Canon, never a mountaineer, was amazed how little fear he felt. My shoes are quite unsuitable, he said to himself. And she's got boots on. She appraised him coolly. You're doing OK, she said. I'm doing OK, he muttered. I should get her to stencil that across my forehead.

They reached the landing. There was less ice. But watch your step, said Fay. Some floorboards had been ripped out, to get at the pipes or wiring or for fuel. Don't fall through. Goat's along here. They passed a couple of classrooms and the art room. Much breakage everywhere, nothing systematic, more an exuberance of beginnings, desks and chairs with only a lid or a couple of legs missing, skirting wrenched off intact. You might pillage for years in this place, the Canon thought. Fuel in plenty till the ice retreats. Around three walls of the art room, quite high up under the broken windows, ran a cast of the Elgin Marbles, scarcely more damaged than they were by the robber baron himself. The Canon stood looking up, the frost light was spectral, the horses, men, women, sacrificial beasts, trooping like ghosts. He stood so long Fay came back for him. The tears on his cheeks had begun to freeze. It's warm at Goat's, she said, having stood with him a while.

Goat's quarters were at the far end of the corridor behind a barricade. He doesn't like visitors, said Fay. Except me. Will he mind me? the Canon asked. No he won't mind you, she answered. I've already mentioned you. More floorboards were missing in this corner but a couple had been laid back loose across the joists. That's his gangway, said Fay. He'll pull it up when we've gone. They crossed, and climbed over the barricade. That's the toilet, said Fay, shining the torch. The door had been torn off and added to Goat's defences. Of the thing itself not only the seat, burnable, but also much of the bowl had gone. Wash basin likewise. Sledgehammer work, by the looks of it. This room with running water was an ice cave now except for some damping on the wall against the study. At least the shit's all in one place, said Fay, illuminating the ruined bowl. And in the ice it doesn't smell. Admirable, said the Canon. In bouts of coprophilia in his final years he would talk for hours, if let, about Goat's convenience, that had once been a headmaster's. Next door is cosier, said Fay.

She knocked, and she and the Canon laid an ear, her right, his left, against the door. Their frost breaths mingled. Fuck off! they heard loudly. Then softly, Unless it's you. It's me, said Fay. Enter, said Goat. They entered. The room was lit with fire and a couple of candle-ends. Goat sat barefooted (and the feet were black) in baggy trousers, a cherry-red shirt and the headmaster's gown, leaning back against the wall, his tobacco and a bottle in reach and a sheaf of paper propped in his lap. He had a broken nose, crinkled and soiled grey hair, some teeth and, yes, knobs on his forehead that might once have been or might be striving to become, horns. His mattress, and on it an overcoat and a stack of papers, lay along the far wall. Happy Christmas, Goat, said Fay. I've brought you some soup. Happy Christmas to you, sweetheart, said Goat. And to you too, Vicar. Peace on earth and God rest the slaughtered innocents. He's a canon, said Fay, taking a thermos, a cup, a bottle of wine and a penny whistle out of her rucksack, I told you. Ex, said the Canon, suddenly driven to say so. Ex, former, erstwhile canon. Ex-man-of-God. I'm going before they unfrock me, later today perhaps. I may announce it publicly later today. Meanwhile, dear Fay, dear Goat, be the first to know. And address me how you like. Once a canon, always a canon maybe. After this speech he rummaged under his greatcoat for the hip-flask which – he told them – he could never get through divine service without. Drink with me, friends, he said, stooping first to Goat.

The room was hot. The frost flowers on its unbroken panes could not survive. Goat was burning the headmaster's desk, a good mahogany thing, all smashed and ready on the hearth, burning it as though there were no tomorrow. And see what I found in his bottom drawer, he said, handing the Canon a wad of photographs. Confiscated, no doubt, said Fay. Give them to me. They curled and blackened and vanished in the flames. Here's soup instead. Here's the blood-red wine. Here's bread. She took off her peajacket. Goat folded his gown over the papers in his lap. Pardon me, he said. My old complaint. Very embarrassing. And how's family life for you, Father? Very poor, said the Canon. And it may end completely this afternoon. There may be an announcement. Herself had enough, has she? She has, said the Canon. My son and daughter married south, they board their children in expensive penitentiaries and with their spouses toil in the Golden Mile to raise the necessary cash. My wife has told me candidly she prefers them to me.

Goat took out his papers, propping them as before, and began to write. The hip-flask circulated clockwise, the red bottle anti-clockwise. Soup, bread; then from a sack, quite absently, continuing to scribble, Goat fetched out a tin of mince pies. The Canon took off his greatcoat and cardigan to reveal, below his snow-white collar, a shimmering purple front. It's a bishop's, he said. I bought it for fancy dress. Suits you, said Fay. Goat looked up and, eyeing her, threw on more splintered mahogany. Fay pulled off her sweater. And that's it, Goat, she said. Heat the room as hot as hell, that's as far as I go. But I will play you both a tune.

She moved to a corner, sat with her knees up and began to play. The flames, already dancing, lit her flickeringly, they moved on her face and bare arms like the ghosts of caresses, released, disembodied, become elemental, living for ever. The Canon saw this at once and might have stared all night. But the reed pipe would not let him be still. Again, as when Fay had described the time before the ice, he heard water. Her playing attuned him immediately to all the hidden ways and energies of water. He felt those biding their time in the frozen pipework of the abandoned school, felt them keenly, from the deep municipal mains up to the stray ends in Goat's own privy, all of them waiting for warmth so that they could whisper, murmur, chuckle and exult in anarchy once more. That intricate life in waiting was made palpable to him as Fay played. But so too was the river under its casing of ice, he felt the sluggish flood still moving underneath over the ooze, the mud and all the deposits of bikes and trolleys, bottles, knives, angry women's rings and bombs from the last war. All that and more, but not just that, also the gnarled streams in the frozen hills to the west, hardened, silenced, clamped into inertia, set there waiting under the sheer ice of the milky way and billions of sharp points of unimaginable cold. That too, but also – the reed was very insidious – he felt in that hot room every highway and finer and finer branching, every thinnest ramification of the liquids of his body, all flowing in him in a sanctuary of warmth in a wrecked colossal palace seized and held fast by ice. He felt himself watered through and through and sensations shot electrically down all the moist conductors in his frame.

Fay slowed, she simplified her playing to half a dozen

repeated notes, rising in interrogation, like a birdcall, again and again, asking, summoning, her black eyes smiling at the men over her pipe and clever fingers. Goat set down his papers and pencil. With the ball of his left hand he rubbed his bumps. The Canon removed his Oxford shoes. Goat began to chortle. Eh, Bishop, he cackled, give us a turn, Holy Father. The Canon began to dance, in a slow twirling at first, his hands raised as though in surrender above his craggy head. Fay's whistle insisted. Goat began to clap, her birdcall and his clapping marking time. Then the Canon was launched. Down came his arms, fists on his nipples, elbows out like residual wings, he tilted back his head and began to stamp and yodel. Now *he* made the beat, Goat and Fay, clapping and piping, had to catch him, and pretty soon, flapping like a dodo, knees up and crooning, he raised the grinning Goat to join him in the firelight. Fay whistled faster, she seemed able to keep both men in mind, to be playing for both, getting to the pit of the belly of each. They linked arms, they turned with time and against time, they parted, bowed, went solo, lumbering like grizzlies. Goat fluttered like a bat in the headmaster's gown, up and out through his flies burst his cheerful affliction, dark as a donkey's, so witless, clownish, helpless, Goat and the Canon laughed to see it. Ghost in the machine, cried the Canon, popping out in flesh. There shall I be in the midst of you, cried Goat. And Fay raised her pipe and with slant notes climbing, with a spiralling and rifling of notes, faster and faster, higher and higher, she led. Then the Canon unbuttoned his immaculate collar, his collar of office, removed it, buttoned it again and with unrepeatable sureness of aim, with the skill suddenly given you in dreams, he hoopla-ed it over the risen vicar of Goat.

Fay ceased. Time, gentlemen, she said. Goat covered himself and sprawled with the Canon on the floor. Fay dressed. Time to go, Canon, she said. Obediently he found his cardigan, his heavy coat, his shoes. Goat sat up, looking sad. You coming again, girl? And you, boss, you coming again? The Canon nodded and shook him by the hand. Very soon, he said. I think I'll be a free man by tomorrow. Fay stowed away the flask and pipe and took out a package. Your Christmas present, Goat. She bent and kissed him on the forehead. He unwrapped his present at once. It was a notebook with black moleskin covers, he opened its white pages in his lap. Write me something, she said. Heart and soul, said Goat, the best I can.

On the corridor, like the cold itself, it struck the Canon into the heart that he must on no account fall and be crippled. I have to dance, he said to himself. From now on I have to be able to dance. He concentrated hard: over the missing floorboards, step by step down the escalade of ice, through the litter of hurtful debris in the yard. Fay watched for him, lighting where his hands and feet must go.

On the street what they heard first was a yowling of drunks from the market place, then sirens, some hastening away, others hastening near. The stars pulsed as though cold were their breath and sustenance, they throbbed like a power, like the dynamo of the remotest orders of life. You go that way, said Fay, pointing up the hill. And you? Through there, she answered, pointing across the street down towards the river. I'll see you around, she said. Yes, he answered. I'll be looking out for you.

That evening, having written a letter to his bishop and made an announcement to his wife, the Canon, unbearably restless, found a torch and his most suitable shoes and went out. At the iron gates he skulked till no passer-by was near, then slipped quickly through into the yard. He was in a hurry, he tripped and skidded, till he mastered himself and concentrated on the guiding thought of the night before. He climbed the first steps very slowly, exulting that he had it in him to re-enter the dream alone. In the vestibule, standing below the hanging swords of ice, he took time to follow some sportsmen and captains by name from school to war, from one roll of honour to the next. This fortified him in his determination to stay alive. With pedantic caution, step by step, gripping the brackets, he climbed to the landing and the corridor. And there was the barricade – but with no gangway. He stepped from joist to joist, then over the desks, chairs and the toilet door. Only now did he wonder why he had come to find Goat. Why had he not roamed the streets in the hope of finding Fay? He knocked, no answer, he entered. There in the hearth squatted a dwarfish man with long arms and very bright eyes. The fire was blazing. He was feeding it pages and pages of pencilled script. Goat's gone, he said. It's my place now. You Little Harry? the Canon asked. A nod. And where has he gone? Dunno. To hell, I hope. Those pages, the Canon said, they his? They was, said Little Harry. They're for my fire now. Faster and faster he dealt them into the flames. The writing sped up the chimney like black butterflies. Give me the rest, will you? the Canon said. Little Harry shook his head. Silly fucker was always scribbling. I'll pay you, said the Canon. Too late, said Little Harry. They were all gone. His book, the Canon asked, he had a new black book. This here? said Little Harry, fetching it out from under him. That there, said the Canon. A tenner? Fifteen, said Little Harry. Hail Mary, the fucker's gone to hell. Tell his tart to visit me, will you?

It was a week before the Canon saw Fay. He sat in a café in the market place, watching. When they closed he sat on the steps under the horse. Then very late and the cold no less she came up unseen and sat beside him and took his hand. Goat's gone, he said. I know, she said. I got you his book, he said. See how much he wrote that night. I haven't read them of course. They'll be for you. She opened the book and closed it again at once. Little Harry hopes he fell through a hole. He laughed like the devil when he told me that.

Between then and Easter Fay and the Canon were often seen together in the market place café, in one or two of the rougher pubs or on the street just walking along. She still did her soup-run. She even visited Little Harry. I can't pick and choose, she said. Walking on the streets with the Canon she would usually take his arm and he, everybody said, looked rather lost without her. Whenever he sat reading or doing a crossword or stood or walked, he looked always to be waiting for her. They were an odd couple; but that northern town had more than a few eccentrics and, had they been let, Fay and the Canon would have done OK. Were their relations carnal? Some said certainly yes, others certainly no, and both camps said you could tell at a glance was it yes or no. All agreed that when Fay and the Canon sat together in a café or a pub they had plenty to discuss. Plotting something, so it looked. In fact Fay had an idea for a piece of agitprop or a happening, she was unsure what to call it but if it were carried through it could not fail to make a difference. Her idea was to gather together five thousand of the county's deserving and undeserving poor, the feckless and the unlucky, the hundreds thrown on skid row by the wars, the rationalizations and the closures. And she, accompanied by the Canon, would play them into the cathedral with her pipe, interrupting choral evensong and occupying the place. Once settled in, they would dance, sing, recite poetry, tell stories, stage plays – and paint banners under which to march out in their own good time and carry the movement into all the cathedral cities. But even as they discussed this venture in ever greater detail the absence of Goat became so palpable their spirits lapsed and they sat and looked at one another dejectedly. I often think he'll pop up again, said the Canon.

The Canon's wife had gone south; he had been evicted from his church house but was living comfortably enough in a bedsit with a view of the railway line.

The cold ended, the river flooded, great trees and dead sheep jostled with floes of dirty ice in the town's lower streets. Bluecoats is a wonder, said Fay, but he hadn't the heart to go and look. Easter was early, so sweetly persuasive with its mildness, snowdrops and blackthorn. Demolition began, the school was trucked away. The Canon found Fay wandering in tears among the market stalls. Goat, his poor remains, had been found in the basement. He had fallen through two floors. In a shroud, they said, curled in a black shroud, otherwise naked. After that Fay and the Canon pooled their funds and began living together but it didn't last long.

In the home just inside the halo of the M25 when anyone knocked at the Canon's door, they heard first, very loudly, Fuck off! Then, very softly, Unless it's you. They went in anyway and it was never you. But he told whoever it was, a doctor, a vicar, a Filipino nurse, that his family, hearing he intended to remarry, fearing he would father better children and anxious to secure for themselves his small estate, had kidnapped him and locked him in a room in hell. And at any least flicker of human interest he would tell the whole story of Goat and Fay, the fabulous cold, the rust- and copper-coloured falls of ice, the dance, the unleashing of the waters. The story was an ever increasing wonder to him. I shake my head at myself when I'm shaving and I think of it, he said.

Strong Enough to Help

BUT THAT SATURDAY morning, end of October, instead of trying to write a poem, he suddenly and without knowing why began to write out all he could remember of the sayings and turns of phrase his mother and her mother and her sister had reached for to colour and solemnify their speech. They came in a rush in no particular order, he heard them in the women's voices, distinct voices, but any of the three women might have spoken them out of the stock they held in common for the family down the generations on the female side. Listening, he wrote: little pigs have big ears, least said soonest mended, enough's as good as feast, face like a wet Whit Week, love locked out, like death warmed up, the ever open door, black as the chimney back, better to be born lucky than rich, pots for rags, he had a good home and he left, like feeding a donkey strawberries, waste not want not, made up no grumbling, rise and shine, sooner keep you a week than a fortnight, I'll make one less, it's as cheap sitting as standing – And there he halted. At the back of his head, or behind him in the room pressing on his neck and shoulders, he felt the vast reservoir of the women's unspoilt language, he felt it would bow him flat on the table top if he sat there any longer listening to those voices and transcribing what he heard. In the dining-room where every Saturday morning he cleared away his breakfast things and folded back a certain measure of the cloth and seated himself at the dark table with his pen and sheets of paper, in that familiar room he was oppressed. Best stop, he said aloud. Better go out now and do my shopping. Carry on this afternoon perhaps. But then he looked at the last thing he had written. He said it aloud in Gran Benson's voice: It's as cheap sitting as standing. And he saw the old woman herself, white-haired, skewed, shrunken in her scuffed armchair by a bit of fire, the light behind her through the dirty windows from the yard, and the dog, Sam, on her right side against her feet. But that wasn't it. Her words were still in the air and he knew with a thrill of something akin to fear that there was a gap before them, a space, and into that space, before he could question it, with a shock of cold, with a starting of tears, came the words that belonged there: Sit thee down, lad. And that was it, her exact tone. The white-haired old woman in a shawl, the friendly mongrel laying its head across her feet, her left side faintly warmed by the few coals, she looked up at him as he came in and he stood there and, having kissed her on the cold smooth forehead, still stood there, at a loss no doubt, seeming unsure, and looking up she said: Sit thee down, lad. And added: It's as cheap sitting as standing.

So he sat at the polished black table in the dining room, among furnishings he had not chosen but had merely gone on living with, and loneliness, hopelessness, deep deep sadness possessed him utterly, froze him, the pen still in his hand, and he seemed to be seeing the opposite wall and his father's copied painting of a painting of Wastwater, not just through tears but through ice.

Then the doorbell rang.

The bell frightened him, it made no sense. In his own house he was elsewhere, facing something he did not feel equal to. What had the bell to do with that? It frightened him, he could not understand it ringing where he was.

The bell rang again. Merely obeying, he went to the front door.

There stood a black woman, wearing gold. Altogether her appearance was radiant. Mr Barlow? she said. – Yes, he answered. I am. – Mr Arthur Barlow? – Yes, he said. – Well my name is Gladys, she said, I'm from the DCMS and here – she lifted her lapel – is my Interviewer Identity Card, to prove it. I do hope I did not wake you, Mr Barlow. You are my first port of call. – No, said Arthur Barlow, I get up at six every morning, weekends included, to read. – Gladys smiled very happily. You read, Mr Barlow? – Yes, he said. Poetry. I read a lot of poetry. Who are you, if you don't mind me asking? You're not an estate agent, are you? You're not a religion? – No, no, said Gladys. Nothing like that. I'm from the Department of Culture, Media and Sport and I've come to ask you how you spend your time and what you think of the leisure activities and facilities available in this town. We sent you a letter about ten days ago, to tell you you were chosen. – Oh, said Arthur Barlow, perhaps I haven't opened it yet. When I'm very busy I tend not to open things like that at once. – It had a book of first-class stamps in, said Gladys, which was our little thank-you to you, for agreeing to be chosen. Do you write letters, Mr Barlow? The stamps will come in handy, if you do. – I send away for poetry books, said Arthur Barlow. So thank you very much, the stamps will come in handy for that.

Gladys opened her bright red folder, but said: Are you all right, Mr Barlow? Would you rather I came back later, or another day? – No, no, said Arthur Barlow. Nothing to worry about. I've had a bit of a shock, that's all. – Oh dear, said Gladys. I'm so sorry. Some bad news? A bereavement? – You mean my suit? said Arthur Barlow. No, I always put this on when I read poetry, or try to write poety, which is what I always do on Saturday mornings only today something else happened and it gave me a shock. It's true I wore this suit to the funerals but when I apply myself to poetry I put it on because it's the best I've got and I do think a person should dress up when he reads poetry or even tries to write some of his own. Mother bought me this suit for my interview and of course I wore it for the funerals but the interview was years and years ago so, as you see, I haven't put on weight, there's that much can be said in my favour. – If anything you must have lost some weight, said Gladys. By the looks of it. So you think you could answer my few questions, Mr Barlow, if the shock you've had hasn't upset you too much? And she opened her folder again and looked him full in the face. – If you've sent me a book of first-class stamps, said Arthur Barlow, I can surely answer your few questions. – Gladys smiled.

But then Arthur Barlow had a thought, his pale eyes bulged, his thin face, the wispy beard, the thinning colourless hair, all his physiognomy expressed unease. They're not private things you'll be asking, are they? he said I'm not one for talking about private things. – Nothing of the sort, said Gladys emphatically. I would never take on a job like that. Only about activities and facilities. Your name and address will be kept separate from your answers. No individual will be identifiable from the results. – Then do you want to come in and ask me? Arthur Barlow asked. Or shall you ask me here on the doorstep? – Entirely as you wish, said Gladys. – Come in then, said Arthur Barlow.

But as soon as he had closed the door behind Gladys and led her into the dining room Arthur Barlow knew that the shock was still with him and if he'd been alone he would have said aloud, Oh dear, this is very serious. By mistake he motioned her to sit where he had been sitting, at the head of the table, facing the wall and the picture of Wastwater, so that he stood uncertainly for a moment and folded back another half yard of cloth before seating himself at her right hand, facing the window and the garden fence. – And these must be your poems, said Gladys, not liking to put her folder down on Arthur Barlow's fountain pen and papers. I've never sat at a poet's table before. Not so far as I know, at least. – Arthur Barlow removed his belongings. It's not exactly a poem, he said.

Now, said Gladys briskly. This won't take long. Your age, please, Mr Barlow? – Fifty-five. – Single, married, widower, divorced? – Single. – And the ethnic group will be white British, will it? – I suppose it will, said Arthur Barlow. – And your occupation, Mr Barlow? – Filing-clerk at the hospital.

Though not for much longer. – A career-move, Mr Barlow? – Not exactly, said Arthur Barlow. They're making me redundant after Christmas. There's less and less call for people like me. – Oh, I am sorry, said Gladys. But at least you'll have more time for your poetry. – That's what I tell myself, said Arthur Barlow. – Now, said Gladys: leisure. Are you more sport or culture? – I suppose I'm culture. – You don't watch football, you don't go swimming, you don't play golf or engage in any other physical competitive activity, you don't go to the gym, nothing like that? – Nothing like that. – Culture then, said Gladys. When was your last visit to the cinema, the theatre, opera, ballet, any kind of concert, an art gallery, a museum? – I don't do any of those, said Arthur Barlow. I go to poetry readings when there's one I can get to on a train or a bus. – And how many hours a week, on average, do you spend watching television? – I don't have a television. I have a wireless and a tape recorder. I listen to poetry programmes and to tape recordings of poets reading their work. – Do you have access to the internet? – No, said Arthur Barlow, nothing like that.

Gladys put down her biro and looked Arthur Barlow full in the face. It struck him that she was beautiful and radiant with life. Weakened by the vision (as it might be called) of Gran Benson in her scuffed armchair and now by Gladys's manifest sympathy, Arthur Barlow shrugged and said, There's not much to me, Gladys, I'm afraid. Only the poetry. Really, that's all there is to me, the poetry. – The public library, said Gladys. You surely belong to the public library, Mr Barlow? – That I do, said Arthur Barlow, animated. Couldn't live without it. Especially the reference section. I use the dictionaries, you see, to try to follow the translations of foreign poets word by word. And from the lending library I borrow things that I can't afford or can't get hold of through the catalogues. And of course it's in the library I find out who's coming to read anywhere round here within striking distance. So at least you can put me down for that, Gladys. I'm a great user of the public library and the staff could not be nicer. They know me in there. They're very kind to me. It's a home from home. I've got my own library here, of course, but I couldn't live without the public library too. Once a week at the very least I walk there and back, whatever the weather, so that keeps me fit, you might say, as much as going swimming would or playing golf.

Gladys closed her folder and began to button up her golden coat. Thank you, Mr Barlow, she said. I don't need to take up any more of your valuable time. – You'll see my books, won't you? said Arthur Barlow. Then you'll have a good idea how I occupy myself. There's some next door, in the parlour, as Mother used to call it. – Gladys followed him through. The parlour was cold; the books lined all its walls; a three-piece suite, a glass cabinet, a stand for a pot or vase, had been moved away from the walls to accommodate the books. This is the third room, Arthur Barlow said. Alphabetically, starting upstairs, my bedroom and the spare room are the first two, it begins with S down here, the anthologies are in that corner by the window. – And all poetry? – And things to do with poetry, the lives and the letters of poets and what they said about poetry. – And not much space for any more, by the looks of it. – No, said Arthur Barlow. And that's a big worry to me. I'm afraid I may have to use Mother's bedroom after all, which I hoped would never happen. And pardon my asking, Gladys, would I be right in thinking that you don't belong in these parts? Are you not from where I'm from, more or less? – Moss Side, where else? said Gladys. But I'd say you were more Ordsall way, across the river, more Seedley or Weaste? – Ordsall, said Arthur Barlow, but with the clearances we went to Pendleton. But the shock I referred to earlier came to me from Weaste. It was Gran Benson in her end-terrace house in Weaste. When I was a boy the trains ran past her gable end, so near and fast they shook the house. But when I visited her just before we left, the line had gone and they were building a bit more motorway and they wanted where her house stood for the width of it. What a noise, day

106

and night! And the dust and the lights! My real gran, Gran Nuttall, was dead by then and Gran Benson, her sister, wouldn't come down south with us. She said she wanted to die among her own people. Not that she had any by then, only Sam, the dog. Her daughter was dead long since and so was her son-in-law. And the grandsons went to Australia so there she was on her own with Sam. Mother kept calling in to see to her and trying to persuade her to come down south with us. But she was adamant. She might have gone into a council home only they wouldn't let her bring her dog. So she stayed put. Not that we wanted to be in the south, you understand. But Father thought we might be better off and the hospital said they'd move him down here if he liked, filing. – I must leave you, Mr Barlow, said Gladys. I have another call on your street, at Number 97. – One last thing, said Arthur Barlow. Did your grandmother or your grandmother's sister ever say, 'Sit thee down, lass' or 'Nowt lost where pigs are kept' or 'I'll make one less' – and go slowly off to bed? – Gladys laughed, such a resplendent laugh. Bless you, Mr Barlow, of course they never did. They said things like, 'Walk-good keeps good spirit', 'Hungrybelly an Fullbelly dohn walk same pass' and 'When lonely man dead, grass come grow a him door'. – Oh Gladys, said Arthur Barlow, you could read me the Caribbeans! I've only got the one voice and it's very poor. If I could hear you read the Caribbeans, how those strong men and women would come off the page and be alive in the room with me! – But Gladys buttoned up her golden coat against the cold and shook Arthur Barlow's hand and left his house.

Arthur Barlow went into the kitchen. It was the time when he made his cup of coffee. He had been on the verge of asking Gladys would she join him, when she left. The place was neat and clean. His use of its facilities and utensils was regular and precise. Never an unnecessary pan or plate or spoon. The vision, still working, resumed in him, greatly intensified by all that Gladys had brought in, and he saw that he would no longer be able to decide for himself how much of his future life he would deal with at any one time. His rota henceforth would not be able to hold out the flood of loneliness of the years still needing to be lived. He might say I will read and write for two hours then make a cup of coffee, same for a further one and half hours, then make some lunch, after which I will at once go shopping and visit the public library, he might say all that aloud in the empty house and raise it as a bulwark against the days and weeks and months and years to come, but he knew the tidal wave was building and might at any time break in and bring it home to him in the here and now what the life of unalterable loneliness would be like. He looked out at the garden. It was rather a dank day. A yellow rose, still going strong, blooming abundantly over the righthand fence, was the one bright thing to see. The kettle clicked off. Top of the list of my New Year Resolutions, said Arthur Barlow, is: restore this garden to its former glory.

The doorbell rang. It was Gladys, smiling. Nobody in at 97, she said. So I've come back here.

Coffee. What a pretty rose, said Gladys. – Yes, said Arthur Barlow, I bought it for Mother on her seventieth birthday. It flowers late and well into November. – I'll have to leave in half an hour, said Gladys. My youngest is only looked after till one o'clock. We moved down here ten years ago. My husband thought it would improve our chances. He was an accountant, working for a charity. But three nights a week he drove a fork-lift in a warehouse and died in an accident, sadly. I thought of going back north but the children were settled here by then. My youngest is eleven but because of a problem she isn't quite that grown-up yet. My kind neighbour looks after her while I do my Saturday job. My boys are big and strong. I hope they will find work they can enjoy. Do you enjoy your work, Mr Barlow? – Arthur Barlow stood up abruptly and answered her staring into the garden. I used to enjoy it in a funny way but lately I've not enjoyed it even in that funny way. They moved me to the cull and destroy programme and, to be honest, I have begun to find that particular job a bit depressing. I have to find the dead who have been dead eight years or more and despatch them to the incinerator. You wouldn't believe it, Gladys, there are twelve miles of medical records just in the place I work. – He turned and sat down again. – It's very good of you, Gladys, to come back in for a few more minutes. Mostly when the bell rings it's the postman with a new volume of verse and I thought it might be him but I was more pleased it was you. Otherwise it's only the gas or the electric. And twice a year two lads come down all the way from North Shields selling fish. I generally buy from them though I don't like cooking fish. The worst are the estate agents. They come asking would I like to sell. They know I'm in this house all on my own. They've got clients on their books would kill to have my house, being where it is, and make bedsits of it. – My mam and dad, said Gladys, looking Arthur Barlow full in the face, when they got off the boat at Salford Docks they stayed in Seaton Street with my aunty and uncle who had come over three or four years before. Next morning they signed on at the Labour Exchange and by the end of the week she'd got a job in a Jewish gaberdine factory in Ancoats and he had started on the buses though at home he'd been a studio photographer. After a while they moved to a place of their own in Darcy Street and that's where my two brothers and me were born. I went back looking for the houses before we left but Seaton Street and Darcy Street and all the other streets round there have gone. Good riddance, I say. There was no nice accommodation in those parts. It shocked my mam and dad to see how poor the locals were. And then the drizzle and the fog and never any music.

Arthur Barlow again went to the window. Gladys, he said, I'm very likely getting worse. My shock this morning said as much. I keep thinking of those estate agents, if that is what they are. One night last month the noise at Number 19 was worse than ever. It was late on a Friday and I wanted to sleep so as to be fit for my Saturday morning trying to write a poem. In the end I thought they'll surely not mind me asking them will they turn it down. And I put my shoes and dressing gown on and walked across. The door was open and I looked inside. I've never seen such a sight and it was as though they'd never seen anything like the sight of me there on the doorstep looking in. I asked them nicely would they mind turning it down or shutting the front door at least because I couldn't sleep. And everybody laughed. Such a din of youngsters laughing at me because I feared I wouldn't sleep. Then one of the lads said – forgive me, Gladys, this really is what he said – he said, Fuck off and die, granddad. Our sort live here now. I was very hurt by that – I mean, I'm not a granddad – and I suppose I must have stood there open-mouthed. And then a very big young man, very big and strong, walked over from among the girls and lifted me up. He lifted me up and held me in his arms as though the weight of me was nothing at all. And he said to the others, Where's he from? and when they answered, Number 2, across the road, he carried me across like that and set me down at my own front door, which I'd left open, and said, Sleep tight. – Arthur Barlow came back to the kitchen table. Gladys averted her eyes and said, And you a gentleman with all those books.

Gladys rose to leave. Arthur Barlow followed her towards his front door. But reaching the parlour, his downstairs library, she stepped inside. – So much poetry, she said. And the first two rooms of it upstairs. And the postman delivering more and more. And you yourself, Mr Barlow, writing and writing. Tell me, have you shown what you write to any living soul? – I did once, said Arthur Barlow, in the year after Mother died. I was all at sea and I fell in love with a young woman in the hospital. I gave her the poems I wrote for her, every Monday morning I gave her a sheaf of them, I'm sorry to say. – Why sorry? – Because she did not want them, because it was bad manners, because she told me to lay off, because I let myself go, because nobody should let himself go the way I did with her. In the end she complained about me and the Supervisor gave me a warning. They moved me out soon after that, to the repository I spoke of where there are twelve miles of medical records. – I see, said Gladys. And when you read poetry, am I right in thinking, from something you said earlier, that you read it aloud? – Oh yes, said Arthur Barlow, it's best read aloud. That way it comes more alive in you, if you see what I mean. And only by reading it aloud can you get it by heart, of course. – You know some poetry by heart, Mr Barlow? – Indeed I do. I suppose like most people I wonder how I'd manage if I were put in solitary confinement or if I ever have to leave this place and can't take my books with me, I ask myself how I'll manage if I don't have a store of poetry by heart. – Is there any for children here? Gladys asked. My Edith is a great one for poetry. You should see her face, Mr Barlow, when she sings one of our songs or says a poem. – Over there, said Arthur Barlow, behind that armchair near the window, there's two or three yards of poems for children. I've always collected them specially, old and new, from all over the world. – And do you have any by heart? – For answer Arthur Barlow straightened his tie, clasped his hands, stood very upright, looked through the window at the ugly street and said:

The Forest of Tangle

Deep in the Forest of Tangle
The King of the Makers sat
With a faggot of stripes for the tiger
And a flitter of wings for the bat.

He'd teeth and he'd claws for the cayman
And barks for the foxes and seals,
He'd a grindstone for sharpening swordfish
And electrical charges for eels.

He'd hundreds of kangaroo-pouches
On bushes and creepers and vines,
He'd hoots for the owls, and for glow-worms
He'd goodness knows how many shines.

He'd bellows for bullfrogs in dozens
And rattles for snakes by the score,
He'd hums for the humming-birds, buzzes for bees,
And elephant trumpets galore.

He'd pectoral fins for sea-fishes
With which they might glide through the air,
He'd porcupine quills and a bevy of bills
And various furs for the bear.

It carries on, said Arthur Barlow, but I think I'd better stop there. – Thank you, said Gladys. And now it's time I went. – Again she shook his hand, again he led her to his front door. He said goodbye, he watched her turn the corner, golden, out of sight. He fiddled with the knot of his dark tie. Late morning, dank.

At the far end of the street the postman was proceeding slowly towards Number 2. Just as well stand here and wait and see, said Arthur Barlow. So he went to the gate and stood on the pavement watching the progress of Naz, the postman, who was always glad for him when his post looked like a book. Gladys, returning, got very close before he turned to see whose the footsteps were. Arthur, she said, if I came back here with my Edith on a day and at a time convenient to you, would you be so kind as to say her a poem and read her one or two out of your anthologies? And if you like, I'll read you some of the Caribbeans in my voice from home so that they come alive in your room, as you put it, those strong men and women. – Naz came up. Good morning, Mr Barlow, he said. Looks like another book for you.

Fault

THERE'S A FAULT through me, he said, a fault-line, and every now and then it moves, or there's a sort of slippage somewhere along it, and that's that. Can't be helped. Anyway, we've arrived. We'll walk from here if you don't mind. Really we should have come all the way on foot. Why is there never time to do things properly?

He parked the car, they got out, he sat by the roadside on a stone among primroses, lacing up his boots. Rain in the night, so copious, kind, steady, she had lain awake listening to it, glad of her interlude of wakefulness while he slept, confident of returning to her sleep whenever she liked. And now their day was mild, scented, scarcely broached. Every slope had its voices of water. Somewhere high up a buzzard was mewling, plaintively, as though tired of circling, solitary watchfulness and the need to keep on killing. Phil, she said, what *is* the matter? He wouldn't look at her, he watched over his hands that were crossing the long laces into their clasps. Nothing, he said. Nothing's the matter. Only me. Colette felt the beginnings of hopelessness, like a clouding over. Why doesn't it work? Why doesn't it do what it's supposed to do? But she took his hand, briskly. Show me the lake, she said. He glanced at her. Again and again she startled him, like a reminder. Yes, the lake, he said. But the undertone in him was muttering that you should not lay the onus of yourself on the natural world, it is not your property, it is not there to serve you.

113

The road, hardly more than a track, climbed glistening wet between stone walls. West flowed the sea, slate-blue, sunlit, unending. Then the road doubled back, to round a spur of the hill, and in the north the mountains stood in their sight, far away but the feeling of them came into him, stepped across the estuaries and the west-east roads a great distance in one swift stride, so that he halted in wonder and shame. It snowed last night up there, he said, when it rained down here. How close the fresh snow brings them. Should you like to go up there one day? Should you? Yes, she answered, of course I would. But this minute I'm happy where I am. She tugged at his hand, as you might a child's. The road turned south again, straight, in a gradual climb, and came out from between the stone walls into a terrain of last year's dead heather, rushes, blond dead grass and the occasional gold flicker of eternal gorse. This is common land, he said. You can step off the road and walk where you like up here. And if you headed east and kept above a few hundred feet you'd cross a road now and then but until you came into England you'd trespass on nobody's land and even if you did you'd never meet the owner.

But the road itself was compelling. Now the man and the woman were taken up into its purpose, the steady climb, bare land either side, and ahead, on a soft blue sky, the moment of going over. She had in her an intensifying presentiment, a mix of foreknowledge and memory, a place, a state out of childhood into which she was advancing with the sureness of a sleepwalker. Imminence! The brink of a vision of freedom! How these things come back to you, how they live in you, biding their time. And when a skylark started up and the singing of it rose to a height and tippled down, it thrilled her like a pure happiness finding its place of resurrection, there in the present, quickened on a scrap of earth and in a shaft and a fountain of sky. This is mine, this is what I have in me and what I am. She glanced at him, and on the strength of her own gratitude swore that all would be well.

He had his eyes on the point of the road's passing over

into emptiness under an empty sky. He knew the lake would be there; but just as convincingly he could imagine nothing there, or nothing that would work. And yet with her help, surely all would come right again, for a while at least and, really, why not for ever? What, in fact, did he have to contend with, what stood against him, where exactly did he locate the threats? He quickened his pace, and she with him, as if to force the issue.

Then they halted, the lake was all in view, just as it had been and, for their lifetimes at least, very likely always would be. And he saw something new, or the familiar thing newly: he saw the shape, the sinuous enfolding space that the low hills made for the water to come into, he saw the water filling that space and finding its own shape in the hollow offered. That felt like a revelation. What is offered, is entirely right: the shape wants filling, the water entering, spreading, rising, entirely wants that determination of itself, that body, those bays, low headlands, lines of straighter shore, the shallows, depths, drifts, that very shape of being and that appearance under the endlessly changing sky. Faith entered him again, he felt abashed by it and did not dare look from the lake to the woman standing next to him.

Below, on the right, the stream brought the night's rain rapidly through rushes and tussocks into the lake. The road descended, the lake became less graspable in its whole shape. That's the way across, he said. There's a sort of ford. They left the road on a muddy track. Now that he was sure of his knowledge, it seemed worth having, he could put it to use. She followed him, his contentment liberated her spirits, she was altogether more at liberty to look around, be where she was. A flock of wheatear, two dozen of them, crossed the drab bog, settling and flitting, they had the colours of the terrain, but brighter. Then, from beyond the lake, she heard the cuckoo, and childhood, from elsewhere, gripped at her heart like a small cold hand. She caught him up, tugged at his jacket, so that he turned. The cuckoo, she said, I used to be frightened of him when I was a little girl. I suppose it was the voice moving around as though it had no body. Perhaps I was frightened that might happen to me – that I'd lose my body, just be a voice, not belonging. It won't happen to you, he said.

They crossed the stream which flowed fast there but through stones, some big enough to step on. The lake was troubled where the new water ran into it and distinct light breezes passed over the surface like shivers over the skin. You can swim from that bank, he said, pointing ahead. I found a way in where you don't have to wade too far for a proper depth. You can strip off and swim. It's very simple. Nobody ever comes. Should you like? – Now? – No, not now. One day in summer. Should you like to come swimming in the lake one day with me? Of course I would, she answered. What a question! And you ask it as though you think I'll answer no. He shrugged. It's a big thing, he said. And my faith is small. I was always on my own, swimming, and I have never asked anyone else. Mostly it was in the early morning. I never saw a soul. I swam out to where I thought the dead centre would be and lay on my back there, trying to float with the least possible movement. I became quite good at it. Several times the heron passed over me. I lay as still as I could on the water, flat, looking up, until I got cold. Then I swam in quickly. Once I did it in the late afternoon, after a very hot day. The water I lay back in, on the surface, was warm, really warm. Then I let my legs sink and everywhere up to my heart felt very cold indeed. I quite like myself as I was then, in boyhood: very self-possessed.

Whenever he spoke to her in this fashion – rapidly, in a low voice, staring hard into her eyes – she could feel him transplanting images into her that for him were of peculiar potency. It felt like courtship: he desired to lodge his words, and the scenes and feelings shaped by them, so firmly in her that they could never be evicted or forgotten. In that way he would win her and hold her. All the same, she had never thought him a calculating man. Rather she felt him to be at the mercy of the things he conjured up. And it was as if he helplessly wished her to be at their mercy too.

After a while, having got beyond the place on the shore from which he had bathed, he halted again and pointed to a small island at the head of the lake and on it a pile of stones shaped roughly like a beehive tomb. There was always a building on that bit of dry land, he said. The story is that many centuries ago a hermit built a tiny chapel and a cell for himself and lived there in peace till he died and the locals rowed over and buried him. But what you see now is what's left of the Englishman's tower.

Here Phil's voice shifted again into the tone of possession. He turned from the lake and, blocking Colette's view of the island, he entreated her with his eyes to witness how the story enthralled him. It was in the 1890s, he said. The Englishman had come up from London and bought himself a house further down the coast in a place frequented by artists. His house stood on a sort of platform above the river where it entered the sea. And one summer morning, waking very early and listening to the water, he felt compelled to follow it to its source. And so he did, as far as this lake at least. For the stream leaving the lake behind the little island flows into the sea where he had bought his house. He swam out to the island, examined the ruins, and decided he would build himself a tower out of them, to visit or even live in whenever he pleased. He had money and was used to getting his own way. At great expense he had a small rowing boat, tools, sand and cement, timber, scaffolding, a hoist, provisions, the makings of a rough shelter and more besides, transported to the shore where the stream ran out. And within a week of his first discovering the place, he had begun to build. Being entirely his own master, he made good progress and had got as far as fitting the joists for an upper floor when two men appeared from nowhere and called to him from the bank. He crossed over to them in his little boat. You can't do that, they said to him. It's common land. No one has a right to build on it. He replied that he was set on building himself a tower on the little island and would gladly pay whatever might be necessary for the right to do so. You can't buy the right, they answered. It's common land. At that, feeling he had made a reasonable offer, he shrugged, rowed back to the island and continued lifting the joists into place. The two men disappeared. A week later, returning from a necessary visit to his house at the river mouth, he saw that all his courses of stone had been knocked down into a mound, the timbers and whatever of his belongings would burn had been piled up and burned, and his little rowing boat had been stove in and sunk. The two men appeared from nowhere and said to him, politely enough, You can't build here, it's common land. If you build it again, we'll knock it down again. So that was that. He went back to his house by the river mouth but the babbling of the water during the night and in the early morning saddened him unbearably and pretty soon he sold up and disappeared.

You seem very enamoured of this Englishman, said Colette. I suppose I am a bit, said Phil. And soon I'll show you why. Quite often when I was a boy I swam out to the island and contemplated his mound of stones. I always thought I'd like to live in a tower and view the world from the top of it. – Imagine a woman building herself a tower, said Colette. You can't. It's unthinkable. – In the 1890s perhaps. But now? I can quite imagine *you* building yourself a tower. – That says more about you than about me, said Colette.

Where the stream left the lake they bore right across a damp expanse and climbed a gate on to a small metalled road. The long hill that had bordered the lake's west shore sloped gradually away, the road cut through this lowering spur, soon crossed another, even smaller, road, and at that junction Phil turned right. Now we make our way back, he said. And the rest that I wanted to show you is near. The road ran quite straight, at first through a tunnel of ash and beeches, the air cool, the greenery still holding the damp of the night's rain. They were close under the hillside which, the road itself running almost level, step by step resumed its steepness and elevation. In a couple of hundred yards they would be out in the open again, in sunlight. The end of the tunnel of trees was very clear. Colette hurried, to be there sooner, out of the chill, but Phil took her arm, halting her. I got the idea about there being a fault through me from here, he said. It only occurred to me last week. I remembered my boyhood passion for geology, couldn't understand how I had ever let it lapse, and at once looked out all my old maps and the handbook for this area. And I saw what I'd never seen before or – is that possible? – had forgotten. This road, with the hill on one side and the flat marsh on the other, runs along a fault. The ruins I'll show you in a moment and the three or four still-lived-in houses we'll pass before we reach the car, all lie on the fault. In truth a small fault like this one is a perfectly safe place to build. The slip happened millions of years ago and you'd have to be very unlucky indeed, far unluckier than I am, for the ground to sink or slide again under your family home. And it's not that the people building here weighed up the risks. I guess not one has ever known a fault ran under his house. They built here because of the springs. Along the line of a fault you'll always find springs. The families sink their own wells. Digging their ground, if they're at all lucky, they'll bring fresh water to light and have it running through their patch of land just as they please. That's what it's like, in reality, living on a fault: earth blesses you.

Phil, said Colette, you know the facts and you twist them to harm yourself. – Only an image, he answered. Not an explanation, just another way of saying it. – I'm cold, she said. Do you mind if we walk on?

They were a hundred yards into the warm sunlight when he halted her again. It's here, he said. The place I especially wanted you to see. Under the hill, very close to the road, were the ruins of a small house. The roof and one gable end had fallen in and everything else still upright looked very near to toppling. An ash had thrust up through the fallen slates, stones, timbers and plaster and was taller now than the house had ever been. A holly at one end, a wild cherry at the other, had been there for the lifetime of the house and were outliving it. This was my Gran's house, he said. I came here every Easter and for summer holidays and in the winter too when I was let. My way to the lake was not by the road we have walked but on a path from Gran's back garden, a steep diagonal. In fifteen minutes I could see the water, ten minutes later I was naked in it. And listen to the streams that come off the hill this side and pass under the road and sustain the marsh. But even better than those, that swell or shrink according to the rain, were the well and the spring. The well is choked now but the spring – come and see – is still there for anyone who knows about it.

He took her hand and led her round the fallen gable into what had once been a garden. All was overgrown by nettles, docks, thistles and many beginnings of ash, elder and sycamore. At a place in the far corner, close by a rusted iron gate, he went down on his knees and first parted and then tore at the covering of dense lank grass. His hands thrust in among roots, into mud, they burrowed deeper. Colette stood over him. His bare hands were like animals desperate for water. She felt an anxiety for him, in case he shouldn't find what he had set his heart on finding and showing to her. But also the haste and violence of his digging and that so much should be at stake, this troubled her, was it not ridiculous, did it not rather repel her that a grown man should go on his knees and thrust and claw at the ground like a beast in the grip of an appetite? Then suddenly he sat back on his heels. There it is, he said, the water. Stoop down and watch closely. She did as he asked and saw the space he had made, of clear water, and in it the faintest, most delicate perturbation, almost aerial, as though breath were entering, as though the earth itself were respiring, but it was not breath, it was water, fine as air but having the subtle body of water and capable of augmenting, filling and overflowing. When I was a boy I cleared the space completely, he said. I made a bowl in the ground and lined it with flat stones. I knew the water's exact point of issue, through a slit of yellowish clay, it fascinated me, I have sat there mesmerized by the whisper of water entering my hoard that was crystal clear and cold.

She stood up and asked in a voice without kindness, What happened to the house? Why isn't it yours? Why do you have to come back to the ruins of it like a ghost and dig in the earth with your hands like an animal? – When my grandmother died, the house went to my parents. They sold it without even telling me. I was their only child and they knew how I loved the house but they sold it for very little money to a man who had no use for it and let it go to ruin as you see it now. I am dispossessed.

Saying this, he had not looked at her, only at the water cupped in his hands. But now letting the water run away and looking up at her standing over him, he said, You do love me, don't you? She flinched, as though he had raised his hand against her. How can you ask? she said. Why must you ask? – At the start I never had to ask. You told me often, as though you couldn't help it, as though it bubbled up out of you. – You liked me helpless, didn't you? You liked me having no more option than your silly spring. And she added, I don't believe I've ever looked down on you before. Your bald patch is almost a tonsure. Did you know that?

He stood up and beckoned her away from the spring, to follow him back on to the road, but through the garden and under the standing gable end that leaned out wide from true; and there, under that leaning wall, he stood, and turned on her again. Say it, he said. It's a small thing to ask.

Seeing him there, she was fearful. She stood further off, under the wild cherry, the tip of the gable came over like a beak, the whole thing, all its fatal weight, tilted over him like a hooded cape. She stood back against the bole of the cherry, her hands feeling behind her at its smooth coolness. He saw her confronting him from a place of safety, with a column of living strength rising behind her spine, and she looked out through the cherry's light blossom at him under the overhang of stone. Phil, she said softly, come away now, will you. Let's finish our walk. Show me the other things you have to show me.

His body had assumed an odd angle, not leaning as the wall did but queerly slant against it. The left side of his face seemed to have slipped, it looked thrown and then frozen into an appalled relationship with the rest, especially around the mouth so that his voice was his and not his, as though rising through the throat and passing between the lips it was refracted. Say it, he said again. With a shock then all she saw in his eyes was a bid for tyranny, not a plea for help and love, and words rose up in her and formed into sentences she would never have thought herself capable of, but they were hers, in her voice, that had become as level, sharp and unbending as a slate. She said, A bully, that's all you are. You want to have me just to your liking. *Have*, that's the beginning and end of it – have! have! have! – and me giving. And she struck a pose under the flowering wild cherry tree and recited: I gave what any woman gives/ That steps out of her clothes. Or – in another attitude – perhaps I'm the rain that gives you the springs and the streams and the lake that you love so very much. Rain, steady rain, that harms no leaf or flower; I'm woman giving as she loves. And you: having! I give myself, you have me.

Then her voice became softer, but still quite audible, still keen enough to cross the gap from her in safety to him in peril. She said, So you're dispossessed, are you? They sold your birthright, did they, for next to nothing? Why didn't you buy it back, cost whatever it might? You loved her, didn't you? She always said you should have it? So why didn't you fight? Why didn't you sell every other thing you owned and raise the necessary cash and buy it back? This place with a spring and a well, this place with a path going up the hill in a steep diagonal so that in half an hour you can swim in a lake in paradise? This wild cherry, that good strong holly tree – we'd have had somewhere to come to, a place with a hearth, a fire, a garden, air fit to be breathed by angels visiting from heaven. Why didn't you fight for it and do whatever was necessary to get it back? I'll tell you why: because you like being a ghost, you like being dispossessed, you like showing me beauties that are not yours to give.

Colette, he said, stepping forward, stooping now, only say it and I'll be all right. There's more than this house which is a ruin and which, as you say, does not belong to me. Just across the road in the bog that belongs to no one there are hundreds of trees: rowans and birches, ash and the willows, above all the willows that grow up out of the wet, out of pools, and their long branches sink down and root in the wet and grow up again and extend like immense candelabra, all soft with moss, all sleeved in green and gold moss, how I loved those families of willows when I was a boy, I climbed in among them, I went from one to the next above the impassable bog that reaches to the sea, I lodged up there, I perched for hours, the jay flashed past me with a shriek, and at twilight the owl, very close, almost silent, a whispering, so close. All those trees and the pools, the lichens, ferns, mosses, the blue, the purple, the yellow flowers that thrive in the wet, in a light like nowhere else, you'll want to see that place. Say the word, and let me show you where I was so happy as a boy.

She too stepped forward. Phil, she said softly, I'm sick of your paradise lost, I'm sick of you telling me of places that would be paradise for children. A safe house, and children. What children? Whose children? You on your own, the only child, climbing trees, swimming out to the very centre of a lake, thinking you'll build yourself a tower on a little island. And then she screamed, Only child! Only child! One of you was enough and more than enough, I'm sure. Turned then and in three strides was on the road, crying over her shoulder, But one would be better than none. He followed her, and halted. Say it, Colette, and we'll be all right. But she strode away down the road, the set of her body entirely angry.

Coming level with the trees he had spoken of, she paused. They were more entrancingly lovely than she had allowed him to try to say. The light among them made and itself partook of the dappling, the shades, the reflections, the shifting glances. Seeing her halt, he thought for a moment she would relent. She looked back to where he stood – jabbed her finger at him, at the ruins of his grandmother's house, at the trees collapsing beautifully into greening pools. Turned from him then – and at that moment heard the cuckoo, very close, in among the trees. He heard it too, and shouted, Hear that, Colette, the cuckoo, there never was a cuckoo in there before, I never heard him in there, not once in all my years. The voice moved off a few yards, further in, a voice on a branch over water that nourished and rotted the willows, the silver birches, the rowans, and the childhood fear took hold of her again, and he saw it, he saw that she was fearful, that the voice of the bird in there, its repetitions, frightened her, and again he felt the start of a shameful hope that in her own weakness, needing him, she would turn and all would be mended. Further in and away went the voice, and it felt to her not like a lure to follow into a perilous zone, but as in childhood as though it was herself, the very soul of her, flitting little by little away and that she would be left on the solid road without the spirit of a life she might call her own. She glanced back at him: he looked boyish and aged, bent and lithe, and as though they were face to face and sharing breath, she knew that in his need to possess her he was helpless. The cuckoo, more remote, sounded more insistent, as though the faintness of the voice was the faintness of herself already in thrall. She turned and began to run down the thin straight road that went almost level along the base of the hill and had springs and wells either side of it and, as he had said, four or five cheerful dwellings and families in them, living their lives.

Charis

CHARIS, ZOË AND Felix, said Zoë, daughters and only son of Prosper and Felicity, christened as they were so that their names should be a blandishment, like calling the Furies the Eumenides, the Kindly-Minded, and just as futile. For in truth, she said, mumble all the apotropaic spells you like, bribe all the greater and the lesser gods you've ever heard of, still they fuck you up, your mum and dad, and in our house, no less than in the House of Tantalus, they do so with a vengeance. Dear sister Charis, third of the firstborn daughters who have killed themselves, I was not at your cremation nor at the Service of Thanksgiving for your Beautiful Life nor at the scattering of your ashes in the Sacred River Alph, farewell, dead sister, I weep for you. Our brother in Jesus, Felix who is full of shit (though he tells all and sundry he had the shit kicked out of him at a tender age by Mama in one of her rages), our beloved brother Felix, who escaped soon as he could to sweet New England to do good works for a Community of Fathers, this sharp-suited executive announces to the world that he has seen you in the arms of Mary Mother of God and that she loves you better than her one and only boy and that you are in the light there and at peace and radiantly happy. No soul among the millions in his Facebook does not rejoice with him at this glad news, said Zoë. Dear Charis, forgive me if I don't forgive you for leaving me in the world with him.

You should see your website! I tell you, one glance at it,

all the anti-emetics available on the NHS would not keep you from throwing up. He calls it his choir of angels extolling you, my sister. And he has posted there the rhapsody he delivered at the Service of Thanksgiving, for the world to see: Charis is in the Light. Charis was brave. Charis prays for us. Charis asks our help to create a Church of Light. Charis is the Butterfly. For after the scattering of your ashes on the effulgent surface of the Sacred River Alph, a butterfly landed on the basket which had contained them and stayed there for a while, quietly. In truth, my dearest, being dead, you have brought out the very best of the worst in him, said Zoë. But this will make you laugh. If you really are safe and sound in the arms of the Virgin Mary this will make the pair of you wet yourselves laughing. Remember that photo of you and me and his daughter Allegra (!) dancing? Was it in Powys, when you returned from the waterfalls? Or at Beaurepaire, before I gave up the unequal struggle, and we were dancing the crane dance, the labyrinth dance, that turn by turn was to bring us deeper into Gaia's mysteries? Oh that dance! There were three of us, Charis, Zoë and the radiant child Allegra, all dancing the crane dance in pretty dresses. And he emails me to say he has airbrushed me out on the grounds that I was looking miserable and spoiled the picture. So now there are two, Allegra and Aunt Charis (deceased), with a hole between them where poor Zoë was till our brother in Christ Jesus disappeared her because she had a face like a wet Whit Week. And that, sweet sis, is how the website opens, on a nice big lie, and goes on that excellent beginning from strength to strength through the ninety-nine delusions with links along the way to multitudes more, said Zoë.

Is there internet in Heaven? Do you spend much time online? I tell you, Charis, Zoë said, it would take eternity and then some to mark and inwardly digest the half of what's already there under your beloved name. The Other Photograph pops up everywhere. I mean the one of you striding purposefully up the long slope towards Seaford Head, all alone, my dearest, and nothing before you but the empty slope, the summit and the sky. Taken a couple of years ago, I believe, in May or June, by that fat holistic potter – Angie? Fran? Isolde? – who told you she could heal you. And there you are climbing out of the busy little town where hundreds of lucky people are having a nice time in ordinary ways. No sooner were you named in the local newspapers, the fat lady emails it, the photo, to our Felix and from him in seconds it goes forth and multiplies and humans in all five continents have it on their screens. Did he weep much for you when you were living, Charis? I don't remember that he did. But now he shows you to strangers on his Blackberry and takes off his glasses and dabs at his eyes with a snowy white handkerchief and says what a comfort that photograph of you climbing Seaford Head in the days of your almost hopefulness has been to him and Father. Tell me, Charis, did you ever understand our brother Felix? Does Mary? Does the Trinity, all three of them combined and thinking hard? In truth though it is an excellent photograph, said Zoë. You are turning away, you are heading off up the long slope alone. I have never been there and I never shall but I imagine the air to be a pure delight and surely there are skylarks and the flowers that love the chalk and all around you space and the feeling of the nearness of the sea. But the white face, the sheerly final face, the flatly vertical height and fall, how could a human being employ a thing so utterly inhuman? Don't worry, big sister, I shan't go anywhere near the place.

That book I lent you about Eleanor because I thought it might fortify you in the locked ward but which you couldn't bear to read, they posted it back to me. I was rather worried that they knew who I was and where I lived, said Zoë. But I'm glad to have her book.

Father skipped the ceremony at the Sacred River, Zoë said. But he attended your cremation and the Service of Thanksgiving, leaving early, of course, to drive back to Ealing and put Mother to bed. To annoy Felix, I asked that she, Mother, be remembered with everyone else among the prayers because if anyone is in hell, in this world or the next, she is. Felix wouldn't allow it, needless to say. He said it would not be appropriate. He said he had consulted the Carmel Fathers and had been told by them that it made no sense theologically to pray for a soul in hell. So I thanked our Felix, Zoë said, for saving the congregation from doing something nonsensical.

Email, mobile phones and the internet are a marvellous facility, Zoë said. Here I am in Swindon miles away all on my own and nonetheless *au courant*. Alas and God help me, it was the last thing I wanted and surely not your intention but doing what you did has brought us closer, me and the blessed Felix. Now the Word comes from him to me in superabundance. As do the images. He sent me one of those slide-shows so I can view you through the years approaching nearer and nearer to that sweet summer morning in the Year of our Lord we are still suffering in. I see you on a trike in Ealing, setting off, and the look on your face is more fearful than hopeful. Your schoolgirl years distress me. By then it was obvious. And you on courses and retreats, you dancing, singing, painting, drumming, weaving, making masks and pots and doing tai-chi and meditating among bare ruined choirs or in a glade. So many stations, photograph by photograph, sent to me by Felix, of your road to Seaford Head.

And would you believe this? (Of course you would.) When he flew in from Boston to visit you on the trauma ward he called at Martha's first and phoned me from the place itself, as he called it, her attic room, with the neighbour who found you, the Good Samaritan, standing by him at the open window. The sill is quite high, he said. You had to put a chair there to climb on to it. He said that beyond the damaged roof he had a view of the garden, the blossom, the little white clouds on a blue sky and to him they were proof perfect of the love of God. He did not mention the psychiatric hospital, whose beech trees, lawns and wards are also visible from that window, just over the wall at the bottom of the garden, as you and I, my dearest, know. But there was, he said, a blackbird

– he thought it was a blackbird – singing from the rooftop above his head. He held the phone so I could hear it, sister.

Flying back next day, said Zoë, Brother Felix emailed me from the airport to say you had told him you were damned but that he had promised you Mary loved you and would lift you down from the Cross into her lap. And he added that the Fathers could not do without him for more than a day or two, however urgent his own family responsibilities might be. He begs the world to google Carmel Fathers. Every hit, he says, feels like a shot of the love of God. And when people see the photographs of the work in progress on that donated land in a glade among the ancient redwoods of New England, when they see the ruined chapel and the cloisters of Beaurepaire, where you were happy, Charis, being resurrected in effigy by the holy work of the Fathers' hands, they put their money where their amazed eyes have been. Charis, by moving from Martha's house to the bosom of Mary you have greatly increased the blessed Felix's fundraising powers, he says. On the ten million dollars he had drummed up already, two million more have come in since you left. He tells me the Fathers tell him he is what they had been praying for: the man abundant in both money and the Spirit. In their Norman and Early-English ruins, by a virgin spring, there will be a place for thinking prayerfully of you, sweet Charis, so he told me, Zoë said. He also tells me he is considering litigation against Beaurepaire for not allowing you to stay there indefinitely and against the psychiatric hospital for allowing you out of their sight. And he has asked the Carmel Fathers' legal advisers to advise him on the soundness of his case.

Felix says you have stepped off a white cliff into universal love, said Zoë. He says you have quitted the Earth of Agony for the Sea of Peace. Stella Maris illuminates you, Mary Star of the Sea illuminates you for all to gaze upon. And Mary has spoken through our brother Felix and said, Go, sisters and brothers of the sister in my lap, go tell the story that must be told and let it touch the hearts of all in all the world. And there is more, said Zoë. Every day he updates the site and emails me and phones me more and more.

How I despise myself, said Zoë. I should shut the system down, drive the whole fat box to the tip and throw my phone in after it and lie still in the dark and see you clearly, Charis.

Charis, when you came back from the waterfalls you were radiant, Zoë said. It was in Powys, early evening in May or June, and although you asked me would I like to come with you I could tell you wanted to walk up the stream alone. Now, if I close my eyes and concentrate, I can see you as you were when you came back and found me reading and watching for you in the grounds. And it is easy for me to remember and imagine what the walk was like out of the grounds, following the stream to the waterfalls that you did not know were there. Though you walked alone you carried with you up the stream the loving fellowship of the house whose trees and lawns and flowers you were leaving. You carried in you the quietness, the expressive dancing, the hours of song and of silent meditation under the stars around a fire, all that and more, as you climbed by the thread of a stream that came down out of the mountains and all the things that made the body and the spirit of the stream, its hurry and abundance, its endlessly varying polyphony, the brightness, the leapings, the passages almost of stillness and the hazels, alders, willows, harebells, ferns, rocks and mosses through which the water felt and expressed itself, all that and more, said Zoë, you carried with you in a joy rising to ecstasy as you stepped out from under the cover of greenery and found yourself at the opening of a large horseshoe, an almost sheer embrace of hillside around a pool into which three waterfalls fell with a steady force and noise and overflowed and ran as living water down and down into the grounds of the house in which you felt at home. And at that place under the waterfalls, so you told me, Charis, Zoë said, you prayed, as you had never prayed in your life before, that having looked and listened hard and breathed the smell in of the thunderous falls and taken a palmful to your lips, you would be enabled to follow the waters down and be for ever in your slight person a vessel and a bringer of love and joy not just into the fellowship of that blessed house but into any house and any company you ever thereafter entered. That was your heartfelt prayer, said Zoë, as you turned your back on the waterfalls and the high horseshoe wall and began your careful descent through the watery greenery to me.

You don't know, said Zoë, unless with the love of Mary comes omniscience, that the only time I visited you during your second incarceration in the locked ward I knew at once, even before you mentioned Seaford and your barmy potter friend, what you were planning, sister. And I didn't try to dissuade you and I didn't alert your keepers. And really I cannot tell whether my conscience troubles me on that account or not. When Felix emailed me his report – from Father – of the hours you spent dithering on Didcot Station and then of your foolish leap from Martha's window my chief thought was, If this must be let it be clean. Naturally he attached his pictures of the hole in the tiles and of the soil pipe, aerial and a section of the gutter hanging off. What a mess you made! What on earth were you aiming at? Quits with Mater? Another dagger in the heart of Saintly Pater? Believe me, Charis, I should not have liked to see you alongside her in a wheelchair and him ministering to you both till he dropped dead. I know about vengeance, I have thought about it and I know there are better forms of it than that. So when in the locked ward I saw how spruce you looked, how mobile you were again, no walking frame, scarcely needing even a stick, and I learned they trusted you to go into town and get your hair done, I had a pretty good idea what you were up to. And when you spoke of Seaford in that lingering way, how happy you had been there with that dippy potter woman, I thought that would be clean at least. Does it weigh on me or not? Worse to bear, said Zoë, would have been your sisterly hatred had I warned your keepers and they took me seriously and stopped your little privileges and put you under obs twenty-four hours a day. You wouldn't have liked that, would you, Charis? Zoë said.

Seeing Felix's photograph on the Carmel website, seeing him among the jolly American Fathers who clap him on the back and call him Jesus or Midas as they please, it struck me again, said Zoë, how strong the family likeness is between him and you, my Charis. You have the same black greying hair, the same thin face, the same spectacles behind which the black eyes look out like insects backed into a corner and expecting to be trodden on. When I left you in the locked ward, a doctor, passing, said to me, Much better, wouldn't you say? Indeed she is, I answered. Sweet, these physicians who think their suicidal patients want a cure. I saw you playing passably the role of a woman on the mend. But behind your spectacles I saw your cowering eyes. You have the eyes, Charis, the family eyes, frightened.

Having announced on the website that you are a butterfly, said Zoë, Felix phoned me to say that in a vision he had seen you ascending through the stratosphere doing bravely on your frail and beautiful wings. And that you had come to the very house of Mary and entered at an open window and settled on the sleeve of her skyblue gown. Then after a silence, said Zoë, he asked me in a different voice did I know about the ichneumon wasp. Yes, I answered, but he told me anyway. The female lays her eggs in the pupa of the butterfly, the larvae thrive by eating it, the butterfly harbours what is eating her. That's it, he said, said Zoë. That's it, the whole story, plain and simple. But resuming his Mary voice he told me he believed the butterfly could choose to die and by dying stop giving sustenance to the killer parasite and so by self-immolation end the curse. Charis was the butterfly, he said. Charis was brave.

Felix tells me Father arrived in his invalid wagon just in time to see you departing in an ambulance. And I wonder is that why you changed your mind at Didcot. Did you think you would be wasted under a train? So you decided you'd give him a nice surprise when he arrived from Ealing with a duvet and bags of shopping for you in your new home in Martha's attic bedroom? Oh, Charis!

I miss you, Charis, Zoë said. I am quite alone. I fear the family will look more my way now. It weakens me that you are dead. We were arm in arm, whatever the distances. Remember our pact to get through childless so the curse would end with us? You kept your word and I will too. Not that there's much temptation. It seems to me I walk with a clapper in my hand and shout, Unclean! Unclean! I feel I have it cut into my forehead, I am of the House of Labdacus, keep away from me! And any I might have loved and wanted children with do keep away from me. What is it about Felix? Did he take a test? Does he have a certificate saying his seed is good? Pity Allegra. Her best hope is that her fool of a mother – whom Felix has deserted, by the way, he emailed me last week to say the Fathers and their phoney ruins need him wholly – will carry her off to a secret place in a forest or on a boundless prairie or in some colossal foreign city and bring her up with never a mention or any clue of our family name. But you know the myths as well as I do, Charis, Zoë said. One day when she's stopped worrying a messenger will come from Delphi or a man on a train will stare at her and say, I know your face, and they'll be back again, back in the mechanism, and the helpless girl will breed.

In therapy once, said Zoë – did I ever tell you this? – they asked what the worst thing was I'd ever seen at home. And I had to answer quick, not giving it any thought. Up popped the image of Mother in her wheelchair in the open lift ascending out of the living room into the bedroom and half way up she stuck. Her pasty face empurpled fast with rage, she swiped at nothing in particular with her stick. Father fiddled with the controls fixed to the wall. I heard him whimpering. Mother by then could not make proper words but clearly the blurtings of her mouth were meant as curses. In the midst of it she shat herself. She was halted half way up, just above my head, I raised my eyes to her, and Father, turning helplessly towards her, did the same. So we stood either side of her thwarted ascension, looking up at her who fumed and stank. Father said he would have to telephone the Services and she would have to be patient a little while until they came or could give him good advice. That was the image that came to mind when they asked me to say, without any searching through my thesaurus of horrors, what was the worst. Mother flung her stick down, trying to hit Father, but of course she missed and when he went to the telephone and left me standing there she slewed her bloated purple face my way and from her mouth, already slavering, she tried to land a gob of spit on me. I'm fairly sure I never told you that, Zoë said. Needless to say, in the leisure of sleepless nights I've thought of much since then to equal or excel what sprang to mind when they said, Say quickly what's the worst.

According to the therapist, Zoë said, some go to terrible lengths to command if it can't be love at least attention. Aiming at paraplegia from an upstairs window is not unheard of, so he said. But it takes two, of course, there has to be somebody you can do it to and you have to be sure on some deep level that he or she is fit material for your scheme. It's quite a risk. In the case of Mother and Father, that particular therapist said, and I agree, said Zoë, she must have known that she had in him a man supremely capable of cruel and abject servitude. Who would not fail or flee however vilely she used him. He was her reciprocity in person, superhuman in his lust to be enslaved, and strong, so strong. I have always pitied Father for his fortitude. Would so much bad have happened had it been obvious he could not bear it? Perhaps he excited the Fates to try him worse and worse by the very fact that he stood so tall and had lived so long. There can't be much pleasure in tormenting a man who will give up the ghost at once.

Possessing Father, that therapist said, Mother possessed the children too. He fed her them whenever she said, Do it. Does that make sense to you? the therapist asked. I shrugged, said Zoë. What do you think, Charis? He fed us to her piecemeal on demand, the three of us? And now there's only two.

Charis, Felix and Zoë, spawned at the confluence of two poisoned streams... I wonder, Zoë said, did the ancestors, dragging their heritage, advertise in the Soul Mates columns of the Daily Telegraph? Clytemnestra seeks an Oedipus with a view to further damage. Thyestes, hungry for children, seeks a Medea.

Charis, said Zoë, I plan to disappear. I know it is said to be very difficult nowadays but I intend to do my best. The day they found you I noticed that my passport would soon expire. I hurried to Boots and photographed myself; got the forms from the Post Office and applied for another ten years, using the Express Service they offer. I can't see why I should be refused, can you?

But what I don't want, Zoë said, is the police out looking for me. Father and Felix, bless them, when they phone and email me and I don't respond, are bound to think, Oh dear here we go again. I don't want anyone looking under cliffs for another missing woman face down on the tide. So I have told Martha, who will surely tell the world, that once I've put my affairs in order I shall walk alone to Compostela in hopes of easing my mind after the terrible events of spring and summer. Of course, she is delighted by this fiction – the first of several I will compose – and agrees I must walk alone. The love feast in the evening and the fellowship of the dormitory will balance me, she says. She drove to see me with a bundle of maps and leaflets and hours of practical advice. Now I could blog my way to Compostela quite convincingly without ever leaving Swindon and this detestable bedsit. But I shan't do that. I'm not sure what I'll do or where I'll go when my passport comes and even when

I've decided I might not tell you, Charis. I expect you'll be haunting Ealing and Carmel for at least a year and I don't want you blabbing to Father and Felix in big-sisterly concern. But whatever I do, it won't be clean, Charis. It won't be the cleanness you got to in the end. Wherever I go, I'll still be among the anniversaries, I'll be in the world of Mother's stick and spittle, of Father's liver spots, his rheumy eyes, his terrible staying power, I'll know that Felix still operates in his dark blue suit, his light blue shirt, his moccasins, his glasses just like yours, his snow-white handkerchief, I'll drag the Ealing torture chambers after me, the soil pipe, the wheelchair and the insect walking frame, my Charis. I'll be in the foul rag-and-bone shop of the heart. For a while at least that's where I'll be, perhaps for the duration of my brand new passport, perhaps for ever, said Zoë, I don't know. It's not what I want, of course, but it's where I have to start.

I shall be all right, Zoë said. And if I'm not I can do without help from Father and Felix, thank you very much. Bear in mind, Charis, that when Mother gets hungry there's really only me to supply her now. Felix is pretty safe, I'd say, in New England among his Holy Fathers and their reproduction Beaurepaire, so it's me our unholy dad will come for down the fast M4 in his paraplegic carriage when Mother says, Get me a pound of flesh and a pint of blood and a dram or two of soul by nightfall, will you, dear. So I must be off somewhere neither they nor you, sweet Charis, nor any other remnant of our blighted tribe can find me.

In my passport photograph I don't look a bit like you or Felix, which must be an advantage to me on my travels, Zoë said. I haven't decided yet what I'll call myself in circumstances where I don't have to prove it with a signature or a document. But it will be something ordinary, something, like Joan or Margaret, that doesn't tempt Fate or raise impossible expectations – Joan Thompson, Margaret Evans, how about that? At nights when I can't sleep I try to calm myself by making up little biographies that in a café, say, or at a bus stop

I could come out with to a stranger, as my own. The most I thought I'd say in the general direction of the truth is that I've recently suffered a bereavement, a beloved sister, and think a change of scenery might do me good. Then last night I expanded on this little scrap in a way that gave me a thrill of pleasure. I'll say that I intend to travel abroad but that before I do, to fortify me, I'm going to spend a few weeks with a dear friend on a smallholding in the north of England, a woman of my age, recently widowed but determined to stay where she is, high up in the snow, the wind, the rain and the sunshine. Yes, she'll stay up there and manage the couple of fields and the animals just as she and her husband together did. And I say how well she is doing, though profoundly deaf. Charis, said Zoë, I love this bit of a story. I get off a bus high up in a village I've never been to before and there to meet me is my dear friend Eleanor and she is wearing the bright woollen scarf and hat and gloves that she knitted herself in the deep mid-winter with wool from her own sheep, wool she spins and dyes herself in many cheerful colours. And how glad she is to see me! And I believe her when she says in the strange flat voice of the profoundly deaf that I will be good company for her and the sheep, the dog, the cat, the chickens and the ducks. She promises to show me things up there on the fells that I will never forget but will cherish for ever, wherever I go, my Charis, Zoë said.

The House by
the Weir and the Way

THEN IN DECEMBER, when the house had lost even the memory of summer warmth and they lived their days in one stone-flagged downstairs room, Odile tripped and fell in the dark hall and broke her right hip so badly the surgeon decided at once on a replacement. All so fast: one day mobile, the next completely crocked and the next laid up and mending. Sabela nursed her, the doctors said she should get over it pretty well.

Still it was a shock. Years of evaded anxieties were suddenly there present, in focus and adamant. The big house would defeat the women, they were too old for it, Sabela herself in poor health and now Odile, ten years her senior, must perhaps wait months for the return of strength. They got help from the gardener, a man in his eighties, who summoned a couple of strong grandsons and moved the bed downstairs to a room across the hall. Both the rooms they lived in now had cavernous and beautifully carved stone fireplaces into each of which, among the dried flowers and the pieces of pottery and sculpture, they set a diminutive and ugly oil-heater. The upstairs rooms, more than a dozen of them with vast ill-fitting windows over the quiet road or the garden, were given up and the stuccoed ceilings and friezes, the weighty candelabra, the rich curtains overhung and enclosed a creaking, scuttering and uneasy silence in which stood massive wardrobes, chests and cupboards and sumptuously

139

draped four-poster beds. Light gathered faintly on the many heavy mirrors. Odile and Sabela housed downstairs in the harboured bit of warmth.

Sabela was a woman of the theatre. She was best known for her dramatic monologues, which Odile wrote for her and which she performed with a good deal of mime and interludes of tunes on her accordion. But even before the accident, that common work, and other things too, had slipped without resistance out to the periphery, upstairs, so to speak, into the chill rooms the women no longer even visited. Now Sabela occupied herself with looking after Odile; wryly the patient observed a renewal of purpose in her nurse.

The cold outside and in the upstairs rooms was brutal. But in their one living room, in a fug of cigarette smoke, cooking and the oil heater, and after a glass of wine or two, Sabela felt life to be cosier than it had been for quite some time. The word 'safe', or at least 'safer', came into her mind; which she did wonder at and knew very well that had she uttered the idea Odile would have thought it risible. In the most obvious matters – the house, money, their health – they were not safe. Sabela, however, there in the living room and ministering to the immobile Odile, felt strangely encouraged. This will make us strong, she said to herself. When I've helped Odile back to health we shall both be stronger and surely the rest will follow as it is needed. After a meal, before she cleared away, while Odile was drinking a final glass, Sabela withdrew to the deep armchair in the corner, sat cross-legged in it and amidst thirty years of common clutter played old tunes very softly on her accordion.

Odile was a difficult patient. At first confined to bed across the corridor – frequently visited and sat with by Sabela – she had insisted on rising and dressing (in a white silk shirt and a velvet trouser-suit the colour of crushed mulberries) for Christmas dinner. Then she inched through the freezing draughts on her walking frame into the living room which Sabela had decorated with lanterns and garlands. Sabela, herself festively dressed, waited on her with affectionate fussiness. Odile, reaching for her glass, said, Enjoy it while you can, darling. It won't last for ever. Sabela, unsure quite what she meant by this, at least did not feel the tone of voice to be unkind. They ate, Odile drank quickly and soon looked as she generally did when the mood was convivial: like Mischief, as Sabela would often say. Her hair was frizzled into a mockery of youthful curls, the ginger lapsing with the weeks after the dyeing. Now all at once she was exhausted, the flushed face haggard. She was old and in pain. Sabela helped her to the frame, opened the doors of living room and bedroom and very slowly accompanied her across the hall whose air was so cold it felt almost substantial, like a river. Now Odile took all the service – all the help getting ready for bed – without grace or gratitude, and when Sabela left to clear away the meal she said harshly, Hurry, come and warm me. Sabela did hurry but there was a lot to do and, exhausted herself, she could hardly fend off her anxieties, Odile's harshness being one of them.

Early in the new year Sabela left Odile at the breakfast table smoking and reading and drove into town for the day's provisions. The cold was glacial, a north wind coming off the snow on the high massif sharpened it into a thing that cut and ached any uncovered flesh. When Sabela returned, Odile was not at the table nor, as on some mornings when she had pain and her spirits were low, was she back across the corridor in bed. Sabela called her name and got no answer. Fear precipitated in her heart. Again she called out, stood at the open door and shouted into the garden, Odile! Odile! Still no answer. She ran across the terrace to the bridge over the frozen muddy water they called the Grand Canal. She stood there, calling. Then she turned. To search any further she would need her boots.

On the terrace, among large and beautiful earthenware pots much damaged by years of frost, Sabela looked up. Odile

stood at a first-floor window looking down at her. Only later
– and how it hurt her then! – did Sabela think, She watched
me anxiously searching for her, she heard me calling her
name, she saw how helplessly I love her. At the instant, the
sight of Odile caused no thought at all in Sabela, only a cold
shock. Odile's face, so familiar (so loved) seemed changed to
a stranger's and Sabela felt looked at as though to that person
in the window she was herself a stranger. And yet so long and
so closely known. Odile, behind the glass, contemplated
Sabela from a height, appraised her, and so coldly and
strangely that Sabela, beginning to try to understand, thought
she must have suffered a stroke and her features were made all
awry and different by it and were struggling to express an
incomprehension and an estrangement suddenly visited upon
the brain. But then, perhaps worse, Odile smiled and waved
flatly behind the glass. So there was nothing wrong – except
that for several minutes she had appraised her friend with the
remote look of a stranger, a look so hard it had set her features
eerily aslant.

Sabela hurried in and upstairs. One or two of the broad
treads were wormed almost through and on the first landing,
as you turned left, a section of the banister was loose. Odile
stood at the window, still looking out. Sabela began scolding,
You got up here, up those stairs, and you can't even walk on
the flat! –The view, said Odile, I wanted to see it again. Sabela
stood by her. Odile's features were tight with pain, she was
leaning all askew and heavily on a stick. The poor sheep, she
said. On a threadbare fall of snow, under the gigantic sequoias,
the dozen mired and draggled sheep huddled together
miserably. How will I get you down again? Sabela asked. Both
women were shivering, in what had been their bedroom.
Look at the river, said Odile. That's really what I wanted to
see. It's the river I miss looking for first thing in the morning.
In truth there was not much to see of the river but through
the large draughty windows often you could hear it out there
on the far border of the property, it came slant over a weir

and the din of that body of water was always more or less loudly present in their room. And once you knew the river was there and you knew where to look, you could see it, turbid-silver, flashing through the lower trees and bushes, especially in the leafless winter. Beyond the river was open country. Help me downstairs now, will you, my Sabela, Odile said. I'm a fool, forgive me. We'll be all right, I'm sure.

By the end of February Odile was moving around quite nimbly with a stick. The frame had gone back to the hospital, the clinic there no longer required her to attend. I'm discharged, she said, with a commendation for good progress. Sabela drove her the short distance into town, sat her in the Café des Sports, did the few errands and collected her to drive home. Apart from that, concerning Odile, she had less and less to do and every day, as the year crept towards spring, her own uneasiness worsened. She said to Odile, I think we might as well stay downstairs, don't you? It's cosy, the two rooms. Odile gave her a look which seemed to say, I know your game, and answered very definitely, Not at all, the sooner we're back where we were, the better. Phone Jean-Luc, will you, and ask him and his boys to move us back upstairs. Sabela said in a rush that she, Odile, wasn't fit enough yet, the stairs were dangerous, they needed seeing to, so did the banister, the bedroom was damp and cold – but in the midst of all this Odile picked up the phone, got Jean-Luc at once, and arranged it. Then nodded to Sabela, So that's that. And by the way, she added, they were asking me in the café was I taking on any work again and as soon as we're back to normal, I shall. Your little job, said Sabela. Yes, said Odile, my little job. It keeps me busy, it gets me out of the house. You'll drive me to the café, won't you, darling?

Sabela fought back. We'll have to sell the house, she said. Buy somewhere smaller. Odile shrugged. So you keep saying, she said. – But this time for certain. You getting crocked. – I'm not crocked now. – Do we have to wait till it happens again? – Why should it happen again? – Because you're old, because we're both old. – Odile was laughing. – Why are you laughing? Sabela said. It's not funny in the least. – You remind me of a part I wrote for you years ago, said Odile. One of your successes, I remember. I must have been psychic, I must have foreseen and foretold how you'd end up.

Next day at dusk Jean-Luc arrived with his grandsons. Back upstairs, ladies, he said. Well that's a good thing. Neither he nor the boys were ever scurrilous on the subject of Sabela and Odile. He liked their company, he had no one at home. He came in for coffee or a glass or two when he worked in the garden or with the sheep or at the weir. He had all the firewood he wanted and more than his tithe of whatever he could persuade the ground to produce. He and the boys took a drop to begin, then they dismantled the king-sized bed, lumbered it respectfully upstairs and in the chilly bedroom put it back together again. He sent the youngest boy for a basket of kindling and logs. Lovely room this, he said. And with a fire it will be warm and cheerful for you, ladies. Old and young then, they wished Sabela and Odile good night.

The room did indeed look beautiful. Lit only by the fire and a bedside lamp, all its graces and none of its defects were evident. There, said Odile. I told you. Now we can start again. The big mirror over the white marble hearth showed them side by side before the blazing logs, Odile smiling, Sabela unsmiling. Sabela's face, from years of miming, demonstrated an inner state, however complicated, with extraordinary clarity. Viewing her, Odile shrugged, which was to say, I can't help you, darling. Then she put her arm around Sabela's shoulders – both in the mirror watched it done – and she, Sabela, looked, as she had done years before, like the woman the older woman would persuade and claim. And seeing that, her helpless face at once assumed the mime-mask of sadness, so that Odile was touched and aroused and said to the mirror woman, Come to bed. All's well. But all was not well, there was no acting it, they slept turned away and as the fire consumed itself and died and the cold inside the house rose almost to equilibrium with the cold outside, even under the eiderdowns they felt the chill insinuate itself into the gap between their backs.

At breakfast – Sabela had risen first, warmed the room, got everything ready – Odile said, Must you line up your pills like that every morning? Sabela felt it as she would have a blow across the face, no warning, from nowhere. I'm sorry, she said. Her contrition was instant and abject. I never knew it bothered you. You never said. – It's depressing, Odile answered. And she added, There's lots of things I've never said. – They breakfasted then in silence, Sabela not looking up. Only at the last, she faced Odile and said, Are you sure you're well enough to go to work? Shouldn't you leave it another week? – Darling, said Odile, I'm quite well enough, thank you, and one of us has to earn some money. So drive me in and drop me off, will you?

Odile's 'little job', an odd survival into modern times, was that of *écrivain public*. She wrote things on command for people who couldn't write or who thought she would say what they wanted to say much better than they could themselves. She sat with her Olympia, a stack of paper and a little bottle of correcting fluid, in a corner, almost a private alcove, of the Café des Sports, not quite out of earshot of the racing, the rugby, the football or the cycling, and with a coffee or a glass of red to hand, received her clients, who were mostly poor, and in a brisk and authoritative manner wrote on their behalf. Needless to say – her fees could not be high and she had her expenses – there was not much money in it. Not in a score of years would she earn enough to mend the roof or treat the woodworm or significantly improve the plumbing and the septic tank. But she liked the work, she was good at it, she was known and respected for it and it got her out of the house.

Most of the tasks were routine and, for her, straightforward. She dealt with bureaucracies; she sent congratulations, condolences and wishes for a speedy recovery to friends and relations five miles away or on the other side of the world; she ordered goods and wrote again complaining if they were faulty. In went the sheet of white paper: she tapped and pinged, the carriage travelled, she slung it back, wound out the sheet, read its black signs aloud and the client, often in a childish wonderment, signed and paid. Good work, she enjoyed it. And now and then came commissions that were more demanding and intriguing. A stranger found her out in her almost-privacy in the Café des Sports; the brief, like a confession, took time; Odile listened closely, made notes, her imagination began to work for the client's purposes. Such a writing could not be done there and then. The client must return the day after tomorrow or next week. Odile carried her notes and her ideas home and worked in a compulsive way till the job was done. Sabela lost her, as she put it, whenever such commissions came along; but had not minded in the years of her own theatre work when Odile was writing with gusto and with love also for her, the mime, the musician, the speaker of monologues.

That first day, among Odile's regular clients, who in her absence had been quite at a loss, was an elderly man, a stranger to her and indeed in all his manner and appearance strange. He wore a black trilby, which he doffed as he approached, and a three-piece suit whose pieces did not belong together. My lady, he said, and laid a script on the café table before Odile. It read: My name is Mister Vlad. I speak and write many languages but not the good one. I am foreign in this land. I love a beautiful lady whose old man is dead. Please you write and say please she marry me. I am a good man. I have a house and goats in very nice place. My friend write this. You please write long and good for me to this beautiful lady. When Odile looked up he smiled at her very winningly – several gold teeth – and took out some photographs from his wallet: one of the lady in question and half a dozen of himself at his place in another country among his goats, fruit trees and flowers. Yes, said Odile. Come back on Thursday. And seeing his incomprehension she pointed at him, at herself and at the table between them and counted three fingers; whereupon he beamed and with his right fist beat gently three times against his heart. And I shall need the photographs, Odile added. To inspire me. She gathered them up, mimed the putting of them and his script into her bag and asked him with her face would that be all right? He closed his eyes, held the trilby to his belly and bowed, which she took to mean, Yes, if it must be, if it will help you to win me the lady without whom my life will be a wasteland, I entrust into your safekeeping her picture, my dearest possession, and these poor proofs of my suitability.

Collected by Sabela, Odile spoke excitedly of Mister Vlad's commission. I shall enjoy this, she said. And he'll pay well. He had more than his precious photos in his wallet. Sabela said nothing until they were back in the coach house that served them as a garage. Then she said, I've often wondered whether you care a fig what these things you write for money might actually do. How do you know he won't murder her? She slammed the door her side and left Odile to manage the bag, typewriter and stick on hers.

The meal was bad tempered. Sabela cleared away, took her drink and cigarettes to the armchair and began to sing Galician songs quite loudly over the accordion. Odile set up her typewriter and laid Mister Vlad's script and photographs by it. He's harmless, she said. You can tell by the way he's smiling at his goats. And I doubt if the lady will need much persuading. By the look of her she is ready for a move. So if my letter furthers his courtship, I'll be glad. I'm sure they'll be very happy together.

Sabela sang. The songs rose in her one after the other. They were archaic, but as they welled up and she uttered them, she felt them to be her own, in her truest own voice. Love and death, the wraiths of both, endlessly coupling, the one story in an infinite variety, Sabela sang her episodes, they were all particular and they all came trailing many ghosts of the general and implacable sadness. Odile hammered at the keys, slung the carriage mercilessly back for more, wound in, wound off, chortling to herself and declaiming in Sabela's direction the bits that pleased her best.

Sabela ceased, she resumed her wine and her cigarette. The skin of her face was white for want of sleep and health and her eyes looked out from blackness. Listen to this, Odile cried. The spirit moved me, I shan't change a word. She read the whole thing, it took a good ten minutes. Whore, said Sabela.

But on Thursday at the Café des Sports when Mister Vlad presented himself in another ill-assorted three-piece suit at Odile's table, he listened bare-headed and enraptured to her reading aloud of the letter to the beautiful lady in his name. He understood not a word, but its rhythms, its variations of tone and pace, its harmonies and, perhaps most of all, its author's manifest sincerity as she delivered it, persuaded him completely that those words in that order and sounding just like that would do the trick. He wept, Odile told Sabela when she picked her up, he thanked me in copious tears, he opened his fat wallet and indicated that I should take what I pleased and when I took a modest two hundred he insisted I take three more. We can buy ourselves a washing machine that works! So what do you say to that, darling? Whore, said Sabela. And more fool him and, if it does the trick, the more fool her.

The weather softened. The house began its annual persuasion: see how beautiful I am, and in strange ways, really like nowhere else. Why would you want to sell and go elsewhere? Sabela answered: because of the woodworm, the roof, the plumbing, because it is draughty because no windows fit, because there is every kind of damp and rot, because we are old. But she stood as she did every spring on the rickety rustic bridge over the Grand Canal and listened to Jean-Luc telling her he could, if they'd let him, transform the muddy trough below them into a thing that purled through cress and mint and kingcups, he would induce the dipper back and the kingfisher, all it needed was to fix the rusted trap at the sluice, wouldn't cost much, he'd get his lads to help. And the damp ground, almost beginning to be warm, widened its hundreds of celandines in support of Jean-Luc's faith. The snowdrops might be finishing but, to continue, so that you could bear to watch the snowdrops die, were there not squills and aconites and the cyclamens? You forget, every year when the cold comes you forget, you side with the dark, you acquiesce in death, and every year at this time, like it or not, the earth that is packed to bursting with many centuries of seed, the black enduring earth reminds you, whether you will or no, of what you'll miss, fools, cowards, creatures of little faith, if you give up now. On the terrace the frost-cracked heirlooms did again what despite any depth of cold they still had it in them to do: they brought forth narcissi and scented the warming air. And the glory – or one of the glories – of the place, the wisteria, from somewhere far below the foundations of the house called up its energies and pumped them through a stock thicker than a hawthorn's into the myriad cords of sap and felt its way irresistibly into the leafiness and budding that would obscure for another summer all that urgently needed doing to the masonry, the sills, the frames, the fascia and the guttering, all of that, bothersome, would be out of sight and out of mind for another few lovely months under a weltering soft purple.

I'll ask Odile, said Sabela. Jean-Luc nodded and shambled away under the vast dark sequoias to have another look at the contraption by the weir he was sure he could fix with a bit of encouragement. And that very day he drove the two worst of the manky sheep in his pick-up to a butcher friend in town. Better to be eaten than be an eyesore, was his motto.

There was no point in asking Odile. Of late, she would agree to anything, very unhelpfully and irresponsibly in Sabela's view. It's your house, darling, she said. Do what you like. She was cheerful, affectionate, almost as steady on her feet as she had been before the accident. But in all this and in her blithe indifference to the problems of money, house and garden, Sabela knew that Odile was letting her go, indeed almost dismissing her, into the freedom she had already taken for herself. Sabela did not want that freedom. So she hated her friend and grieved over her insouciance. Odile sat in an old duffel coat on a broken chair in a patch of sun and beamed out benevolently over the flowery terrrace and the still wintry rough grass, towards the river that now, empowered by many tons of melted snow and ice, hurled itself with a joyous din over the weir and through the greening trees and bushes, away, away. Nice bit of sun, she said. Things are looking up.

At the Café des Sports Odile was enjoying herself. Enough work came in to keep her busy and, as often in the spring of the year, at least once a day some person she had never seen before asked her for help in a private story. It was as though having got through a hard winter these strangers woke and in the twilight before the beginning of quotidian life said aloud, If not now, when? And remembered they had heard of a woman who would write what your heart dictated, things beyond your own small powers of speech. Mister Vlad had not returned, from which Odile serenely deduced that her magic had worked and that by now he and the lady were settled together among his goats and vines just at the season of lust and sprouting when there is work to be done and two pairs of hands are so much better than one. Sabela's sardonic disbelief made her laugh. That's your problem, darling, she said. And Sabela's face, so adept at showing more than words could tell, agreed.

Every late afternoon Sabela collected her friend who was full to bursting with other people's stories; and every evening, having cleared away and retired to the armchair with her drink, cigarettes and accordion, she must watch and listen to those stories being gaily and noisily developed by Odile and her Olympia in a tempest of bright ideas. She wrote a letter for an absconding wife to leave on the kitchen table; another for an illiterate monk who had run off to live on a narrowboat with a girl barely above the age of consent and wished to tell the abbot how much he abominated him and all his trade; another for an old man who, nearing his end, wanted to make a clean breast of things to his wife, mistress, children and grandchildren and who urged Odile to be truthful and not indulgent. Odile read her concoctions aloud, enjoying their pathos and her cadences, and Sabela sang in Galician of a girl who hanged herself in the apple tree and a soldier boy who deserted and was found at his sweetheart's house and shot in her yard. Strangest in this strange passage of the year, Odile took on and conducted all three sides of a triangular entanglement: a woman in love with a girl, the girl in love with a man, the man in love with the woman. She saw each in turn on separate days, nine so far, and was, even she, beginning to have doubts about 'playing God', as Sabela put it, when events overtook her and she sent word to the *patron* of the Café des Sports that for the foreseeable future she would not be needing her table in the semi-private alcove and on no account must he divulge where she might be found, she would not be there anyway, she was travelling. Summarily all her characters were left to their own devices.

Sabela stood at the weir. Odile was in the Café des Sports, Sabela had hours to kill. She had thought again of Jean-Luc's annual suggestion that he fix the trap and restore the Grand Canal to its former glory, she thought of it only as an item of worry and sadness, one among many, still it drew her, or the weir itself did, the noise, the thought of the weir, off the flowery terrace over the rough grass through the sheep and the grove of immense sequoias, nearer and nearer, till she stood there, at the weir.

A weir makes evident how strong a river is. A weir is a man-made step going over which the river displays a section of its body and lets you know how little a leaf, a log or the carcase of a sheep or human would bother it. A river smells more at a weir: you smell the underside, the under-body that has dragged the muddy bed, and the water, under the whiteness of its surface going over, is the colour of the smell of the ploughed bed and of the lives that can live in that peculiar zone. The din of a weir is frightful. Stand close, it batters every other thought out of your head. It is *steadily* thunderous. If you listen very hard and close you may begin to believe you can distinguish some peculiarities, some slight fluctuations, of the weight, force, pace, but really your hearing is not fine enough, or rather not strong enough, your beginnings in the art of distinguishing are soon battered to death by the general roar. The weir makes a roaring, it no more abides your questions than an avalanche would. It is just itself, overwhelmingly, just that, an all-obliterating weight of noise. The eyes can't comprehend it either. For the weir lies slant not straight across the flow so there is always a feeling, through the eyes, of a willed deflection of the body of water towards the bank. The water may want to get over the step all in one hurrying piece, full on, but the thwart obstacle slews it so that – to the eyes and so also to the attending consciousness – much water seems to run along the brink, fleeing, so to speak, towards terra firma, whilst the bulk of the force and velocity takes it over in a diagonal fashion which to the mind focusing just on that feels worse than headlong, it feels like a residual and ineffectual will of one's own, overwhelmed, and the most you can say for yourself, good or bad, is that you did not go over without demur, some lingering poor wish you might call your own held you back at an angle and making for the bank till the very end.

Sabela stood there close in the din and stink of the weir and its slanting topple mesmerised her. At this time of the year the whole phenomenon was at its most violently self-assertive. This was what the river did in spring and by the weir the nature of its deed was made most manifest. The river ingested the mountains' snow and ice, bulked itself up with them and ran full tilt for the distant sea. Sabela shook her head, and tried to concentrate again on Jean-Luc's annual idea.

For their Grand Canal water had been taken off in a leat out of the river's left side and conducted around the rough meadow and the big trees to pass before the terrace of the house and, in former times, to be useful downstream at a mill. The enabling sluice gate, long unused, was rusted shut; but Jean-Luc thought he could induce it to open again, if not the whole thing, which might, he conceded, be perilous, at least a small hatch or trap half way along it. That would give them all the water they wanted and he, or some other trustworthy person, would operate it just as the ladies decided, for their canal. But that afternoon Sabela saw only the ferocity of the river in spate and the very thought of bleeding its body for their amusement terrified her. And as to amusement... Odile had no more interest in such schemes than she had in supplying Sabela with new monologues. The soul had leached out of their living together in that beautiful and enchanting place. And in Sabela the residue was only material worries and a fear of worse.

By the sluice gate, over the muddy leat, was an iron footbridge. Sabela crossed, climbed up three steps, and stood on the river bank. Upstream the view opened north, to the massif and the resistant snow. And from under that bulk came the pilgrim path, heading south, following the river for a while then leaving it to insist on the south and the Pyrenees, the climb into her own Galicia. A young woman was approaching on the opposite bank. At the weir she halted and turned to face Sabela across the river.

Sabela fetched Odile from the Café des Sports. It was the girl today, said Odile. She brought me the letter I had written in the woman's voice to her. She asked me to read it aloud. She wondered should I answer it for her or not. – We have a guest, said Sabela. A pilgrim. I put her in the Red Room. Her name is Béatrice. She has just been made redundant. So she is walking to Compostela on the money they gave her. – My word, said Odile. A pilgrim in the Red Room. – Yes, said

Sabela. Jean-Luc lit her a fire. Only a girl really, free as a bird. She'll stay two nights, maybe longer. Things are looking up.

They sat in the car in the Coach House and watched Béatrice. She had her back to them and was standing with outstretched arms flat against the biggest of the sequoias. She could encompass very little of its girth. Then, keeping as close as possible, her palm flat on the bark, she set off anti-clockwise, in large strides, over ground that was massively ridged by the upsurge of the tree into the sky. She went out of sight. They waited. Her orbit seemed to take a long time. Then she re-appeared, still touching the trunk and making large ungainly strides. They could see that with a childish concentration she was counting aloud. They waited, so as not to distract her, until she reached her point of outset.

Béatrice came over the rustic bridge to meet Sabela, with the shopping, and Odile, with her typewriter and paper. Nineteen strides, she said. Nineteen! – I will show you a photograph, said Sabela, of seven of us holding hands to encircle that tree: Mother and Father, their mother and father, my twin brothers and myself, but you can only see us, the children, and only my face because I looked over my shoulder at the camera, all the others are facing away or hidden behind the tree, and all of them are dead now, long since dead, except me, I was only two and a half in that photograph. Odile stood awkwardly aside, her hip was paining her. She could not take her eyes off Béatrice's face, its almost rapt attentiveness. The girl seemed helplessly given up to what Sabela was saying and in Odile, who had seen the photograph many times and many times had heard Sabela speak of it, old feelings revived but their cause and focus now were less the woman she had lived with for thirty years and more the girl, a stranger, the beautifully attentive listener. So she felt no irritation nor did she interrupt, as she often had, when Sabela continued to talk about the great sequoias and that tallest of them in particular which was, she said, at least 165 years old and nowhere near maturity yet, let alone demise. The grove had been planted on the land at river level, well below the house already ancient then, for an anniversary, before her great-grandfather was born; and now their crowns were higher than the house by far and still pushing skywards. Odile listened to Sabela solely through the wonder in Béatrice's face and stood there entranced, only dimly aware of a weight of things in her arms and the pain in her hip, and wondered herself at the expressiveness of beauty. It was Sabela who broke off, saying she must cook and inviting Béatrice to eat with them.

Also during the meal, for which Odile and Sabela dressed as festively as they had for Christmas Day, Odile was mostly silent, as though abashed. She drank, as did Sabela, a couple of glasses quickly, then watched the conversation. Sabela spoke, fast and animatedly, as Béatrice questioned her and by an entranced attentiveness led her to speak more and more, so that Odile, never looking at her, saw again the richness of Sabela, her passionate life, but more as it was revealed in Béatrice's face than carried in Sabela's own words which she, Odile, had heard many times before, often with impatience, whenever they took in travellers to be some slight help in the struggle to make ends meet.

My father didn't want the house, Sabela said. His father wanted him to take over the business and live in the house as the family had done for generations, but he wouldn't, he spent a lot of time on the riverbank fishing, just above the weir, where I first saw you, Béatrice, he sat there whenever he pleased, fishing, and waved at the pilgrims passing by on the other side, month after month until he got sick of his father nagging him and early one morning without a word to anybody he crossed over and set off himself to Compostela though he wasn't a religious man which made it worse in the eyes of his father and mother, he was nothing but a runaway, they said. He sent them a picture postcard from Roncesvalles. Before that they had no idea where he was, he might have drowned in the river for all they knew. The next they heard he was in Compostela. He sent them a card of the cathedral saying he'd arrived and would probably stay down there because he had fallen in love and was getting married. When he reached Compostela, so the story goes, said Sabela, he didn't like the look of the cathedral and all its trade so he never went in but found a bar in a back street and that's where he met my mother, she served him his carafe of wine, love at first sight, very romantic, Sabela said.

Odile, contemplating Béatrice, was obliged by the look on her face to consider Sabela, the teller of the tale. Odile sat, so it felt, rather to one side and looked from the face of her friend to the face of the stranger, Béatrice, and back again in a silence that seemed to last an eternity, slowly from one to the other and by each powerfully attracted, and for all that time neither Sabela nor Béatrice looked at her. Sabela, the mime-artist, there at the dinner table having fallen silent, wore a face that looked whitened thick with chalk, the eyes smudged in with charcoal, cavernously black, a face made simple to say one simple thing over a welter of complexities: that's the fact, my father and my mother in Compostela a lifetime ago, and here I am now in this house this evening and this now is the face of it, how it looks now in me as I tell it to you. And Béatrice stared, in the silence, after the words, taking in the face of it, and Odile's eyes went between them, dwelling on one and being pulled back irresistibly to the other.

Béatrice turned to face Odile, and not (this was obvious) as a courtesy, to include the other woman, but in the palpable desire for something more to wonder at. Sabela told me you write things for other people, she said. – Yes, said Odile, I'm an *écrivain public*. We call it the oldest profession. – Yes, said Béatrice, I was wondering whether there's anything you would refuse to write. – You mean however much they paid me? – No, I didn't think money was at the heart of it. Sabela told me you charge poor people very little or nothing at all. I meant do you ever feel you shouldn't write what they ask you to write? – No I don't, said Odile. And it's worse than that. I write things they never knew they wanted to say, then when they hear it they say, That's exactly what I meant. I put words into their mouths and they thank me for it and pay me if they can. – I see, said Béatrice. – But I never do anonymous, Odile said. Whatever I write for them, if they want it they have to sign it in my presence. They have to agree it's really theirs. So I never do poison-pen letters. They sign, I type the address on an envelope and post it. That's the deal. What I write they have to put their names to and stand by. Then she turned to Sabela and said in a tone of voice Sabela had not heard for months, Tell Béatrice a bit more, my love.

I was born the day Franco started the Civil War, said Sabela. My twin brothers were two and a half by then. Father went away, fighting. When it was lost in Galicia he went to Catalonia and when it was lost there too and everywhere else he came back for us in secret and we got out over the mountains into France. So we turned up here, without warning, as strangers, asking for shelter in the family house, the house he had not wanted to inherit. I know this from my mother who gave me the photograph of the seven of us holding hands around the giant sequoia and she told me how we had got here and how we were not permitted to hold on to one another. Father went away again, this time with the French, fighting in the north, and when it was lost there and they took him prisoner and found out that he had fought against Franco in Spain they sent him to Mauthausen in Austria and of course he never came back, nobody got out of there except through the chimney in the smoke and ash. Soon the police came here looking for my mother and my brothers and me but we had a warning and went away and hid. Later we were in a camp and my twin brothers died of typhus. Then when the war was over my mother took me home, as she put it, back to Galicia, but we were not welcome there, it was not home, but that is where I grew up and in the end married and had my own children, Sabela said.

Odile stood up. Sabela said, It's hurting again, isn't it? Let me get you your stick. – No, no, said Odile. I shall go to bed now and leave you and Béatrice to talk. – Béatrice said she would help Sabela clear away but Sabela refused, saying she wanted to be on her own and when the room was cleared and ready for tomorrow she'd play and sing a bit to herself. So Béatrice stood uncertain until Sabela said, Help Odile upstairs, will you, if she'll let you.

Odile climbed slowly. Half way up she halted. Admire the ancestors, she said. They go on and on, up another flight of stairs and around the landings. Gloomy buggers, the lot of them, the men and the women just the same, on and on, dozens of them, miserable long faces. And her mother and father, the only exceptions in this dismal family, the only ones you and I would have have liked, Béatrice, needless to say they are not here. When I am cruel to Sabela I tell her she lives in the past. I tell her I live in the moment, now, and that she is stuck in the past with her miserable ancestors. That is how cruel I can be.

The Red Room was across the landing from Sabela and Odile's bedroom. At the open door Odile halted and looked in. The fire in its hearth of dark pink marble had burned low. Above the bed the flat ceiling-light cast down a faint red radiance. How strange it was, and absurd. Veils were hung from the light, drapes as frail and diaphanous as webs, and they made a canopy over the double bed as airy as mosquito nets but faintly blushing. Brothel lighting, Odile observed. The wallpaper had a large motif of poppies. Opposite the fire, reflecting it and the bed, stood a dressing table with a large tilting mirror; and towards the window, in shadow, a massive wardrobe, and a piano on which was set a red musical box in the form of a merry-go-round with a conical roof and a pelmet of mirrors. I'd forgotten that, said Odile. She limped across, wound up the mechanism and let it play. The tune itself creaked, the painted horses and their riders rose, sank and revolved in a laboured and halting fashion, but the circling frieze of mirrors caught what was left of the firelight and of the faint red luminance shed from the ceiling and wafted these glimmers to the big mirror over the dressing table which helped them into a continuation of their life.

This house, said Odile, more to herself than to Béatrice who stood by the bed, watching. Sabela tells our guests this house came to her when we fell in love, she and I, and had no home to go to. Nobody else in her family wanted it – you can see why – and the lawyer for the estate wrote to Sabela saying it was hers for the asking. That very day we had sworn to spend our lives together. Fate, Sabela says, we were given the blessing of Fate. She gave up everything to come with me, neither her husband nor her children wanted anything more to do with her, they swore they would never speak to her again and they kept their word. Then came the lawyer's letter and we moved here. This house, we decorated all the rooms, one by one, every one different, we gave them names, this is the Red Room, where we sleep is the River Room, we won them back from the cold and the damp, for fun really, for guests now and then, for travellers, for passers-by, but not for any family, of course. And one by one these last years we have lost them. Good night now. Sleep well. That scallop on your rucksack, how beautiful. Take the torch with you to the bathroom. And watch your step. Put another log on the fire when you get into bed. The firelight reflecting in that mirror is a lovely thing to contemplate till you fall asleep. My hip hurts again. What a nuisance, I thought I was over it. If you leave your door ajar I expect you will hear Sabela playing and singing. You might walk all the paths of the earth, you'll never hear anything sadder. Good night, Béatrice. I'm not sure I can take another year.

Odile turned to leave but halted and there in the doorway turned again and asked, Are you a religious person, Béatrice? – Sort of, said Béatrice, who had picked up her washbag and the big torch and was standing by the mildly lurid bed. I mean, I don't believe in God or in an after-life but – she smiled, Odile nodded, Béatrice continued: I'm glad I was made redundant, I believe since I started walking that everything has mattered.

Odile nodded. Tell me, Béatrice, what manner of people do this walk? – All manner of people. – Old people, people who can't walk especially well? – Oh yes, most are much older than me. – Old as Sabela? Old as me? – Oh yes, said Béatrice.

Next morning Sabela took her pills before the others came down. Breakfast went very cheerfully. The sun poured in. They sat back. Odile announced that she would not be going back to the Café des Sports, she had written a note, one of Jean-Luc's boys would take it. Then Béatrice having said again how well she had slept and that the room was beautiful, so strange and beautiful, with the fire and Sabela's singing, quite unforgettable, said she thought after all she'd better only stay the one night and would get ready now and settle up with them and be on her way. Sabela's face assumed the mask of tragedy, it seemed to be instantly palmed upon her by the passage of an invisible cold hand. Odile said, Sabela, my darling, you are looking particularly witless all of a sudden. And she rose, limped from the room, they heard her in the hall putting on her duffel coat and then, through the window, saw her making across the terrace for the bridge over the Grand Canal. She's got that silly cap on, said Sabela, but where's her stick? Sabela ran after her. Stubborn, she said, coming in. But I made her take it.

Sabela sat at the table, desperate. Must you go? she said. Why must you? Why can't you stay? Why must you go to Compostela? Compostela is a horrible place. All of Galicia is horrible, so bigoted and oppressive. Why can't you stay with us here? It would be like having a daughter again. We could adopt you. You could have this house. Surely we could make enough money, the three of us. We could put things right. We wouldn't have to sell. Jean-Luc says he could make the Grand Canal flow with lovely clear water again. A day's work, he says, not costing very much. The dipper and the kingfisher would come back. Imagine that.

Béatrice looked to be back in the first enchantment.

Odile told me you left your family to be with her, she said. – She made me, said Sabela. I had no choice. She is stronger than me. She left someone else, a woman she had been with for many years, who had left her family to go with Odile, and Odile left her just like that, from one day to the next, and has never spoken to her since, because she decided she must have me. She rented a cottage close by where I was living with my husband and my two children. Three nights a week she made me stay in the cottage with her. Then she would come and sleep with me in my house. She made me make my husband sleep in the spare room and she would sleep with me in our marriage bed. Then when she had done enough of that, of showing him who was boss, she said we should go away and find a place of our own. – And that day you got the letter from the lawyer, Béatrice said. – She told you that? – She said it was Fate, she said it was proof that what she was asking you to do was right. – She said that? I loved her, you see. I had no choice. I still love her. Only what she wants of me – the sex – I can't any more, and when I say, Aren't we good companions? she says she spits on that, all that cosy stuff, nodding by the fire, she's not going to die like that, she says, she says she'll dance with Love and kick Death in the balls and dance and dance until she drops. Passion, she wants. She's mad. And now where is she? I must go and look for her. Come with me, will you, she'll have fallen down somewhere, you'll have to help me pick her up. Why must you go? Stay here and inherit the house. I think if you stayed we might be jolly again. We might be very happy together, all three. Surely she would write for me again and I could speak what she wrote and mime it and play my accordion for the two of you in a nice warm room or on the terrace in summer with lanterns and we'd hear the nightingales. She wrote me lovely things. She said she was writing what she wanted me to hear and say. Listen, for example – Sabela stood up, assumed the face that was hers and not hers, the young woman's face, as old as love and sorrow, she put on the appearance of youth in a

161

chilly shroud, she composed herself, stared hard at Béatrice and in a chanting speech began: 'Many are the things a woman may wish for/ Under the eternal sun in the years of her fleeting beauty/ Many and very different things will beckon her looks/ Here on the black and flowering earth, but nothing/ Not honour, nor wealth, nor the hearth and abundant home/ Swerves her wherever it will, whenever it wishes, whatever it does/ Like love. Therefore, my Anactoria…' Sabela broke off, saying, She'll have fallen down, her hip is worse again, the ground is very rough, come with me and find her and help me bring her back.

Odile stood on the river bank, just above the weir. The day was persuasive, so mild and scented the air, so headlong the waters carting away the melt of the vast massif. The pilgrims who had left their beds an hour or so upstream were passing now, always one or two approaching, saluting across the water, passing beyond and below the weir into the trees and out of sight. And true, just as Béatrice had said, there were more elderly than young and some were old and more than a few crept by on needed sticks. Odile saluted them. She thought them ridiculous and magnificent. Herself she had not the least desire to be a pilgrim; but she did passionately desire not to die just yet. She was thinking about Béatrice, her look: rapt, fascinated, quite without prejudice. All that mattered to Béatrice, so it seemed to Odile, was that things should matter. Odile supposed that must be what Béatrice had meant when she said she was glad to have been made redundant. It released her, she was passing through and, as though absolved by this from customary judgement, things fascinated her along the way, and so intensely she felt they mattered. Perhaps she would always be only passing through. How persuasive, how very seductive. Footloose Béatrice. As Odile understood her look, she, Odile, might dance and howl as she pleased and never be disgusting, always be only a wonder to Béatrice. The thought thrilled her, like an invitation.

Singly, in pairs, in groups and always far slower, even the fastest, then the river sliding slant and eagerly to the weir, the pilgrims passed. You could tell the ones who were already a week or more *en route*. They wore the abstracted look of an increasing eccentricity. Whatever their idea of themselves, they had taken leave and were now at an angle, ambling or striding by, accoutred modernly or mistakable for Saint Jacques himself, they had a bias now in their course of life. Holy fools, said Odile into the drowning roar of the weir, I'd rather croak your side than mine.

It was then, in a longish gap when Odile was alone with her thoughts in the din of the weir, that she saw the woman on the donkey led by the very pretty adolescent. It was as though the stage had been vacated for them. Throughout their passage, from first sighting to final vanishing, no other character entered to be a distraction. Odile stopped thinking, heard the weir and felt the pain in her hip only as background, and stared. The woman, a hefty figure in a scarlet skirt, silver blouse, black jacket and jet-black wide-awake hat, bestrode her tough mount comfortably. She was swarthy with dirt and weather; the girl-boy, under a tousle of black curls, was pale and clean as a water sprite. Over her right shoulder, so that it rode on her left hip, the woman wore a leather satchel on which was affixed the scallop, the Venus shell, the comb and *mons veneris* luscious salty bivalve, the sunrise emblem that so snugly fits the palm. Drawing level, unsmiling, gravely benevolent, she inclined her head and raised her left hand in a Pope Joan blessing. The donkey plodded, indifferent. The boy-girl grinned and danced a few steps of a jig. In their own good time they passed by and went out of sight beyond and below the weir. The din and the pain resumed. That's it, said Odile. If she's not gone yet I'll buy a donkey and she can lead me. And if she has gone, I'll catch a bus and waylay her with a donkey further down. That's what we'll do. That's how it will be.

Sabela and Béatrice had come through the safely grazing sheep and the black gigantic sequoias to the river and the weir. Halting there, they saw Odile on the bank at a distance above them acting, as Sabela thought, very strangely. She had seen them and looked to be shouting something important but in the deafening noise of water they could not make out a word of it. She knew this or she didn't, her mouth continued to work, she gesticulated, wagging, pointing, jabbing and slashing with her stick. She's mad, said Sabela. She's gone madder. But Béatrice's face had assumed the expression of slightly absent and unconditional fascination. Odile on a brink just above a constant and inexhaustible avalanche of turbid water, in the apocalyptic uproar of it, was acting something out, for her spectators to grasp. Getting nowhere, she mimed a woman bethinking herself of the need to be clearer. She flung her stick into the river, after it her red baseball cap and after that, with a struggle, her duffel coat. This last caused Sabela a lurch of terror in the stomach, the coat in the flood looked so substantial. Odile herself however, disburdened, stood sideways on now, widened her legs, crouched and bobbed up and down on an absence, on thin air. We must go up and get her, said Sabela. She will have to have some sedation and be put to sleep. Odile, continuing to bob, glared down at them and across her body with her right hand repeatedly beckoned Béatrice and swatted Sabela away. Oh, said Béatrice, oh Sabela, it's the donkey, she has seen the donkey. Everyone in the refuges said a woman on a donkey was coming with a beautiful black-haired girl or boy. They were behind us, coming up slowly, along the way. Surely Odile has just seen them. – And she wants you to go with her, said Sabela. Help me, Béatrice. – But Béatrice, crossing her arms on her breasts, had absented herself into pure watching. Odile began to jig and caper – a few steps backwards along the brink, then a little run forwards, her hands rolling or suddenly flung up, her eyes glaring only at Béatrice, she smirked and perhaps in the din was also yodelling. In the gaze of the girl's fascination, the waters overwhelming all her human sounds, she jigged and footed it lamely forwards and backwards, she twirled, slapped her thighs, cavorted, perhaps hearing cymbals, tambourines and pipes. With her fingers she mimed a poking and a feeling, with her loins she thrust like a goat. Sabela wept and raised up her hands, imploring. Béatrice, steadily as a gorgon, gazed and smiled.

Lewis and Ellis

BEYOND ONCOLOGY, BEYOND the Hospice where the normal people die, quite a bit beyond in a separate unit on what looks like wasteland or it might be Nature, suit yourself, there's the place they send you, when the time comes, if you belonged in a locked ward before that time. Crake's House, the place is called, after a benefactor.

Lewis and Ellis were not close friends. Neither Ellis nor Lewis had any close friends, as such. Funny phrase, 'as such'. People add it to all sorts of statements. He wasn't a success, as such. He did not have a happy life. Not as such. Meaningless really. Anyway, Lewis and Ellis, though not close friends, played chess together most evenings, in Ellis's room or in Lewis's, in the safe accommodation at 473 East Arboretum Street, and they were pretty evenly matched. Sometimes one man won, sometimes the other, but more often than either of those two results put together, a long silence ensued, both men stared at the pieces, couldn't make head nor tail of them, couldn't remember whose go it was, until at last Lewis, or it might be Ellis, said, Call it a draw? And never once in their three years, seven months and twenty-three days living together in the safe house on East Arboretum Street did either say, No.

Life seems to last for ever, at times. To Lewis those evenings playing chess with Ellis have often, since they ended, seemed an eternity. He drank, Ellis smoked, neither spoke a word except Check, Check mate, Call it a draw? The house was silent and if the streets were noisy neither player noticed it. Two or three times Lewis went out for a leak, but Ellis never moved, he smoked, lit the next, tamped out the butt he had lit it from, and stared at the black and white things on the board. Peaceful really, dying, as it seemed, very slowly, all the time in the world. Though not a sentimental man (as such) Lewis has looked back on those evenings fondly and some days worse than fondly. He feels a gap. He still has the chess set and he knows it is possible to play against yourself and he has that up his sleeve as a last resort, and in the meantime gets through till bed by drinking more.

In their vices and eccentricities Ellis and Lewis were pretty equal too. Ellis smoked, Lewis drank. From old newspapers and magazines Lewis cut out photographs of heroic women – saints and goddesses of all the mythologies, suffragettes, filmstars, great society ladies, novelists and poets, that sort of thing – and pasted them on the sloped ceiling above his bed. Ellis, who, in addition to the usual pension and benefits, received an allowance from a rich brother, a Professor of Experimental Psychiatry in Santa Barbara, passed as helplessly as the moon through a cycle of sudden getting and sudden dumping of the classics of world literature. He woke, the need had entered him overnight. No breakfast, unshaven, he took the first bus down the long road into town and was there on the doorstep, smoking and trembling, when the one bookshop opened for business. Then in half an hour, hurrying, he assembled again the works he could not live without: good editions of Homer, Virgil, Dante, Chaucer, Shakespeare, the King James Bible, and so on, to the *Four Quartets*. This last he took with him and the rest, on his account, he had delivered before sunset to 473 East Arboretum Street, and arranged them chronologically around him. A week or so later, sickened to the point of vomiting, he binned them all. Then he lay on the bed, smoking. At least I'm constant in my smoking, he said to himself. The sloped ceiling was stained dark brown. On the bedside table he had always a cup of cold black coffee. He woke in the night, sipped, smoked, thought.

Lewis, moving in after the death of Fat Babs, got wise

to Ellis's compulsion one morning when he went to tip his empties and some pizza into the container. All the books! He fished out a few, cleaned them up the best he could, and sold them for very little money to a man on the market half way into town. When he and Ellis became friends, friends enough to play chess, he did think of asking him would he mind, when the disgust came, giving them clean to him, Lewis, so that he might improve himself, but never quite dared. So he fished them more or less filthy from the bin. He never mentions my women, he said, so I'll not mention his classics.

The end, or the beginning of the end, came in winter six weeks after the lung cancer Ellis had been breeding for many years finally outed itself and by all his physicians he was given at most three months to live. Given! Ellis shared the news with Lewis in such a voice and with such a look that Lewis didn't rightly know how to respond. Merriment almost, a certain satisfaction, his eyes very wide and bright: They've given me three months! Lewis nodded then shook his head and offered Ellis a queen concealed in either fist to decide who would be black. So they played on, in Lewis's room or in Ellis's, fairly evenly winning and losing and with the customary greater number of games they called a draw. Lewis drank, Ellis smoked and coughed and the eyes in his head burned brightly. Then one evening getting towards Christmas, Lewis went out for his third leak and Ellis, weakened perhaps, went and lay on Lewis's bed under the sloped ceiling papered with heroic women.

Lewis came back. Ellis stood before him, yellow and shaking, his head bonier, the skull very apparent, the eyes glaring. You bastard, he shouted, waving his nicotine hand vaguely behind him towards the bed and the papered ceiling, oh you bloody bugger! Lewis had a morbid horror, far older than Ellis's cancer, of people shouting and waving their arms. He had no idea what was upsetting his friend. Fat Babs, Ellis shouted, you put my Babs on your ceiling. Where did you get her from? Where have you been snooping and thieving? How dare you put Fat Babs on your stupid ceiling? Lewis shook his head. He had fallen into the state he always fell into when things came at him too fast and hard. His failure to understand a particular item enlarged at once into a total incomprehension so that he did not understand even the flattest sense of the words that made up the question. Ellis grabbed him by the arm. How bony, he thought then and has often thought since, were Ellis's stained fingers when they gripped. Ellis dragged him to the bed and jabbed with the other hand, just as stained, at one photograph among the hundreds on the sloping ceiling. There, he said, you fiend, my Babs! Ellis peered. It was a photograph of a very fat woman sitting on a low garden wall, behind her a drooping buddleia. She wore a long red skirt in the lap of which lay a bag of chips. She had small eyes and even her mouth, which was smiling, could not assert itself amidst the fat. All around her, and parts of the nearest obliterated by her, were photographs or pictures of Mrs Thatcher, Aphrodite, Lady Ottoline Morrell, Marie Curie, Boudicca, Messalina, the Virgin Mary, Freya Stark and many more. My Babs, said Ellis, some spittle at the left corner of his mouth. God's truth, said Lewis, I never knew it was Babs. On my mother's grave, Ellis, I swear to you I'd no idea who it was. I took a drawer out and she'd fallen down behind. I thought she'd look well on the ceiling with my other ladies.

Ellis let go of Lewis's arm and swung from rage into an equally violent grief. The last photograph I ever took of her! he cried. She sent me out to get her a bag of chips. She sat on the wall – that's our wall, did you not recognize it, you damn fool? – and when I came back she looked so happy I photographed her. It was a warm evening. A blackbird sang. Next day she was dead, lying here against the door. I couldn't open the door when I came to take her orders for the day. The doctor had to climb in through the window. Ate herself to death, he said.

There was no holding Ellis now. He began to blub and howl. The cruise! he howled. Oh she broke my heart when she made me book her in for that cursed cruise. Took all her benefits and all my allowances for three months or more. The arrangements, the change I had to find for the payphone, then the taxis. It will be worth it, Ellis, she said. It will be worth it in the long run. It was a health cruise, specialist doctors and nurses were in attendance, she swore she'd come back as skinny as Perdita. One card I got, one vulgar card from the Bahamas, saying I'd hardly know her she was doing so well. But she came back fatter than ever, the doctors and nurses could not withstand her, she easily defeated them. The taxi-driver was at his wits' end. And no sooner home, she sent me out for a take-away.

Lewis shook his head. Steady on, old son, he said. But Ellis was foaming, and coughing bloodily through the foam. To conclude, he ran out in his shirt sleeves into the sleet and shouted his love and sorrow at the traffic. Somebody phoned the emergency services and he was taken away.

Lewis was very miserable that night. He drank a couple more than usual and lay on the bed under the heroic women. He blamed himself for hastening the end of his companion. I should have recognized the wall, he said. So the following days and nights passed miserably for him. Already he missed the games of chess and the slowing down of time in the evening. He did not expect to hear from Ellis again. He supposed officials would come and clear his room. So it surprised him greatly when the postman delivered a card from Ellis written in frail capitals that said: PLEASE VISIT ME. I'M IN CRAKE'S. YOU GET THE 135 TO THE CEMETERY. CROSS THE ROAD AND ASK THE WAY. E.

The next morning it was raining. Lewis borrowed a yellow-and-red-striped golfing umbrella from the hall, bought a packet of ginger nuts at Patel's next door, caught the 135 as far as the cemetery, alighted, crossed the road and began to ask the way. Beyond Oncology, they said, beyond the Hospice. Keep going. Keep asking. Lewis was a small man, not much of a walker, and he would have been an odd sight to anyone, a consultant, say, looking down on him from one of the glass towers, a bright thing, an exotic pest, crawling along and frequently halting in the steady rain. In himself he marvelled at the vastness of the precinct he had entered – so many buildings, some named after an ailment, some after a philanthropist or famous physician, all given over to the business of keeping you going as long as possible. The walk seemed interminable to Lewis. His feet hurt. Very likely he went wrong. Very likely a visitor who knew exactly where Crake's was would have got there in half the time. Lewis asked, did his best to understand, crawled onwards in the general direction of the pointing, among ambulances, catering vans and any number of other visitors. He counted seventeen carparks. Then finally he came through, he was quite alone, he asked last at the Hospice and they pointed further on into the rain, that way, to Crake's.

There are no trees at all on East Arboretum Street. On that road in living memory there has never been a tree; but on the open terrain between the Hospice and Crake's quite a few old thorns and even some small youthful oaks still survived, their ground not needed yet. Crake's House itself was new and bright. Wherever it could be painted it was postbox red. At reception, collapsing his large umbrella, Lewis said who he had come to see and a nurse with many keys through one door after another conducted him into the Day Room.

Ellis sat in an armchair with his eyes closed and the tips of his stained fingers raised together so that the two indexes touched his chin. In the few days since his abrupt departure from the safe house on East Arboretum Street his clothes had become too big for him, his dentures had gone and the skull had almost entirely replaced the living face. His shut lids, showing black, camouflaged his eyes in the darkness of the sockets. A few faces turned without much interest Lewis's way. Silence. Then Ellis showed his pale blue eyes and spoke. His voice, though roughened and impeded by his illness, had become yet more itself, louder, more accentedly posh. See

172

where I am now, he shouted. Look at the people I am among! Not even Charterhouse was as bad as this. Nor the Church Army, nor the Sally Ann. I've brought you some ginger nuts, said Lewis. Then I'll need a cup of tea, said Ellis. Can't eat a thing unless I make a sop of it.

Trish arrived with the trolley and among at least some of the old men there was a stir and a focusing of attention. Behind Trish, who tilted painfully at the hip, came three younger women, Saba, Ranata and Mila, and they were the animators, they had come to brighten up the terminals with talk of children, journeys, home and Christmas. Theirs was hard work. Everybody said at Crake's the women were angels. Saba rubbed Freddy's cold hands. Ranata buttoned Alf's cardigan right. Mila gathered three before her and sang to them in her foreign language. They stared like owls. Meanwhile the tea did the rounds. Bless you, Trish, said Ellis. My good friend Lewis surely deserves a cup as well. He has brought me some ginger nuts. In the unhappy place between the legs there were stains on the trousers of two of the men and a man called Basho was rocking with a small groaning noise to and fro, to and fro. A very large man with no lenses in his glasses came and helped himself to five of Lewis's ginger nuts. You see what I mean? said Ellis. But what can I do? At least they let me smoke, so long as I go out in the cold.

Lewis wished Ellis would not talk so loud. No other voice in the room was at all like his. He sounded far more foreign than Mila, Ranata or Saba. And his head, said Lewis to himself. So big. I'll have to be going now, he said to Ellis. It's a long way back. But I'm glad to see you comfortable and well looked after. I'll come again. Listen, said Ellis. Then he began to cough. He could not stop coughing. Trish came over with a white napkin. She laid her right arm around his shoulders. She held the napkin ready by his gasping mouth. There now, Mr Ellis, she said. There now.

When Ellis could speak, he said, They give me a week. Don't come again. The books in my room, they're for you. It's a new lot, all the classics. Many good women in there, Helen of Troy for one, Lady Macbeth for another. And Perdita, welcome hither, as is the spring to th'earth. I saw her at school, acted by a boy I liked, so slim. And Maggie Tulliver. George Eliot is a woman by the way, not a man. I know, said Lewis. He nearly said, And if you hadn't gone fucking mad about Fat Babs you'd have seen her in the top right corner with Sappho, Emily Brontë and half a dozen others – but he bit his tongue, so as not to leave any bad feelings in his dying friend. Parliament of Monsters, said Ellis very loudly indeed. Look around you, see what we are like. Look in my Wordsworth, *Prelude*, Book VII, Bartholomew Fair, the Parliament of Monsters, alive with heads, all out-o'-the-way, far-fetched, perverted things, the horse of knowledge and the learned pig. There now, said Trish. Lewis was staring almost fiercely at Trish, to get her by heart, to imprint her on his retinas, so that he could lie on his bed in the dark, a can to hand, the long night to get through, and see her among the others on his ceiling, in pain on her slewed hip, still holding Ellis around the shoulders, her white napkin ready, willing him not to cough again, not to give himself unnecessary pain. The big man, whose name was Michael and whose trouble was in the oesophagus, came again for the ginger nuts. Basho rocked to and fro but had ceased his groaning. Behind him Mila, Ranata and Saba were taking it in turns to sing, each in her language, what might be carols or might be lullabies. There, there, Mr Ellis, said Trish. Lewis took his friend's stained and freezing hands in his. Best of luck, old son, he said. Then he collected his stripey umbrella and was let out through three or four locked doors to find the 135 back to the safe house at the far end of East Arboretum Street.

Leaving Frideswide

WORD CAME BY a thin Somali boy on a mountain bike. Suddenly he appeared at the open door, braking hard and behind him the brazen sky. Letter for you, Miss, he said. He stood there offering it over the handlebars. Beth noticed that his trainers didn't match. Well I hope they fit at least, she said. She had taken to uttering her hopes aloud – softly, below the hearing of anyone more than a yard away, but aloud, and her fears likewise. Said, they were real, she owned up to them, the things she hoped and the things she feared. The messenger wore a blue football strip, kingfisher blue. He could not be more than seven or eight. He wore his importance proudly and fearfully. How white his eyes.

Beth came out from behind her desk and took the letter. What are you called? she asked. – Barnie, Miss. – Would you like some apple juice, Barnie? – Yes, please, Miss. – She took a jug from the fridge and poured him a glass. The generator died half an hour ago, she said. But it should still be all right. Barnie gulped it down. Beth poured him another glass. Not much this year, she said. Not much and the last.

The letter, on county council notepaper, was handwritten in beautiful copperplate at which Beth marvelled, before she read:

Friday 30 September

Dear Ms Atkins,
The buses will come for your party tomorrow, 1 October,
at 10 am. Please be ready to leave at once. According to
your submission of 15 September, you have 43 people in
your charge. We shall send an ambulance for Mrs Eaves,
to bring her to hospital here. On the buses there will be
space for 5 wheelchairs. Luggage is limited to one suitcase
and one handbag or shoulder bag per person. There will
be space also for your boxfiles. Before leaving, please
make the office, the school, the Big House and all sheds,
outbuildings, stores and workshops as secure as possible.
I wish you a safe journey.
Yours sincerely
Thomas Cartwright
Health and Social Security.

Below this was scrawled: PTO. Beth turned and read: Dearest,
admire the script! Harry's dad – he used to sort our post –
offered his services. There's another talent we never knew we
had! Be brave tomorrow. I'll follow when I'm let. My love as
always. Tom.

Beth looked at Barnie. He was staring at her, almost
imploring, which choked her throat with pity. Oh dear, she
whispered. What will become of him? Barnie, she said, will
you take a note back to Mr Cartwright, please? I will write
it quickly. Yes, Miss, said Barnie, his stare never quitting her
face. Beth wrote: My darling, please send Barnie to me with
the buses tomorrow. I will have written you a letter by then.
Tell Barnie he must carry my letter to you. I couldn't bear to
leave without being sure that you will have my letter. But it
is too sad for words. Beth. – She sealed and addressed her
note. Barnie tucked it down his right sock, and vanished into
the heat.

They had known they must leave. At least, those in charge and those in their care whose wits still worked that way had known it for weeks. All the same, Barnie's word was very sudden. Beth stood in a vagueness, staring out into the flickering heat. The air itself was hot, she could scarcely have said where the sun shone from, its heat had entered the air that people must look at, feel, smell and take into their lungs for breath. Perhaps it will rain, she said. But that was an out-of-date hope, not big enough. Very likely it would rain. It might rain next week, tomorrow, before nightfall. So what?

Kingston stood in the door. That kid ride like the wind, he said. Oh, Kingston, said Beth, they sent him to say the buses are coming tomorrow. I knew him for a messenger, Kingston said. That boy's a born messenger. Kingston advanced, as out of a fiery furnace. Nobody at Frideswide could say how old he was: maybe sixty, maybe ninety. He had been there for ever. Kingston was where he had come from and what he was called. That was the one sure thing. Beth and everyone else at Frideswide who thought about Kingston supposed that something bad had happened to him early on. Or not just bad – the worst; so that nothing so bad could happen to him again. That seemed the most likely reason for his calm, stature and gentleness. His hair was a dirty white, he wore soft and faded clothes, walked slowly, looked around him a good deal, stooped his height benignly over all who spoke to him. Then we better get moving, Elizabeth, he said.

The office was more or less packed up already – in boxfiles 1-30, year by year, a record of who had come and who had gone, the aspirations, deeds and disappointments of the place. Tom Cartwright, who had come visiting more often than strictly he needed to, said one day, if he was let, he would write a proper history of Frideswide, from the leper hospital to the new woodshed with its solar panels, from Sir Philip Swithamley to Ms Beth Atkins. Beth put on her wide straw hat and went out with Kingston to tell whoever had to be told.

Alfred was standing at the school gates with his photograph. He been standing there too long, said Kingston. He won't come in, said Beth. I've tried. He's having one of his bad days.

Beth's office was in the old school, facing the front yard. The juniors had moved some years before, to a bright new place, but the infants still attended, or had until July, when the schools, this and the rest, finished for the summer holidays and no new year would begin. For a while, daytime and evenings, the hall and the classrooms continued to accommodate courses, events and meetings of one sort or another. There was art, Keep Fit, IT, local history, yoga, English as a foreign language, first aid, a creche, a playgroup, twice a week the CAB were there, once a week the MP, there were discos and talks on global warming, the WI held their AGM, the Allotments Committee met, so did Crisis at Christmas, all the usual things that people arrange for mutual aid, instruction and entertainment continued for a while in the hospitable old school till one by one in the gathering heat they ceased, they gave up, they were terminated, the foyer still said, Welcome! in thirty-five languages, the classrooms harboured their equipment and materials, the charts, the paintings, the photos, all the bright paraphernalia, but the humans, infant and adult, were gone and already from the roofspace to the cellars the emboldened rats had the run of the place, up and down the stairs, and Beth, working late, heard them at her back, the risen and rapidly multiplying population.

The old heart of Frideswide, the leper hospital and its chapel, once some distance outside the city walls, had over the last hundred years or so been taken in; but from above, from a police helicopter, say, the whole domain looked to be feeling for the lost country still. In a ragged fashion it reached beyond its own boundaries for connection with like-minded terrain: an unkempt graveyard, a park, the backs of gardens, an allotment, the dark corridor of a stream or a disused railway line. Even before the heat, the very thought of this thriving greenery was a refreshment. It lingered in parched minds now as an after-image: terrible loss, commensurate longing.

Wherever you went in the territory of Frideswide you had heard the rumour of the city, faintly the traffic on the motorway, trains passing west and now and then a big military plane came over low, heading for its base in the open country, concrete enclosed by wire. But these sounds of the outside world, if heeded at all, had only ever deepened the feeling of sanctuary. Now silence pressed upon the quiet of Frideswide, you hearkened at it far more than you ever had to the din of the streets, you listened to it.

Frideswide's workshops were clustered behind the school, by the entrance to the market gardens; and across these gardens, next to the main orchard, stood the ruins of the chapel and the leper hospital and close to them the Big House, once the workhouse, and there most of Frideswide's people lived.

The first workshop was still busy. They were assembling wooden toys – engines with trucks and carriages, farm buildings, dolls' houses – and painting them and the humans and animals to go with them, in bright colours. Beth sat down at one of the benches. She had no wish to impart her news. Kingston sat against the wall, very upright, and closed his eyes. He withdrew. It was like sleep, but deeper, further away, blacker, in the substratum of himself, beyond consolation and asking for none. Even in the heyday of Frideswide when there was much to do and the bright things they made for children passed quickly to the shop and into the outside children's world, even then, suddenly, in any company and on any occasion, Kingston might retract himself and sit against the wall, showing the face of a sadness as old as thinking man. Nobody intruded upon him.

Beth said her news matter-of-factly and watched it home, from face to face. The same at the other two working benches. Leaving, she said, Supper's at six-thirty. And to herself, in the undertone: Candles and oil-lamps.

Bench by bench in the other two workshops Beth told the people they were leaving home next day. After that, entering the gardens, she sat in the doorway of the nearest shed and pulled her straw hat down over her eyes. The faces appeared, all of them together, pressing to be seen again as they had looked when she spoke the news. Hardest among them to bear were those like Sammy who had not known what to make of it, was it good or bad? and looked, for example, to Albert who knew it was bad and expected no better, or, for example, to Ethel, who smiled on the world, never learned but forgot and reverted always to her incurable bent in favour of trust. So Sammy looked at one or the other and back again at Beth, again and again he looked hard at Beth. He rested his big hands on the red roof of a dolls' house and his eyes like creatures at bay implored her to promise nothing bad would happen.

It was late afternoon. Between the shed and the Big House lay the acres of cultivated land, all manner of plots, all shapes and sizes, with osier hedges, and the paths passing under rustic arches. There were coops and trellises, cane wigwams for beans and sweet peas, small families of apple, pear, damson and plum, a scrap of old woodland with beehives in, there were troughs, waterbutts, sheds, here and there a wicker statue, a scarecrow, so much work year after year, so much wit, care, inventiveness and delight, all the loving craft, ending. No one was working. A dozen or more of Frideswide's own people and a dozen at least from outside come in for respite and to learn, they should have been here, among the statues and the scarecrows, you'd have seen people picking, tending, pruning, clearing, getting ready for next year, there'd have been a slow bonfire or two, and from the far corner you'd have heard the Dixie Band practising for Apple Day. Really, there was nothing much left, no chickens, no ducks, nothing much had come through, scarcely enough for their own needs, very little for the shop, nothing in store, the glacial days in May, then the heat, the searing, the hail, the dust, the hail, deluge, tempest, heat, heat, heat, had left wreckage, blackening, blight and putrescence and over all, till the next sweep of rain, lay the fine red dust.

Beth watched the red kites. They came in up the quiet motorway and, unless the weather was furious, congregated over Frideswide, twenty or thirty of them, spying down, tilting, gliding lower for a closer look. You might come across one on the earth itself, tearing at a find, not at all perturbed by your arrival. They would clean the place up. The deer came in too, fallow and muntjac, along the parched corridors, for any remnants of succulence. And stray dogs, once or twice already a pack of them, and lone cats ranging out of town. After three days of hot south winds, with the red dust many thousands of butterflies blew in, they clouded the brassy sky, the local birds fell upon them gratefully, they drifted the earth, the wood-chip paths, the asphalt playground, the roofs, the gutters, the sills, in a soft litter and it was only then, fallen and finishing, that you saw how beautiful they were, how delicate their structure and fabric, how various their symmetries, countless thousands of creatures, flocking, whirling and settling as softly as snow.

At the Big House they were laying the two long tables for supper. The fare would be what they had rescued from the freezers when the generator gave up the ghost. Quite a feast really. The day's cooks had switched to gas cylinders and half a dozen camping stoves. They were pleased with themselves. There won't be another supper here, said Beth. Barring miracles. So yours will go down in history. As it happened, two of the shift did believe in miracles. They were a couple called Elsie and Carlo Viti who, in earlier days, had walked the roads from Cuthbert's house in Durham to the Black Madonna's in Viggiano and back again. Bless you, said Elsie. The Lord will return us to our garden, when it is time. Carlo beamed at her and then at Beth. They carried on setting candles and now and then a silver oil lamp down the centre of the tables.

Beth went to tell Mr James. His job was brushing and mopping the hall and when he had done it he returned to his small room at the back of the house, to work. The time before supper was the best, in his opinion. Beth told him the news. He said nothing, only turned away and looked through the window at the orchard that year after year, till now, had never failed, month by month, even week by week, to be differently beautiful. He sat at a small pine table on which was a Liddell and Scott, a fountain pen, an HB pencil, a pencil sharpener, a rubber, an open exercise book and *Oedipus at Colonus*, the Greek text, in an edition that had belonged to one Eric Johnston of Wadham College in 1912 and that now lay open at lines 669-95, which Mr James was translating. Self-taught and too late (he said), he worked very slowly. First, in pencil, he copied out the Greek, leaving a good space between each line. He loved this stage of the work, took infinite care over it, rubbed out and corrected any mistakes. Making the letters with their breathings and accents pleased him inordinately. Next, after hours of pondering and consultation of his text's notes and glossary and of his own Liddell and Scott, he entered below each line, in ink, a very literal version of the Greek. And only then, again in ink but on the facing page, after days of struggle and staring into the orchard, did he write out a version in verse, accompanying, as he said, but not faithfully matching, Sophocles' metres. Later still, having let it lie for a week, he did a final version in fair copy on a new page. What do you think of this? he said over his shoulder to Beth. It's only a draft still, I'll have to let it lie. Beth stood by him, looking into the palsied orchard. Mr James read:

> Famous for horses, there is none
> More beautiful on earth
> Than this place you have come to, stranger
> Bright Colonus where
> The many nightingales sing loud and clear
> Amid deep greenery and under the wine-dark

Berried ivy, down
The untrodden ways that no storms shake
Nor fierce sun burns
The god comes, Dionysus comes
For revelry
With the undying
The ever-fostering nymphs.

Here in the dew of heaven
Day upon day narcissi thrive
Whose clustering beauty
The goddesses have always worn for crowns
With the golden shining crocuses and never
Do the unsleeping streams
Of Cephissus dwindle but they roam
For pasture and every day
With undefiled waters
Over the swelling land
Give easy birth. The Muses
Love to dance here and the golden-
Reined Aphrodite rides…

Beth put her hand on Mr James's shoulder and left the room
quickly.

The casseroles and the jugs of apple juice passed down the
table. The undexterous and the people sitting back in
wheelchairs were served first. The mood was more gay than
sorrowful and those who, like Sammy, had not known what
to make of Beth's announcement sided now with cheerfulness,
followed the banter this way and that, and the fear, the
apprehension of ill, withdrew from their eyes. Before the
crumble – made from last year's plums – Beth had the lamps
and candles lit and with them came a solemnity, the face of
every person present shone in a new light in a unique character,
and in that lay the seriousness and poignancy, not in virtues or

vices, not in good or bad looks, but in uniqueness, every person, each herself, each himself, so that Beth said aloud in her undertone, They all matter differently. What will become of them?

Beth went to the sickroom, where Lucy Eaves was dying. The nurse, Marija, stood at the open window. The air outside was not as it should have been after sunset. Beth looked at Lucy and shook her head. Then to Marija she said, You go and eat now.

Beth set a small table under the window and between two candles began her letter to Tom. Only her own breath moved the candleflames at all, the air outside seemed to have lost the gift of breathing. The dying woman behind her breathed perforce, mechanically, not yet allowed to cease.

Beth wrote: My love, I am sitting with Lucy Eaves, the woman you are sending the ambulance for tomorrow. I hope she will be able to die by then. Marija must go back in the ambulance with her. How happy I should be if you and I were leaving Frideswide together. I should hardly mind what happens, if we were together. Lucy is one of the oldest people here. Nobody knows anything about her. She never said much, except, Thank you. She often said, Thank you, and asked other people how they were getting on. In normal times perhaps we should have found some relative of hers when it came to this. As it is, nobody knows of one. I'm sitting at the open window but it makes no difference. Is fresh air a thing of the past? What a strange expression that is! I could make quite a list of things that are 'things of the past'. Love isn't one of them. Is wanting a baby? When I saw Barnie this morning, when he suddenly appeared in the doorway, so brave and scared, my feelings tore at their captivity again. So wanting a child is not yet a thing of the past. Marija is from Croatia. She was going to get married. She only came here for a year to make a bit of money. And now she's stuck.

Lucy's breathing got louder. Beth went and sat by her, took her hand, closely regarded her face. Inhalation was hoarse and laborious, but worse to attend to was the holding of breath. It looked, each time, like an exertion of the will to die by not breathing out, the effort being grotesquely at odds with the woman's slight frame. Her face became hectic in the pause. So long it lasted, each time so very long. It is mechanical, Beth said aloud. She is not suffering. But that was not how it looked and sounded. The release, when it came, was like something ruptured and no sooner done with, the next heaving in began, deep, deep. So you might open a window and breathe in the breeze riding in on the sea. But the air in the sickroom was leaden, like a forbidden planet's.

Marija came back, Beth left her, promising to send another woman up as soon as they were done in the hall. Kingston and three of the younger men had locked what of Frideswide's outbuildings could be locked, but Beth still had much to do before morning. She was late to bed.

Beth woke hearing owls. She drifted there on the borders, between sleep and waking, hearing the owls. All night in dreams and in near-the-surface monologues she had laboured through an oppression and anxiety in which were compounded her duty to lock up Frideswide and Lucy Eaves's imprisonment in breathing. But now she woke, listening to the owls, she lay wide awake in the dark and the bad feelings lapsed away from her. She remembered with relief the many gaps in Frideswide's fences, the bed of the stream, the over-reaching trees. There were many entrances for any creatures seeking nourishment and shelter. She lay awake, watching the window and listening to the owls calling to and fro. When light became faintly certain, they ceased. Beth rose, dressed, lit a candle and went to the sickroom.

Madge sat by Lucy's bed. Just gone, she said, just a moment ago. Poor soul, such a struggle, but see how she looks now, so peaceful.

Beth went back to her room, brewed coffee on a camping gaz and in daylight which had become sufficient she continued her letter to Tom. Dearest, she wrote, Lucy has died. We have to be glad it wasn't sooner or before she reaches a mortuary she – her body – would have suffered too much heat. My love, I have to tell you a strange and beautiful thing. When I woke or half-woke this morning it was still dark and I heard owls, quite close, calling and answering, one from the old leper hospital, another, I am sure, from the dead orchard. And it was just then, Madge told me, that Lucy was at last allowed to die, just as I woke and lay listening to the owls. I felt they had conducted me to the borders of my sleep, they had piloted me in, to the very edge of daylight, and there they fell silent and withdrew, back into the darkness where, for their safety, they belong, and I was left feeling very honoured and blessed. If I close my eyes now I can still hear them calling and answering, so ghostly and real, so frail and persistent, and I am encouraged. They brought Lucy to where she had to pass over into death and me they brought into daylight and wakefulness with the courage to leave this beloved place. I wished – how I wished – you were in my bed with me listening to the owls but at least you will learn about them in this letter that Barnie will bring to you and so you will know that I feel braver than I did and you will be encouraged too. Goodbye, my dearest, for now. Come after and find me when you can. Beth.

PS I have decided to give Barnie my lapis lazuli.

Everyone was waiting in the playground. The buses arrived on time, one was an open-topped tourist bus, the other was a minibus from the Sunshine Club with most of its seats taken out to accommodate the wheelchairs. The promised ambulance pulled in after them.

Beth was watching for Barnie; couldn't see him, and had to supervise the embarkation. Kingston went in the ambulance to the Big House, for Lucy Eaves. At the sight of the red tourist bus many began to laugh and shout. Suddenly the departure seemed a jolly affair, like an outing to the seaside. Well this is all right, said Sammy. Eh, Bert, eh, Mrs Winters, this looks all right, wouldn't you say? Mrs Winters lolled forward in her wheelchair, asleep, and Bert, who years ago had appointed himself her valet, stood over her, all decorum, with a parasol. The fittest, embarking, clambered upstairs and opened the big bright umbrellas provided there against the heat which was already severe.

Beth was in her office, seeing the files out. Everything else would stay. Still no Barnie. She locked up. The ambulance returned, depositing Kingston, picking up Marija, and leaving at once with the body of Lucy Eaves. Alfred stood facing the school, his photograph in one hand, his suitcase and a Fairtrade shopping bag on the asphalt either side of him. Kingston handed Beth the keys of the Big House. All the keys were assembling. No Barnie, she said in her undertone, Kingston being close enough to hear.

Beth carried her case and shoulder bag to the tourist bus. The driver took them in. With all the keys and her letter to Tom in a plastic bag she rejoined Kingston. From nowhere, very fast, skidding to a halt, kingfisher-blue, Barnie arrived. Letter for you, Miss, he said, leaning forward, handing it to her. This boy's some messenger, said Kingston. And Mr Cartwright says please to give me the keys and is there any message? Barnie said. There is, Barnie, said Beth, handing him the plastic bag. See, Miss, I got a satchel, he said. Mr Cartwright give it me. He stowed the letter and the keys safely into it. As last time, he looked awed by his importance. There's no apple juice, said Beth. Stay here with Kingston, I'll bring you some water.

Alfred came over, set down his bags, and showed Barnie his photograph. My wife was at school here, he said. That's her, that little girl. Would you believe it? And do you know, I think that's why I came here when she passed away. Kingston picked up Alfred's bags and led him to the bus.

It's not very nice water, said Beth. But drink some now and take the bottle. Even drinking, Barnie could not take his eyes off her face. And this is for you as well, she said, giving him the lapis. It was my mother's. Wear it round your neck. It will bring you luck. Perhaps you'll be my messenger again one day. Then he was gone, she watched him out of sight, a dwindling brightness on the dirty air.

The buses pulled away. Beth sat with Kingston downstairs, across from Mr James who was on his own, gripping a briefcase tied up with string, in it his writing materials, his texts and his Liddell and Scott. Upstairs and downstairs there was a good deal of hilarity. They were trying on the tourist headphones, some worked, some didn't, you chose among fourteen languages for a commentary. Beth clutched her letter. They were passing through the outskirts, that had been rich and leafy, the roadside trees were all dead, scacely any traffic, scarcely a soul to be seen, a pack of dogs, the heat. Mr James put on a headset, it worked, he chose a language. Beth glanced at him. He was listening, he was crying. Never had she seen a person cry like that, so quietly, so helplessly, the tears drenched his face and fell on to his hands and the briefcase. For a whole tour of the city he was leaving, its churches, the dwellings of poets, the botanic garden, the museums, the art galleries, the site of a martyrdom, the ancient places of learning, Mr James listened and wept. Beth felt she must cross over and comfort him but Kingston, in an undertone, said, Mr James is all right, Elizabeth. You read your letter, I'm going to sleep.

Doubles

You and your doubles!

It's all very well for you, she answered. I live on my own. Naturally, I think too much, I have no one to distract me. And then I see things.

Which are only in your mind.

No, no, she answered. Everything I see is real. It's not at home that I see these things. I see them when I go out, on the street, in a park, under a bridge, wherever I happen to be. And they're not things, they're people. Doubles. And lately only yours. To be honest, since I got to know you the way I know you now, it's only your double I see. And not often. I've only seen it – you – three times since I got to know you the way I know you now.

Always on your own, you live on your own, but you don't like it, do you? And this is your home, this beautiful house on stilts, on a platform over the flatlands going away into the sea, the between-lands, neither salt nor sweet, sometimes more one, sometimes more the other, so lovely, so interesting, but you can't stand it, can you, being on your own, though there's nowhere you love better than here.

She was upset by this. It's not fair of you to say that, she said. Even if it's true, it's very unkind of you to say it. I do all right

189

on my own. I'm sure I manage better than you would. You don't know what it's like having nobody.

Well, I'm here now, you've got me now.

For a while you are, she said, suddenly tearful. I have you for a little while. But you'll leave when you please. I won't be able to make you stay even a minute more than you want to. Anyway, she said, after a pause during which she collected herself, I get around as much as you do, probably more. I know all sorts of people, they let me into their homes.

But that's just it. You're only there when they're not there. You go in when they go away. You house-sit, you feed the cat, you forward their mail.

And I listen to their music, she said. I read the books on their shelves, very slowly, a little at a time. Then I close my eyes, listen to the music, think about the lives in the book and the lives of the people whose house or flat I am in. That's not nothing, is it? Surely in that way I know an awful lot of people.

You look at their photographs. Any house or flat will have photos of the children on the walls or of the owners themselves when they were younger, perhaps when they first met. You surely go from room to room looking at those. I've even wondered do you read their letters. Often when people receive a letter they throw the envelope away and leave the letter open on the desk or folded in a rack with all the others they mean to answer one day. It's extraordinary what personal and private things people leave lying around for the cleaner to see or anybody looking after the house while they go off on their travels.

And that's unkind as well, she replied. Why are you so unkind this evening? I only look after places for people I like. They trust me. I am their friend. Why must you say I'd go prying into things that are private?

Some people like the idea of others finding out about them, as it were by accident, by accidentally on purpose leaving things lying around. I knew a woman who left her diary open on the kitchen table. You'd sit down for coffee and she'd go and busy herself over by the window and then suddenly pretend to remember her diary and be embarrassed. I think some people like the idea of being haunted by another person who knows their private affairs.

She stood up and, turning her back on her unkind visitor, looked out over the sunlit marsh. In late spring and throughout the summer and for part of the autumn nowhere was more home. It's only in the winter I have to go wandering, she said, still turned away. And it's only in winter, when I go to London and stay in a hostel or look after somebody's home, that I ever see the doubles. That must surely mean I possess myself and am an intact person for much of the year, and only when it's dark so early and so long am I not myself or can't hold on to myself and go for shelter into the nooks and crannies of other people's lives and see some I love who are not actually there.

Do you ever see him? When did you last see him?

I don't see the dead, she answered, turning to face her questioner. I see the living every now and then in places where, as it turns out, they cannot have been, they can prove, when I tell them, that they were somewhere else. But him, the one you are calling 'him' – she became animated, her face took on a light like that of the evening sun on the corn-coloured reeds of the wide marshes under the sky – Listen to this, she said, something I am pleased about, something I feel proud of myself for doing, I haven't told a soul, I've had it in my heart all to myself, still wondering over it.

Go on, then. Tell me. I shall always be glad to hear of anything you are proud of.

Yes, she said, there's precious little, but now there is this. Every year these many years, in spring, I've felt the longing to go back south, to the island where I was in love with him and we walked together through the red anemones and he spoke to me in that low hurrying voice of his and easily persuaded me I was indeed the girl he saw in me. But this year I understood how foolish that return would be. I'm so much older now and he is long since dead and it suddenly occurred to me that I should go not to where he was already old, old to me at least, the girl in love with him, but to where he was young, young as I was then, the place he used to go to as a boy, from the school he hated, and then as a young man from the war. I decided I would go there. I was flat-sitting in Hampstead, a place overlooking the Heath, and I went online on their computer and worked out the trains and when my friends came back, I left, not saying a word about my plan. If I was a poet I should think it the best idea I had ever had – to go back to the house he stayed in when he was young.

Such a long journey. I sank at once into a deep thought of him and concentration. I felt sure of my purpose, I was finding my way towards a better understanding, among strangers on public transport I was excited, attentive and patient, following my own desire. She sat down at the table again, facing her visitor whom, she had said, she would not be able to detain. Are you listening?

Yes, I'm listening.

So she continued, speaking in a low voice, and felt her account to be, as the idea itself had been, utterly compelling, persuasive, a thing to enthral her listener for as long as she wished. Mile by mile, she said, first travelling north into the midlands, then from there across Shropshire towards the sea, the idea clarifying in me was how beautiful our country is and how passionately you would love it if you came back into it from somewhere foul and how cruel that love would be if you expected soon to die. So first I was thinking of him travelling in the holidays to the place that would feel like paradise after the hell of school and over that I laid his going there as a soldier on leave, back to the place of his boyhood, only a few years older but from the war, from the foulest places the earth in those days had to show, loss upon loss and the brief recovery of paradise all the more sweet and cruel. You do see very ugly things through the window when a train slides into and slides away out of a town, the backs, the things let go beyond repair, the slovenly mess, but even all that, I thought, you would fasten your eyes on it and wish not to let it go, because nobody wants to be shut up dead while the world, good and bad, continues without them when they are young. And besides, I felt all that ugliness to be very little, there is still, especially once you get in among the ancient hills, so much that delights and satisfies your eyes. The fields, orchards, houses and kitchen gardens, all the habitations and the works of human beings look to belong there as they have for more than a thousand years. Oh I saw more, much more, and felt it much more keenly than I can get across to you.

Don't try. I've been there too. We can take it as read that Shropshire and the Borders and Wales are beautiful.

She felt this to be discouraging and when she continued it was as though she must now persuade herself that her story mattered and she felt watched more than listened to in this endeavour. She felt her doubting visitor to be watching whether the faith in her would hold. Well anyway, she said, looking down at her bare hands, it was magical whether you believe me or not and when I changed trains for the second time at the junction on the flood plain and we crossed the river and made slowly north around the great sunny bay and the mountains stepped up on the right and we crossed a couple more wide rivermouths on old bridges, the idea became so clear and lively in me I felt possessed by it, I felt I could offer it another passage of life.

Does it matter whether I believe in your journey or not?

I won't let it matter, she replied. I will try not to let it. I got off at the station underneath the castle which centuries ago had the sea lapping at its rock and now stands inland more than a mile. That is where he was met, as a schoolboy and as a soldier home on leave, they sent the trap for him and so he was conveyed up the steep road into the village and from there, turning north, the half mile or so along the level through the trees to the family house.

But you walked, of course. Pilgrimages have to be done on foot.

This wasn't a pilgrimage, she answered. It was a haunting. I doubled up – I was the haunter and the haunted. I begin to think you will not understand. But yes, I walked, I found myself a nice B&B by the church, I made a cup of tea, lay down for half an hour and when I set off to visit the house it was late afternoon.

I had never been there before but I had read what he wrote about it and what they wrote about him there when he was dead. Besides, on the island when I was in love with him and we walked through the anemones under the olive trees, often he told me how much the house had meant to him that had the mountains behind it and a view of the western sea from its front windows. But that afternoon when I left my room and set off on foot as a visitor into his boyhood and early manhood suddenly I remembered a terrible thing I had read: that when he came home on leave and they met him with the trap at the little station under the castle, they gave him the *Times* and he read the latest casualty lists and wept all the way to the house over the names of his dead friends.

So you arrived in tears…

So I arrived in tears at the house and like a dreamer walked without hesitation up the steep drive and knocked at the side door as though they should be expecting me.

And got no answer…

No answer, so I went round to the terrace and peered through the big French windows into the dining room but there was nobody. I had the sea far below and far away behind me but it was the house I wanted to enter and so I went further round, to the back door and knocked there.

Again, no answer…

No answer, they were not at home, pehaps they were in London or had gone to the island itself, to that other house with its anemones and olive trees, and I felt the idea I had been so sure of now beginning to fail in me, the faith began to go out of me as though winter were approaching already and I should have to leave my home and go looking for shelter in somebody else's, to get me through. She looked up at her visitor, for some understanding, and the face, although unsmiling, was not contemptuous. She heard the mouth in it say:

Go on. Go on with your trespassing, finish telling me how you trespassed.

Was I trespassing? I felt I was dreaming, I felt that a dreaming ghost had a perfect right to go anywhere and enter wherever she chose. When my courage began to fail me I felt I might be waking and that I should stand there on somebody else's land like a person who has sleepwalked and wakes among strangers in her nightclothes, laughable. But then just at that rise of panic at the feeling of waking I saw the gate and I was saved, I inhabited him wholly again or he inhabited me, I saved my idea back into life and I got the understanding I had come for, it was not in the house, it was at the gate, an ordinary rusty little iron gate, half-open, stuck fast half-open, out of the strip of back garden, half-open for ever on to the path that runs behind the house. It was the path I needed for the complete incarnation of my idea, not the house, I needed the back way out of the property.

A rusty iron gate and a path?

Yes, she said, very sure of herself again. I understood what I could not have understood when I was in love with him as a girl. It has taken all this time and I had to go there in person to the house where he was a young man and find the path. Don't you think that is strange and wonderful? That I have to wait so long but I get there in the end by having an idea and following it all the way like a dreamer? Her visitor shrugged, seeming not interested, perhaps about to leave, so she hurried to say the rest, not wanting to be left all night with the thing to say and nobody to say it to. She said: The path runs level immediately behind the house, you step on to it in a stride through a rusty iron gate that is stuck for ever half-open, in a trice you have left the house and garden, which were never yours anyway, the mother owned them, you are at liberty to leave, you have your path. The path that late afternoon was densely bordered with stitchwort and wild garlic, above it under the trees the slope was streaming with bluebells. No wonder he loved me and the others the way he did, in that peculiar fashion. He had come out of the pit, out of a place that festered and that was coarse on the touch and foul in the nostrils and on the tongue, an abomination to the eyes, it seethed with worms in the flesh of his dead friends, it writhed with gas and the vapours of putrefaction, and here behind the house ran the path, Olwen's path, no wonder he loved us, we were clean, fresh, scented, our skin was smooth, we were as sweet on his smirched senses as are the trails of flowers from that gate along the path.

Is that it?

Yes, she answered, wearying. Except to tell you – then you can leave – that the path, Olwen's trail, led somewhere. It went through the bluebell woods and bore away left, climbing, and would bring you into what he called the country of his choice, into the mountains where there are wild goats and ancient stone circles, the rowan, the whortleberries, the heather, the small lakes under the sky. And I thought of him – no, I *became* him, walking up there on leave, knowing he would be recalled into the filth and expecting to be killed. And I believe he loved me and the others for the rest of his life as though he were briefly reprieved and that his craving for the beauty of young women was always that of a young man, hardly more than a boy, who had been left for dead under corpses in an unspeakable foulness. And we, the young women, and the wild land were for him an order of life in which he could never again be commanded to kill and be killed. We were the counter-order, the world of his own making which he set against the world of lies and unfreedom he was drafted into at birth as a male child at that time and in that class. And now long after he is dead and now I am so much older I don't at all mind having been loved like that. I loved him in my way, passionately as a girl knowing very little, and he loved me in his way which only now, having stepped through the half-open gate on to the path bordered with the clean white flowers, do I begin to understand.

So that really is it, still him, only him, all your wandering years only for that?

And what if it is? she answered, her voice now also failing her with her spirits. That's not nothing, is it? Surely it's not nothing that I have come to understand? He was like Septimus, he fell on the railings, they were all like Septimus, their dead friends, their dead enemies who might have been their friends who kept rising up at them out of the stinking mud, they fell on the railings and were pierced through for life. He survived by loving, he followed a trail of white bryony into the hills, he lived in despite of the modernity of lies, orders and poison gas. And that's not nothing either. She paused, white and exhausted, looking hard into the eyes of her visitor. Listen to this before you go. Some years after he had moved on from me when I was elsewhere living my own life of sorts I heard from another young woman that he had stopped speaking and would sit in a chair for hours on end staring into space in terror. When he stopped speaking and had no power of words any more the terror came up in him invincibly. He had nothing left in him to oppose being buried alive under terror.

Yes, if that is all, I shall leave you now.

Yes, go, she answered. But there is one final thing. I wasn't quite honest when I told you earlier that yours is the only double I have seen since I got to know you the way I know you now. Last week in London, in Tavistock Square, the day before I came back here, I saw my own double, I saw myself, a much younger self, a girl becoming a woman, on the street. I followed her across the square and into the florist's which is on the corner. She had her back to me but I could see that she had taken to the counter a bouquet of three or four kinds of white flowers. It was myself, much younger. I stood a couple of yards behind her. Then she turned. She knew me.

She blushed. She knew I was herself, albeit much older. Then she smiled and made one step towards me, holding her white flowers. We were a yard apart, knowing each other, smiling, almost about to embrace. Then a voice called her name – my name – from the door. We both turned that way. All I could see was a shadow on the street outside, a dark shape, I couldn't say whether man or woman. I reached out my arms but my double looked at me as if asking my forgiveness and ran to the door, leaving me.

That's bad.

I knew you'd say that, she answered. Go now at once and let me be. I knew you would say that seeing your own double is a bad bad sign. But I do not think so. Not in this case. I will not allow it to be so. I won't listen to you giving me examples of how bad a sign it is. I want you to go. Tonight I am not being left, I am telling you to leave. I have ideas of my own, I give them life, they work.

Ev's Garden

FOR A WHILE Ev helped at the old slaughterhouse. It was the Warden's idea. Something for you, Ev, he said when he heard what they were doing. The first day, since she was nervous, he went down with her. After that she went on her own. She liked the place and everybody there. In the bad old days the slaughterhouse drained straight into the river and the gulls came upstream and the crows came out of the woods and fought like souls in hell over the slops. Then it stopped being a slaughterhouse and but for the rats stood empty. The Council didn't know what to do with it, it was an eyesore, and when a group called Seed Corn asked could they have it for a fruit and vegetable co-operative they were mightily relieved and answered, Be our guests!

So that was where Ev helped out. She was in at the beginning, doing her bit, in there helping with the clearing and the cleaning and the whitewashing over the spattered walls. For all important next moves the co-operative held a meeting and anybody could speak. And though Ev never did speak she was there at these meetings watching and listening, turning her face with very bright eyes from one speaker to the next. It was decided, for example, not to remove the hooks from which the animals had dangled upside down but to clean them, paint them in rainbow colours, and hang great panniers of fruit and veg from them instead. It had been a small and local slaughterhouse and where the slaughtering was done, the long stone shed with the rail and the travelling hooks, this became the store itself, the trestle tables ran the

201

length of it and behind them stood Seed Corn, male and female, all young, cheerful, engaging, a joy to behold, said the pensioners, poor, decrepit, dressed like extras in a pit-disaster film, when they crept shyly in on opening day. The antechamber, where the shitting beasts had been received and penned, became a little café serving nourishing soups. A joy! The Council smiled. But then they sold it to a developer who, after a bowl of soup and a quick look round, saw possibilities undreamed of by Seed Corn and after a spot of bother and a bit of bad press he got them evicted.

Ev when she worked at the old slaughterhouse had more happiness in her than anyone looking at her pinched-up face and bitten fingers would have thought her capable of; then more sadness when her work there stopped, more than looked possible in so slight a creature.

Ev went back to her old haunt between the Vicarage – as they still called it – and the derelict school and sat there most mornings doing nothing, only looking. It was an overgrown terrace with gravestones, some broken, poking through. You had a good view west from there over the street, very steep at that point and just re-opened, in the interests of commerce, to through traffic which made such an effort getting up, it shook the shop fronts and even the terraced graveyard above and behind them, where Ev sat. Opposite, on the far side of the street, stood the Majestic, which had just closed down. On benefit days and on any other days when they got hold of any money, four or five men from the Vicarage might come and sit in the graveyard with a carry-out. They were never especially rude to Ev but they did make a lot of noise when they'd had a few and began finding fault with the system and the world in general, which spoilt the good of the place for Ev and she went back to her room at the very top of the Vicarage from where she could see across the street and across the river to the far western edge of the town and beyond that to the empty hills and the sky.

What you going to do with yourself, Ev? the Warden asked. He liked Ev, she was no trouble at least and no one ever refused to sit next to her at meal times. Dunno, Mr Sykes, she answered. Then after a silence, the Warden looking at Ev and Ev screwing up her face, she said, Thought I might make a garden for the dead people. Make it nice for them.

At once the Warden, himself near to despair much of the time, said, Show me, and Ev led the way across the abandoned Vicarage garden on a path she and the drunks had made through a rank luxuriance of nettles, brambles, elder and bindweed to a breach in the brick wall between it and the burial ground. Over in there, level with the Majestic, feeling the tremors of juggernauts, the Warden sank yet again into the sinful love of ruin. Let it all go, he murmured, and me with it and all my hapless charges. But Ev was looking up at him, the way a sparrow might at a man eating bread and dripping, for a smeared crumb. Take a lot of work, he said. He kicked at one of the cans. And the carry-outs will have to move into the school. I've told them that before. With any luck it will fall in on them. But why not? It's a Quaker ground. My father was a Quaker but I lapsed even from that. Quakers aren't fussy what happens to 'em after they've gone. If it was Mainstream or the Fatwahs or the Hallelujah Mob, there'd be hell to pay.

That evening over tea the Warden asked for volunteers to help Ev make the graveyard into a pretty garden. He got none. Thank you, he said. Sliv said the Lord would crucify anyone who meddled with Christian dead folk even if they were only Quakers. Drinking and pissing in there is fine, he said, but disturb the holy ground itself and you're asking for it. Nobody else said anything. Thank you, said the Warden again. I'll phone the Castle.

The Castle stood on a very solid mound above the Vicarage and for seven or eight hundred years had been just that: a castle, monstrous at first, no doubt, but less and less so as enlightenment advanced and latterly quite harmless, of interest to tourists and in the care of the Ministry of Works. Needs must, however, and the Castle had been sold off to Jails UK and at the time of Ev's plans for the Quaker burial ground it was being converted to house five hundred asylum seekers, their present accommodation, a hulk in the estuary, having been found unfit for purpose. Jails UK already had their offices in the Castle along with their sister company, Alternatives, which, at a price, would supply services to the community below.

The Warden phoned them, knowing very well that on his budget he would get poor-quality personnel. The six sent round the following Monday wore the company's smart red uniform – motto: Firm and Fair; logo: handcuffs with eyes in and a smile underneath – but really were a disgrace to it. The Gangmaster, delivering them, said as much. You get what you pay for, he said, and they don't come cheaper than these. I doubt you'll need the leg-irons but buzz me if you do.

Ev led the way, the Warden brought up the rear. It was a dampish day and to the scaffolders on the Castle and to a meeting of Planners on the roof of the Majestic this passage of Alternatives through the Vicarage's rank garden perhaps looked like a trickle of life blood. At the tumbled wall, never a problem to Ev and the carry-outs, came the first objection. Finn, still 373 hours to do, said it was ridiculous to expect a man with knees like his to climb that wall. Everybody knew he needed flat terrain. Nell (93 to do) and Ali (773) also objected, the former for psychiatric reasons, the latter on principle. The Warden, unsurprised, said briskly, Objection accepted. This morning we clear the way in. Pile the bricks over there. They'll come in handy. And he added that they looked to be eighteenth-century.

Ali, a young man, was full of resentments. Born among the poor, when he began thieving he thieved off them, they had less security and he knew from home where in a house he'd find their few valuables. He got by, he was never caught, but then one day he met a holy man on the road who told him that his life was a scandal, robbing the poor, his own kith and kin, was a sin for which he would surely burn in hell. Then next day, in a pub, he met another man who told him burglary was for idiots, he should get into identity fraud, all you needed was a few rich people's bills. This made sense to Ali. But next day he got caught with his head in a recycling bin on a very good street with a view of the cathedral. Hence his many hours. His world fell apart. Why the minute he mended his ways should he get caught and punished? It made no sense to him. Listening to this life-history, the Warden knew there was no hope for Ali. Get stacking, he said. You'll feel better once we're working as a team.

Ev climbed over the tumbled wall and sat on a terrace among the dead people. She wished the Warden hadn't hired the Alternatives. They would only spoil it with their grumbling. She wished she was back in the slaughterhouse with Seed Corn, never a cross word, everybody cheerful. Ev had the gift, if it is one, of becoming at any moment the manifest living epitome of whatever state she was in and when the Warden saw her sitting up there among the weeds and the empties with her chin in her hands staring away west over the condemned Majestic, he shook his head and wondered how much more he could bear. He climbed up to her with a dozen black sacks. Come on, Ev, he said. Make a start with the empties and be glad you're not Ali or a planner.

So Ev made a start and before long she was joined by Eric, a poor white-collar offender in his sixties whose hours were all but done. He brought a sickle and a pair of loppers. God's work this, he said. It might help me later. Ev said nothing. She had a sackful already and dragged it to one side. Eric bushwacked his way to the top wall, behind which a ginnel, skirting the Castle mound, linked the Vicarage and the derelict school. Hogweed, said Eric. Very nasty. I'll deal with you later. Ev brightened up. Ali, Finn, Nell, Petula and Daft San had formed a line along which the Warden, at the breach, passed brick after brick.

The morning proceeded. At coffee time – Alice from the kitchen appearing with a tray – the Gangmaster called by, Ali began complaining, the Gangmaster offered the leg-irons, the Warden declined. Suit yourself, said the Gangmaster, we can always add to his hours instead. Ev was glad to get back through the wall with Eric who sang spirituals as he worked, in a deep voice. Then just before dinner there was an accident. Eric, a heavy man, trod too close to the edge of the top terrace at a place where the coping was missing. The edge gave and he slid on a chute of earth ten yards or more, uprooting plant life and coming to rest at Ev's level, two terraces down, the debris settling around him. Much jeering from the Alternatives below. Not funny, said Ev to herself, for she saw that Eric, sitting very still, had a skull in his lap and more human bits and pieces beside him in the black dirt.

No matter, said the Warden, hurrying up. That was bound to happen. It is after all a graveyard and, as I said, the Quakers have an idea of resurrection which does not entail their being physically pieced together. Eric had the skull in both hands and was contemplating it closely. I know a lot of poetry about things like this, he said, a lot of quotations, poetry and prose, and quite a few songs I have by heart that deal with things like this. Would you like to hear any? The dead people, said Ev. Another curious thing about the Quakers, said the Warden, speaking rapidly, is their refusal to use the pagan names for the days of the week or the months of the year. See there on the headstone of Joseph Harrison: Died third day of the first month 1818. Same day and month as my mother, said Eric. She did her best for me against the tyrannical wishes of my father but he prevailed, needless to say, and sent me at great expense to his old school with the consequences you see before you now. Sliv, in drink and carrying more in a bag, approached through the breach with two men the Warden did not recognize. Seeing the skull in Eric's lap and more remains showing dirty-yellow through the ripped-out ground elder, Sliv went white and said, Back off, lads. This is no place for a harmless can or two. The end I foretold is nigh. God will strike these bleeders dead before morning. You weren't coming in here anyway, said the Warden. You must go round by Piss Ginnel into the school. And be careful, when you're in there, it doesn't fall on you.

The Gangmaster returned, took one look and said he was pulling his people out. It was more than his job was worth to have them rooting around among bones. Suppose they got religion? What use would they be to Alternatives then? Eric sighed, looked the skull in the sockets and laid it down reverently on a fallen stone. I'm sorry, he said to Ev. I'm bad luck wherever I go. The Gangmaster ushered him through the breach and away with the others.

Ev ate her dinner in silence, frowning hard. Cheer up, sweetheart, said one of her rough companions in that place. What will be, will be. Ev scowled fiercely at this comforting, well meant no doubt, and when she had finished eating and had taken her plate to Alice at the hatch she went straight out again and sat on the top terrace from where Eric had fallen. The low sun, rounding the Castle, now mildly illuminated the overgrown slope and a determined hopefulness came back to her such as she had felt on her first day working with Seed Corn at the old slaughterhouse. She took up another black plastic sack and concentrating solely on the empties worked her way down terrace by terrace until she reached the bottom wall behind which was an empty premises, once a printer's, that fronted the busy street. Seven full sacks of cans and bottles she lugged to the breach where the Alternatives had reduced their sentences by three grumbling hours.

That evening a policeman called at the Vicarage and said to the Warden, It has been reported you have dug up human remains. We expected to, said the Warden. We are restoring a graveyard, making a memorial garden of it, so that some of our elderly residents may sit there of a summer's evening, enjoying the view and reflecting on the successes and the failures of their lives. – You got permission? – Not as such. But this is a Quaker burial ground, early to mid-nineteenth-century, and I am a Quaker. No Quaker minds being dug up accidentally or in the interest of some greater good. And we shall re-inter every surfacing relic with proper respect. Forensics want a bone, said the policeman, to test how old it is and check it's not some murdered person of the recent past.

Two ticks, said the Warden. He returned with a dirty fibia and, seeing the officer's distaste, kindly wrapped it for him in page three of the day-before's *Sun*. There now, he said. Please bring it back when forensics have done. Quaker or not, I have a sentimental wish to keep everyone together in that plot. Next morning he saw Ev at the breakfast hatch and said to her, You carry on, Ev. I don't think they'll bother us. Thank you, Mr Sykes, said Ev. I done the empties. Today's needles and condoms. Gloves, said the Warden. Then leave everything by the wall. I'll get Alf and Chloë to shift it.

This will be a nice place, Ev said aloud. Early March and the Castle for most of the morning blocked the sun; but beginning her search for sharps and slippies and gathering them into a thick plastic bag, she saw aconites and snowdrops fighting for breath in the brambles and ground elder. Don't give up, she muttered. Ev will help. Against the earth-tremoring din from the choked street all manner of birdsong hurled itself. A wren popped up from a prickly undergrowth and perched and churred in plucky rage on the headstone of one Mabel Evans who had died on the fourth day of the third month, 1857, aged 83 years. Alice came out to Ev at coffee time, the Warden in person called her in for her dinner, and by then she had reached the printer's wall and her sack of brief pleasures was securely tied and set with the empties at the breach for Chloë and Alf to hump away.

Ev went back after dinner with the loppers, the sickle and the whetstone that Eric had been using before his accident. This work was tiring. The purple brambles were almost tibia-thick and deeply resented being snipped and dragged out of the entanglement they had holds in. Any rampant feeler might be ten yards or more and as for their roots, they were down among the long dead Quakers and determined to live for ever. Same with the nettles: you might sickle them level with the earth but the roots, yellow as chicken-legs, clung in deep. And against the top wall, higher than it, overlooking Piss Ginnel along which the carry-outs crept like disgruntled trolls the extra hundred yards to the derelict school, stood the hogweed, utterly baleful. This is where a man would come in useful, said Ev aloud – and at once, as though her wish were some kind god's command, there stood Eric at the breach, wearing gauntlets, knee-pads, a yellow hard hard hat and cradling all manner of tools across his lifted arms. I'm here in my proper person, he shouted. Not as an Alternative. Warden says OK. OK with you?

Eric climbed up to Ev's level. She heard him muttering, Tread softly, Eric. Arriving, he said, These poisonous chaps – jabbing an elbow towards the ten-foot hogweed – I was thinking in the night we'd have 'em out and plant sunflowers instead. Imagine that, Ev! A baker's dozen of sunflowers, their backs to that vile alley, looking out over the Majestic to the moors. Ev glanced up at him from under her bit of fringe and screwed her mouth up tight as though she mustn't laugh. Gently, knowing their poisons, Eric took a pruning saw to the hogweeds' thick stems. In ten minutes he had felled them all and one at a time, very circumspectly, he dragged them to the breach. Their vast dead slithering heads scattered in self-preservation several galaxies of seed. Eric, however, dug out their roots and lobbed them over the wall into Piss Ginnel.

When I was little, said Eric, just before my father sent me away to school, I began hiding in a field he had bought to develop one day for a good return. It was called the Ladywell Field, it had an old stone fountain at the centre and nothing whatsoever grew in it but giant hogweed whose touch would burn and blotch your skin. And I crept in there, into the dried-up fountain, and read Biggles with nothing around me except those poisonous plant-creatures, three times my size. I reasoned that nobody would come looking for me, first because the field was private (many notices said so) and secondly because its only life was noxious. So I've always had mixed feelings about the giant hogweed. I could imagine nicer company for a little boy whose only desire was to fly away with his mother in a Sopwith Camel. How about you, Ev? Did you get on with your Pa? Never had one, said Ev. Nor a mam neither. I was found in a toilet, the nurse called me Ev. And who's to say that wasn't a blessing? Eric said.

By tea-time Eric and Ev had cleared the top terrace. Give the nice things a chance, said Ev. Eric set three fallen tombstones upright against the alley wall. Very striking they'll look through the sunflower legs, he said. Each terrace had a retaining front and a coping of gritstone blackened by the local smoke; but over the years some slippage had occurred, some bulging and tilting. We'll have to watch that, said Eric. His own slide had deepened an existing route down which little by little some burials were making their way. Altogether, as is natural with terracing, there was a desire to slide and settle finally as low as possible.

The policeman called again. He handed the bone, in its same wrapping, to the Warden and said, Forensics say about 1825 but they're keeping an open mind. You find anything funny, you phone us at once. Will do, said the Warden. And to Ev at breakfast, passing her the bone, he said, Green light, Ev, dig and delve. Eric all right, is he?

Ev added the tibia to a pile she and Eric were making. Of course, not being experts, they couldn't say for sure how many dead people were contributing; but they treated every piece with equal respect and covered over the pile with a tarpaulin at nights. Whenever she caught Eric mumbling to a skull, gently Ev took it off him. She saw that he had a melancholy streak. Best to keep him chatting – she did not need to answer – or singing from his store of spirituals.

Agreeable days. Ev was even happier than she had been in the slaughterhouse, for this garden was her idea. Eric never failed, now and then the Warden lent a hand, and one or two of the other residents, Lanky, it might be, or Corporal Bob or Ethel the Tooth, stood in the breach some afternoons and smoked and offered advice. The trolls passed along Piss Ginnel to the derelict school, came back for tea bawling the old songs and cursing God. The scaffolders fitted up the Castle; traffic, with the usual accidents, laboured up and came too fast down the Western Hill and sent a shiver through the soles of the Planners who, most days, met for an hour or two on the roof of the Majestic.

One morning Smiff from Seed Corn appeared head and shoulders over the Piss Ginnel wall. Hi, Smiff, Ev said. You've grown! Hi, Ev, he answered. I've not grown. I'm standing on Tibbs. He says Hi as well. We heard you were up to something. Wanted to see what it was. You doing a garden then? Yes, said Ev – for the dead people. Good thing, Ev, said Smiff. We're into gardens too. We're called Slurry now, not Seed Corn. We bought a couple of old dung squirters and filled 'em with the stuff they squirt along motorways, seed-soup, wild flowers, you know. We trundle around and squirt where we think things need brightening up. You should come with us one night.

Ev's garden was taking shape. Stones upright or leaning picturesquely were left as they stood; the fallen were raised and supported; the pieces of any broken were assembled and the Warden himself came up with some ready-mix and made whole where he could. He liked to read out the names and dates. He shared with Eric an interest in how long people lived. See how well the women do, he said. Mary Hemmings, 87. Alice Beveridge, 93. And that's without a health service. But the men were finished at fifty. Still are round here, of course. How old would you be, Eric? Sixty-seven, said Eric. And still gardening! said the Warden. Ev tells me you sing a lot. Perhaps that's the secret.

Ev was sitting between Eric and the Warden on the top terrace at ease, legs over the coping at a place where it looked solid, late evening, full in the sun. Much beauty in the form of primroses, stitchwort and bluebells had come up already, allowed to by the removal of what had choked it. In addition, Ev had thoroughly seeded the earth with purchases from the indoor market. Here and there, on the germination and the jostling of shoots towards the light, more human remains poked through. Ev's policy lately, and Eric agreed, was to mound over them with good tilth from the workings of moles and to pack these little tumuli with poppy seeds.

Should be nice, she said. Very colourful. But for the longer and more substantial pieces already thrust or tumbled into the daylight she and Eric had dug a new plot at the midpoint of the second terrace and planted the best possible ramblers, climbers and trailers, the idea being that these would well up and riot over the edge and tumble on down and be so mixed and various in their colours, scents and manners they would do some justice to the miscellany and uniqueness of the human lives whose fragments had been dispersed and recollected. I see it already, said the Warden, the cascade! What a sight it will be from the roof of the Majestic! I'll suggest it to Planning, who are very short of good ideas. Make safe the roof space and let the people ascend and behold the glory of Ev's garden! Ev put her hand over her mouth so as not to laugh but it was like the ground itself in her when the Warden spoke hopefully like that, a great pressure in her to laugh.

The Warden leaned across to speak to Eric who had been 'a bit under the weather' for a couple of weeks, in the pit, in hell, in hell's ninth circle, in the ice, his head clamped in the black ice, his spirit compressed into a ball of black lead, his voice flattened, sunk, emptied of tones, but who was, he thought, possibly coming up again. What do you say, Eric? said the Warden. Won't Ev's garden be fit to be looked at from the roof of the Majestic? Eric nodded. I don't blame my father for committing suicide, he said. He had embezzled himself into a corner and what else could he do? But I do blame him, in fact I curse him, for taking my Biggles books, my hamster, Sam, and my mother with him. It was close to the beginning of the new school year, always a bad time, and though he must have known he couldn't pay the fees and I wouldn't be going back, he hadn't told me. Had he done, I'd surely have been home with Mother and Sam and would have perished with them. Instead, I was hiding with *Biggles Sees It Through* among the giant hogweed in the Ladywell Field when I heard the explosive roar of the fire and then the engines. After a while, wondering, I crept out and watched from a safe distance. Then I went back and hid in the dried-out fountain again, all night, and presented myself at the police station towards evening the next day. They were amazed when I said who I was, naturally they had supposed me ashes in the ash, and to one another, above my head, they said I would never get over it, no child would ever get over a thing like that. Well, I don't know. I'm sixty-seven, I've repaid my debt to society and, as you said, Warden, I'm still gardening. Anyway, I don't know what getting over it means. I have a recurrent dream in which I'm crawling through an impossibly thin slit, I'm slobbering with terror and would retreat if I could but I can't and have to go on trying to make myself flatter and thinner so as to fit through the slit and pretty well the first shrink I ever saw, when I told him about that dream, he said, Oh that's nothing to worry about, millions of people have that dream, it just means you didn't want to be born, but quite honestly who the hell does and who wouldn't backtrack and curl up tight again if he could and some say nobody ever gets over that so all in all I don't think I've done so bad but I was very fond of my mother, she did her best for me, and why I mention it again on this lovely evening in Ev's garden I've no idea.

That night before trying to go to sleep Ev, as she often did, counted her blessings, beginning with her first foster-mother, a Mrs Evans, and continuing with Mr Sykes, Alice, the people in Seed Corn, quite a long list, she had always thought, and now there was Eric too and the garden, Ev's garden, they were calling it, but in her mind it was the dead people's garden even if, without a doubt, it counted as a blessing for herself, Ev. Up there in her attic room when she couldn't sleep Ev listened to the owls and the foxes who lived their lives at night between the Castle, the Vicarage, the burial ground and the old school. They were friendly. On the steep street often there was shouting and crying, things getting broken, sirens and even in the deadest hours always some heavy pieces of through traffic. She preferred the owls and the foxes, and on any night after rain quite clearly she could hear the trains, the long slow goods trains and the one night express, the comet with its long tail of sleeping people and their dreams. But that night after Eric had told the story of his survival Ev felt certain she would sleep. Counting her blessings had brought her to the garden which she was sure would soon make Eric cheerful again and he would carry on being her friend every day for ever perhaps. And alone in her room, where nobody could hear, she let out a strange chortling and gasping for breath such as had come up in her when Mr Sykes said how wonderful the cascade of flowers would be to anyone looking across from the roof of the Majestic. What a sight! From terrace to terrace, a waterfall, one flouncing step after another of honeysuckle, clematis, aubretia, white rock, everlasting pea, rambling roses and anything else that cared to join in and be colourful and scented and a delight to the dead people out of some of whose remains it all sprang. Ev's garden! On that vision of a life already planted and germinated, already muscling up, budding, opening and getting ready to topple and multiply, Ev with a smile on her face was ferried into sleep.

A couple of hours later, into Ev's dreams, an articulated lorry, carrying nine colossal blocks of granite from Shap to the east coast for the new sea-defences, ran out of control as it began the descent of Western Hill, jack-knifed half-way down and launched the rear two of its blocks very fast through the old printer's shop. The crash woke everyone in the Vicarage except Sliv. Living in the expectation of imminent apocalypse, he slept on. The others, in an appalling silence, struggled in their various ways to comprehend what had happened but before they had got very far with that relatively simple task, the rest happened, slowly at first and quietly, as a tremor, a slithering, a rough susurration and during this first phase all the woken, from Ev in her attic to Corporal Bob curled in the cellar round his still, just had time to wonder, guess and quail at what then duly followed: the groan, rumble and roar of the collapse and slide of the whole slope from Piss Ginnel to the printer's, all the terrraces, all the bones and headstones, all the whole and peaceable or already scattered skeletons, the black grit copings and facings, the total seeding, planting, sprouting, mole tilth and humus, went in relief, after centuries of holding, headlong into the street. Silence again, with after-shocks, with little after-trickles, the outriders, the stragglers, all following the natural wish of things to fall, if let, as far as they can. And that was that. The woken sleepers, the interrupted dreamers, put on a little clothing, came out under the moon and viewed the street now barricaded with a lorry, Shap granite, debris of a printer's shop and many hundreds of tons of the garden Ev had dedicated to the dead people.

The earth stirred, the driver was pushing through it on hands and knees. When he could stand, he did so. A skull and some yellow vertebrae rolled off him. He removed his cap and flung it down, unbuttoned his overalls and stepped out of them. These garments lay there like a sloughed-off skin. Then, nodding to the witnesses and tapping his nose with his right forefinger, the driver walked briskly up the hill and disappeared.

At first light there was a meeting of Planning on the roof of the Majestic. Nobody had much to say. We saw some good films here, said the Chief Planning Officer, stamping gently. 'The Sound of Music', 'Planet of the Apes', things like that. My wife and I used to like coming here. He went to the edge and looked down, his committee following. The lorry itself, with its cab slewed back as if on a broken neck, had entirely blocked the street. The granite toppling off had doubled the barricade. And on top of all that came the burial ground. The Planners looked across: Piss Ginnel, without its wall, crept along a precipice above a void. The Planners glanced at the Vicarage – wondered; glanced up at the Castle – wondered even more. Just because a thing has stood for a century or for seven or eight centuries does not mean it will stand for ever. Then one of their number pointed down. Rats, he said. Below the barricade, on the town side, rats were running in multitudes out of the narrow alley that led from behind the vast and derelict school through the shop fronts into the street. The rats emerging turned left without hesitation like dirty water and streamed at great speed downhill towards the market place. So many! Far more than all the generations of pupils who had ever learned their lessons in the school, far more than them plus the drunks and dossers who since the days of schooling had drunk and bawled and fitfully slept in there, a multitude of rats, enough for a whole town you might have thought, came out of that narrow alley out of their underworld and headed intently down into the market place and on towards the new developments along the river. Then they were gone. The street sloped empty in the morning's innocent and merciless light. Now I wonder what that means … the Chief Planning Officer murmured.

The school collapsed. From the roof of the Majestic they saw it suddenly succumb. It gave up all of a piece, fell in on itself with a loud noise, fell down and lay there in a silence out of which rose the vast and substantial spectre of itself in dust. That's it then, said the Chief Planning Officer after a pause. That really is it.

The Vicarage was condemned. Fortunately the Council had several more empty vicarages at its disposal and on a sunny morning early in June the Warden, wearing a wide-awake hat and carrying a staff, led his charges, some in wheelchairs, up the hill, their few belongings following on a brewer's dray, to a new place with an even larger view west from the attic, which was to be Ev's room, and with a fine derelict garden on a slope which, the Warden said, to cheer her up, could surely be made very nice. In truth Ev was in low spirits, kept to her room, lay on the bed, did not look at the view, would not come down for meals. The Warden brought Eric to see her but she shook her head. She was thinking of the dead people, all slid into the nasty street. She's wasting away, the Warden said. Word came that the Western Hill was closed for good. Your garden's flowering nicely, Ev, said the Warden. Planning are saying the crash was a blessing in disguise. Even as he said this, his heart misgave him and a week later came further word that the Council had declared Ev's garden a heritage site and sold it to a firm called Bloomers. How could the Warden tell Ev that? He sat in his office, once a vicar's snug, and whispered to Despair that she could take him when she liked.

Smiff came in without knocking and asked to see Ev. She has turned her face to the wall, said the Warden. And who can blame her? Ballocks, said Smiff. And climbing the stairs three at a time he entered her attic and said, Get up, Ev. You're needed. His eyes were fiercely bright and his blond hair seemed quickened by a violent static. Bloomers are enclosing your garden – or they think they are – at six tomorrow. But you're manning Jumbo on the south side with Tibbs. Me and Father Jeez are on the north side with Baba. We squirt the bastards silly and poppies come out of their nose holes. That's the plan. Can't fail. Press will be there. Sunrise is five-twenty-five, we need you on site by three-thirty OK? OK, said Ev.

Smiff withdrew. Ev got dressed, Alice brought her up some soup. Back downstairs they found the Warden phoning. Smiff had swung him on the point of five seconds from abject despair to ecstatic revolutionary confidence. He kissed Alice and Ev, called them his beautiful comrades and thumped the boards with his staff. I've done the bands, he said. There'll be jazz on the barricade itself, from about four. Then brass, half a dozen of them, coming in from the villages, just after six, *behind* Bloomers, very clever that, north and south: they're kettled, Baba and Jumbo squirt 'em. Smiff's given me a list. Amazing! Did you know there were Diggers in Hetton-le-Hole and Levellers in Pity Me? Well there are. Anarcho-syndicalist Morris Men, Tai-chi Leek-Growers, Dahlias for Peace... The list goes on. Now I'm doing Faiths. Slurry are doing the Communities, on bicycles. Ev was staring at the Warden. You've gone funny, Mr Sykes, she said. You wait, Ev, he answered. Just you wait. At three tomorrow morning I lead this lot back down the hill. I've had thirteen volunteers already and the rest we rope to the wheelchairs. Whose garden is it? they ask. Ours, they answer. Sliv says he always said God moves in a mysterious way and it was his idea all along. Corporal Bob says he worked his balls off in that garden.

The Warden's vision was luminously clear: at dewfall, at first birdsong, the silvery-grey first light spilling like mercy over the soiled and bartered town, in that pause under the sky's soft precipitation, quietly on the barricade the jazz starts up. Sunrise, and the abundance of Ev's garden becomes apparent. Her cascade has worked its way back into the light and spills over the north side and the south. The dead are flowering. Poppies everywhere, such a thorough red success. And assembling almost as abundantly there will be a field of folk, the recalcitrant, the surviving, the life living in the cracks and shadows, the odd, the unmanageable, the unasked, they well up from the quarters that await development, they push in from the abandoned estates, they trail in after their remnants of music from the ruined villages.

Eric will be there, said the Warden. So will St Bridget's Flower Ladies. And did you know there's still a Darby and Joan in East Hedley Hope? They're coming. Meals-on-Wheels are doing the catering. Really we can't lose. I said to Smiff, Why don't we take back the slaughterhouse? One thing at a time, he answered. Tibbs and Smiff are cranking. You and Father Jeez are on the nozzles. You'll be all right with the nozzle, Ev? Aim low and work up 'em, Smiff says. Will do, Mr Sykes, said Ev, stopping with her fist the welling of laughter in her mouth.

Mr Carlton

AFTER THE CREMATION Mr Carlton's two daughters invited people back to the house for tea. Not many came and there was none of the hilarity – relief – you sometimes get on these occasions. After an hour or so only the daughters and their families remained. They washed up, cleared everything away, put the table and chairs back where they belonged. Then Mr Carlton said, You go now. I'll be all right. His daughters weren't so sure. Yes, yes, he said. I've got to be on my own. Best start at once.

As soon as they were gone Mr Carlton went upstairs and stood for a moment in the bedroom. Then he took the bag he had packed two days before, locked up the house and drove away north. It was midsummer, the long evenings. At the first services, sitting in the car, he sent a text to his daughters: I'll be out of touch for a few days. But don't worry. All will be well. Love. Dad. Not knowing, not wishing to learn, how to send a message to two people at once, he composed his text twice and dispatched it west and south. That done, he got out of his car, fitted the phone under the nearside front wheel, drove slowly over it, reversed, drove over it again. Should be enough, he said to himself. But, to be sure, he retrieved the thing, which was indeed flattened, and walked across to the nearest bin with it. Getting back into his car he noticed that he was being stared at by a woman parked twenty yards away. That's one witness, he said. No matter. And having filled up with fuel he drove off, north.

Mr Carlton feared and hated motorways. He kept to the nearside lane and only moved out if absolutely necessary. In the middle lane, enclosed in ranks of metal travelling very fast, he felt as vulnerable as a snail among marching men in boots. Rarely did he cross further right; but that evening, just north and west of Manchester, he was obliged to and from there, the fast lane, he noticed that no traffic whatsoever was coming south. As soon as he could, Mr Carlton crossed back left. Ahead of him warning lights blinked, the whole vast speeding entity slowed, clogged and stopped. In no time at all many miles of track were plated over with many thousands of vehicles come to a standstill. Rapidly the solidifying continued south, every minute another mile of it. The engines idled for a while, then hushed; and this hushing extended down the lengthening lines. A helicopter hurried over, north. Fire, police and ambulances went by on the hard shoulder as fast as they dared. But the stronger feeling was of a gathering silence. Whatever could be done further north was being done. In the long repercussion behind that violent point there was no movement. The evening was mild, stretching itself towards dusk and a distant nightfall. People got out of their cars, lorries, coaches and walked where pedestrians are not allowed to be. They climbed into the central reservation and gazed in something like wonder at the vast and empty southbound carriageway. Others strolled along the hard shoulder, leaned against the crash-barrier, smoked, chatted, phoned.

Mr Carlton stood apart at the barrier. That stretch of the motorway is raised up on columns. They carry it over a flat moss whose chief beauty once was birchwoods, of which there are still remnants. You can also tell which parcels of land had once been drained and farmed. But first Mr Carlton looked half a mile or so west and saw the feeder road, also raised up and its traffic halted solid and shining in the sun. Had you stood at the junction of that road and the motorway and looked back, your sense of the moss might have been of its opening, widening and escaping; but from Mr Carlton's viewpoint you saw it narrowing and stopped. But the strange silence and stillness and the mild westering light lay over this segment of surviving land like a blessing or a reminder or a haunting. Mr Carlton orientated himself in relation to the silenced roads and the moss, felt the queerness of the time and place, and only then looked nearer and down.

Below, barely thirty yards from the nearest concrete column, was a house and home. It was a brick house, it stood in its own close, hedged all around, a comfortable rough square, with a gate on the far side into a kitchen garden, more raggedly fenced and a scarecrow hoisted and tilting over the produce. In the far corner of the close there was an apple tree and a swing by it with a green iron frame and a red seat. Washing hung on a line down the dandelion lawn. And there was more, oh much more. Mr Carlton felt himself presented with something he would not have the time to take in. It was an interlude, he would have to leave, he would never come back, his knowledge of the place would be small and so poorly ingested how should it do any lasting good? What do they grow there? He could distinguish runner beans and broad beans and at least four rows of potatoes. Those might be beetroot, those were surely carrots. Raspberries and currants in a coop. That was the toolshed, with a pipe from the guttering into a water butt by which stood the can. A wheelbarrow, a compost heap, a patch of nettles and docks. What fuel do they burn? Behind the house Mr Carlton saw a coal bunker. Who would deliver to such a place? Mr Carlton found a track, it departed from behind the house and proceeded, with many right angles, towards and then alongside the feeder road, south. Would a lorry manage that track? In the wet, in snow and ice? Perhaps the man of the house had to fetch the sacks himself. From where?

Mr Carlton had just noticed a means of transport, a squat black car, parked outside the south hedge of the kitchen garden, when a man joined him at the barrier and pissed through the bars of it steadily in a bright gooseberry-yellow arc, towards the house but falling far short, of course. That's better, he said, zipping up. Then: Fucking silly place to live. I suppose they were there before the motorway, said Mr Carlton mildly. I suppose they were, said the man, pulling up his white tee shirt to wipe his neck. But who in their right mind, he wanted to know, would stay? He had a hairy belly, over-folded. That there, he said, pointing at the black car, that there is a Ford Popular 103E. I know a man who collects them. Mebbe I'll come back here and buy it and sell it him.

An old woman came out of the house with a basket and a bag. She wore a floral dress and heavy shoes. She moved the foot of the pole back just far enough to bring the line down within her reach, then worked her way along it, clothes into the basket, pegs into the bag. When that was done she turned, holding the full basket with the bag of pegs on the top, and looked up to where the traffic and the spectators stood. But she gave no sign of any thoughts or feelings, only turned and went back into her house. As though we're not here, said Mr Carlton to himself.

An old man came out. He wore boots, faded and quite baggy blue trousers, a smock of a darker blue and a brick-red cap. He took away the clothes pole and laid it flat and close under the gable end; came back, untied the line from its two posts, coiled it and took it to his wife who was waiting at the door. She took the coiled line from him and went in. He crossed the close into the kitchen garden, fetched a hoe out of the shed and with his back to the motorway set to work.

You married? asked the fat man who had pissed. Yes, said Mr Carlton. Yes I am. He said this aloud in answer to the question, said it without any hesitation, feeling it to be true. And having said it, he felt he must abide by it, in a sort of reservation within himself, and certainly mustn't try to be more exact, in the world's terms, with a stranger. I was, said the fat man. Still am, sort of. They were side by side leaning on the barrier, watching the man below at work in his kitchen garden. Swallows flashed out from under the concrete of the motorway, dipped up under the eaves, adhered there briefly with an audible twittering, and flitted off hunting again. Heavens, said Mr Carlton. Swallows live here too. The man in the garden leaned his hoe against one of the six wigwams of canes that his runner beans were climbing and went to fill the watering can. She fucked off and left me, said the fat man at the barrier. Mr Carlton turned to face him: his eyes were bulging and watery. Took the kids as well. – I'm sorry, said Mr Carlton, face to face. Thank you, said the deserted man. You meant that, didn't you? – Yes I did. – Dozens of people I've told it to and never one till now, till you, ever said they were sorry. Mostly they look at me and it's as clear as daylight they're thinking, Can you blame her? Why wouldn't she fuck off and leave you and take the kids? And they're dead right, of course. Why wouldn't she? But at least you said you were sorry and I believe you when you say you meant it.

The man in the kitchen garden was watering his beans. The water showed pure silver in the lowering sun. Plainly the job contented him, he took his time over it, so much time he had. Mr Carlton felt he had never before witnessed such leisurely and contenting work. Three times the man went to fill the can again. The sound of it filling, the changing tone of water filling a can, lifted like a memory of itself as far as Mr Carlton at the barrier. And the man in the garden stood with his hands on his hips watching the water leave the green tub through the black tap and enter the green can. He watched; it entranced him. The deserted fat man offered Mr Carlton a cigarette. No thank you, said Mr Carlton. The fat man lit one for himself. I'll toddle over and see what's doing, he said. And he added, leaving, Before she left me I wasn't this bad. I didn't always look as bad as this.

The woman came out of the house and walked through the close into the kitchen garden. Now she wore a dark shawl over her shoulders. She stood with her husband. If they spoke it was too softly for anyone on the motorway to hear. The swallows came and went, at speed, intently, with a clean skill and grace. A blackbird sang from the apex of the roof. Was it so or similar, changing with the seasons but in essence just so, all fitting, all in place, all pleasing, was it always so even under the usual traffic?

A helicopter flew away south. Did that mean anything? Mr Carlton wondered whether the swing meant grandchildren visited now and then. The colours were bright, the seat and the ropes looked strong. Would children mind about the noisy motorway? Was there anything to interest them outside the house and its bit of land? Mr Carlton began to look for paths. Towards the south, where the moss widened, he thought he could make out a way which, like the carriageable track, advanced in right angles, perhaps to find bridges over ditches. He saw a couple of trees that did not have the appearance of birches. They might be ash or sycamore and a house had stood there once. If the children had been his grandchildren he would have taken them looking for frogspawn in the ditches. Surely the man and his wife knew where to find whortleberries and mushrooms. A moss was a rich place if you were born there or if you came in as a stranger and got to know it.

The old man had finished watering. He put the can back by the water butt and the hoe back in the shed. The light coming over out of the west was golden now and almost level. All visible things partook of it and became truly themselves. Most astonishing, from under the motorway itself, the route the swallows were familiar with, half a dozen fallow deer appeared. They paused and were illumined; then moved sedately in single file around the north edge of the close and at greater speed bore away south. The old man and woman, her arm in his, watched them out of view and continued standing there in no hurry to leave the light.

A young woman came up to Mr Carlton at the barrier and said, You wouldn't lend me your phone, would you? I'm very sorry, said Mr Carlton. I don't have a phone. Oh, said the young woman, so you haven't told anybody you're stuck, you'll be late, they needn't worry? I had already told them,

Mr Carlton replied, that I'd be out of touch for a few days. I was speaking to my husband, the young woman said. Then my phone gave out. It frightens me being stopped up here. My husband was telling me not to worry. But what if we're here all night? I've never left him for a night before. Perhaps that helicopter was a good sign, Mr Carlton said.

The old man and woman had left the kitchen garden. They were crossing the dandelion lawn towards the house. They halted, looked up, the old man pointed. Bats, said Mr Carlton. It's not us he's looking at. He has seen the bats. The swallows have roosted, the deer have gone to where the moss is wider and perhaps there is still woodland for them to hide in. Did you see the deer? I've been watching the swallows. And now the bats. All those creatures have come out from under the motorway. I'm pregnant, the young woman said. I only found out yesterday. I went to tell my mum and dad. I wanted to tell them face to face. And now I'm stuck here. I don't want to be away from home in the night.

The old man and woman went into their house. In rooms to the left and right of the door the lights came on. Oh they've gone in, said the young woman next to Mr Carlton at the barrier. They've shut the door. In the room on the left, on view, the old woman busied herself for a while. Then that light went out. She appeared at the window of the room on the right, stood there for a moment, now without her shawl, then drew the curtains.

The young woman at the barrier took Mr Carlton's arm. I'm frightened, she said. You don't mind, do you? What do you think has happened? It must be very serious to close both carriageways. I heard a man say it was a fire. And somebody else said ten minutes earlier we'd have been in it. My husband said not to worry, they'll clear it eventually, if we're here much longer they'll bring food and water round. He's right, said Mr Carlton, patting her hand that was gripping his arm. We're quite safe here. How still it is. I was wondering do they have grandchildren who visit occasionally. I hate it when you're on a train, the young woman said, and you stop in the middle of nowhere and after a long time they tell you there's a fatality on the line. Yes, said Mr Carlton, that is a horrible expression. And everybody's only wanting to get home, the young woman continued, and they don't care about the fatality in person. But it's horrible sitting there knowing that someone is chopped to pieces further up. And this is worse than that. It has blocked both carriageways.

The after-lingerings of a midsummer sunset last for ever. Infinitely slowly pallor passes towards blackness. The vanishing light edges north, smoulders on earth long after the source of it has gone below. But with an utter abruptness the light went out in the old couple's downstairs room. They're going to bed, the young woman at the barrier said. Mr Carlton shuddered. The bedroom light came on. The old woman in her floral dress stood at the window illumined and looking out. Perhaps she stood there every night, every soft summer night at least, and looked down on the close and the kitchen garden for a minute or two, taking it in. She drew the curtains. You're crying, said the young woman holding Mr Carlton's arm. What is it? You're crying? What's the matter? No, no, Mr Carlton replied. I have two grown-up daughters, older than you, with children, a great joy, as yours will be. No, no, all is well. The light in the bedroom went out. They're going to sleep, the young woman said. Is it that? Is that why you're crying? Yes, said Mr Carlton. It's that.

The southbound carriageway opened. Down it in a flickering torrent of blue lights the police cars and the ambulances screamed. After them, bulkier but quietly, came the fire engines. Carnage, said Mr Carlton. A few minutes later the normal traffic followed, three lanes of it, headlong, heedless. Now we'll be moving soon, said Mr Carlton. Do you want to go back to your car? I'll stay here, if you don't mind, until it starts, said the young woman still gripping Mr Carlton's arm.

Romantic

3 MARCH, COMING home from work, pushing open the gate and stepping down into the yard, Ruth finds him (Morgan) asleep in the angle of the wall and her front door, wrapped in the civil defence coat she bought him six months ago, his knees up, his boots showing beneath the hem of it, his arms hugging a cloth bag. Her cry of shock wakes him. That bird, he says. Hark at it. Yes, the blackbird, twilight, there is some grey in his hair. She shakes her head, You again, and leans over him with her key to open the door.

Inside he says, I was in a bad dream but when I woke I heard your voice saying that line 'And twelve hours singing for the bird' and at once I heard the bird, a thrush it was, very close, perhaps on the apex of the gable, and that decided me. I walked twelve hours. I see, she says. Then he asks, Shall I light the fire? Yes do, she says, it's laid in, I don't always bother. He goes on his knees on her hearth rug wearing his big coat still and the soles of his boots showing, his head bowed, his hands quickly making fire in the black range so that in no time there are flames and he is reaching for the brilliantly shiny small lumps of coal to feed them with, little by little, just what they can take and not be overwhelmed. He sits back on his heels, she sees him staring in a trance into the coals and flames and hurrying smoke, and, Not again, she thinks, but says, I'll cook, you'll want a bath, and when she comes in ten minutes later with the clothes he left last time washed and ironed and piled up neatly on a big folded towel, he's still there kneeling upright, staring into the fire, so she kicks his soles and says, Wake up, go and have your bath.

In the clean clothes – collarless white shirt, soft black

227

trousers, thick red socks – he comes down into the kitchen where she has set the table and is cooking with a glass of wine to hand. He moves about, touching things, lifting them up, even the most fragile things, and setting them exactly back in their places. For perhaps a minute, his longest pause, he stands next to her by the stove, she smells the clean clothes and his clean skin and hair, then he turns away and again kneels at the fire and feeds it more coals but cannot rest even there, stands up abruptly and goes through into the unlit sitting room which faces north across a wide valley to the railway line along which at that moment a train is hastening north, a trail of lights, into the night, through fields under the stars. Ruth calls, Now you've come, come and talk to me, and he goes back in and does as she bids him, sits at the little table, but sideways, uncomfortably, on the chair, leaning back against the wall, and she pours him a drink which he will only sip at, as it were to keep her company, and nothing occurs to him that he might say, so, Ask me something, he says, I've not been talking much lately, not aloud at least, or not to anybody when it was aloud, so ask me and it will mebbe come back. But then Ruth hasn't the heart, he may have walked twelve hours from wherever it was, from a thrush to a blackbird, but she has worked all day with difficult people, how difficult they all were, why couldn't he, now he has appeared again, be nice, ordinarily nice, and say a few ordinary pleasant words to her, but she knows he can't, can't or won't, so she loses heart and goes on with the cooking, drinks her wine at a gulp and leaves him to lean his black curls and the grey in them against her kitchen wall.

But when she serves him and sits down at the table, close and opposite, and sets the bottle between them, she takes pity on him and on herself, raises her filled glass and tells him he is welcome and he blushes, he is ashamed, he drinks to her and says in a voice so soft she can hardly hear that her house is the place he loves best in all the world and tells her in a rapid whisper how he had woken from his bad dream, the one that at certain times will lay itself upon him like a coffin lid, night after night, but then her voice had reached him, saying the line of verse which was in the book she gave him, does she remember? Of course she remembers, why does he suppose she might forget? Where were you going? she asks. He shrugs, Nowhere special. Further north. So he turns east, she thinks, into the bloody rising sun, no doubt, and arrives here twelve hours later with it setting behind him and falls asleep on my doorstep. She shakes her head at him. Really, it won't do. Eat, she says.

Ruth makes up the spare bed for him, in the little room over the yard. Have a lie-in, she says, I'm gone quite early, I'll leave you some breakfast and a bit of lunch. When her alarm goes off she realises that in the night she has been aware of him, she tries to piece him-in-the-night together as you would a dream: certainly he got up two or three times, she heard him moving around, and once, she is almost sure, he cried out. Coming downstairs she feels a draught in the hall. The back door is open, he is standing there in his shirtsleeves looking out, she turns left into the kitchen, he has set the breakfast, boiled the kettle. Does she mind? Is she glad? He comes in, he is clean and shaven, she can feel the cold off his face and his bare neck. That tree's still there, he says. You remember, that tree I always liked, on the horizon, and the lane going up to it and over. She looks away from his face, off which, with the cold, too much excitement, joy with an edge, is radiating. Six months, why shouldn't the tree still be there? And that lane doesn't go anywhere special, he knows as well as she does, only to Newton's, a brutal sort of farm, and Finchale with the nasty caravan park, if the mud lets you. But yes, it's the tree itself, still in place, on the other side of the valley, on the brow of the hill, the sky lightening behind it, the lane visibly climbing up and going over. Ruth knows.

Ruth has to go to work. I'll bring something in for tea, she says. No, I'll see to it, he says, let me. She looks at him, OK, that would be nice. She roots in her bag for her purse. I've got money, he says. She looks at him, he lowers his eyes, mumbles, Mother's dead, I sold the house, I've got money, I'll do the shopping. Ruth nods, I see. Some days he wouldn't go out, some days he wouldn't have the nerve to go and buy a newspaper. Very well then, she says, if you're sure. She must leave for work before he raises his eyes. This is not the moment to look him in the eyes. The spare key's hanging up, she says. You know.

Again it's about six when Ruth gets home. She opens the gate, steps down off the street into the yard, sees a stack of chopped logs under the window box and indoors the light on and the fire lit. She lets herself in, calls, Hallo, he doesn't answer, she goes past the kitchen, the fire burning brightly in the black range, on down the hall into the sitting room, where he has laid in the fire and set a few logs on the marble hearth. She stands at the window and sees him by the elder in the far corner, stooping over the bank of earth that ends her garden. This man, his intentness. For some time she watches. The sky is nearly white, the dark seeping into it, there's a train heading away north, the carriages are lit, they will appear brighter and brighter. She goes into the garden, still he does not notice her, birds are singing, they do indeed sing while the light lasts, from two or three rooftops of the small terrace, from the gable of the nursing home below on the right, pure song over the nervous scuffling, chattering, bubbling of sparrows and starlings. She is halfway down the garden before he becomes aware of her. You're busy, she says. You don't mind? he asks. I'm making a way down. Those hawthorns below will be so lovely, I thought you'd like a way down to them. Yes, I might, says Ruth. And you found your old clothes, to work in. Yes, he says, where they were, in the big cupboard, where you said they used to keep a pony, where they kept the coal once, where there are still some bright grains of coal between the floorboards. Yes, there. You don't mind? Then: You had a good lot of snowdrops. Ruth shrugs. And all these daffodils coming up. Across the valley just to the right of him Ruth can see the tree he likes. It means he will go away again.

After tea Ruth has some reports to write. I'll wash up,

he says, you go in there, I'll put a match to the fire. I usually stay here, she says. She keeps telling him things he knows. At once he looks so disconsolate, she says OK, she will do what he seems to want her to do. He hurries away, to draw the curtains, light the fire, put the lamps on. She can't make him out, is it for her or for him, is it amends, is he just about holding together? But the room is so beautiful, lit and with a fire. The logs burn up in a scent of smoke and resin. She turns to her notes.

Morgan takes his time. The washing up is too soon done. He looks for other little jobs. He is glad she cannot see him. He has drunk two glasses of wine and should be feeling better than he does. He puts his boots together neatly on the hearth, in front of the bread oven that is never used. He opens its door, the flues are choked with soot and rust. Perhaps if he stays he will clean them, perhaps he'll make the daily bread. Such abilities come to him sometimes like a memory, sometimes more like a way of imagining faith and hope. He hangs up his overalls in the big cupboard. Evenings are often bad and the nights are something to get through. He has met people, women, who look forward to sleep not as oblivion but as a pleasure they will be deeply conscious of enjoying as the night passes. Morgan would be glad of oblivion, a quiet passage. Or if there must be nightmares, to wake nevertheless strong enough to brush them off, as you might the dead leaves in a forest you have slept in.

He goes through. She has not quite closed the door, on stockinged feet he enters silently and sees her in the big chair under the lamp, papers in her lap, her hands on them, her eyes shut, her face wet with tears. He is so quiet he has knelt and taken her hands before she knows.

These people, she says, what is it in them? And I have to write something. The little girl, she's three, and they tie her by the leg to their bed and go out for the night and most of the next day and when they come in he kicks her in the ribs because she's dirty. What is it in them? What can I say about them? The bedroom was like a dossers' squat, their filth was everywhere and the little girl was in it, tied up so she wouldn't hurt herself, they said, and when they come in he kicks her and she, the mother, says serves her right, so he says.

Morgan says nothing, he can't think of anything to say, he holds her hands. After a while Ruth stops crying. You go to bed, she says, I'll finish this, good night.

Ruth sleeps at once. Then wakes. It is only two o' clock. Is it better or worse with somebody in the house? The hole in the night, the next day lamed before it starts. But this has happened before. She composes herself, crosses her arms on her breast, by force of will beginning to breathe deeply, by force of will she is inducing herself gently back into her necessary sleep. Then he screams. So it is worse having somebody in the house if that somebody is him. He screams again, a different note, more pleading, more like begging something not to happen. Without further thought Ruth puts a dressing gown around her nakedness and crosses the short distance from her room to his.

The street lamp is shining through. He has left the curtains open. He is awake. I'm sorry, he says, I woke you and you need your sleep. She sits on the bed, his eyes are still wide with the sights and feelings of the dream. Can you tell me? she asks. He shakes his head. I'll be better now. You go back to bed. Will you sleep? I might, but don't worry now, you go back. Ruth stays where she is, he moves to give her more room. You didn't wake me, she says, I woke before that. But for the job I wouldn't mind not sleeping. Most nights there are trains. I suppose it's freight, I suppose they send things through when there are no people travelling. Especially if we've had rain you can hear them rattling away north or south, long long lines of trucks. My bedroom's best for listening to the trains, they sound quite near though it's far across the valley, and then fainter and fainter till they're gone. But you know that. I'm forever telling you things you know already. If it wasn't for the job and having to get up early I wouldn't mind lying there not sleeping for an hour or so. I would, he says. That's the trouble and the difference, I fill up with bad thoughts and wish it would hurry and be daylight so I could walk. Unconsciously, rather as though she were asleep and he were falling asleep also and this sleep gave them a licence, she has been looking for some time into his eyes in a way you hardly ever can in daytime. Then he says, Would you have married me? How do you mean, she replies, 'would have'? I mean when I nearly asked you? When did you nearly ask me? Last year, last October, I very nearly asked you. Did I know that? I thought you did, I thought it was very obvious, I felt sure you knew I was very near to asking you. Strange, says Ruth, I don't remember that I knew any such thing. Anyway, he says, would you have? Neither looks at the other's lips, each looks only at the eyes, into the eyes, so that the voices, little more than whispers, seem to be continuing a private colloquy elsewhere. Well yes, since you ask, says Ruth, yes I would have. You would have, he says. And would you now? How do you mean, would I now? If I asked you now will you marry me, would you say yes? I don't know, says Ruth. Now isn't then. But perhaps I'd be no more likely or unlikely to say yes or no than you would if I asked you. Ask without if. It won't do, Morgan, will it?

Morgan closes his eyes. Shall I sit till you're sleeping, she asks. No, no, he says, you go back now, I'll be OK. You'll be OK, she says. And will I be OK? I'm sorry if I missed it last October when you very nearly asked me to marry you, it's possible I wasn't paying close enough attention and I suppose it's also possible you weren't giving me quite enough clues that you were very nearly on the point of asking me something so important so now please open your eyes and listen very carefully because I'm going to ask you something without an if in it as clearly as I can. Will you come and sleep with me in the big bed in there? If you want time to think about it, I shall understand, and if you want me to say please and give you seventy-seven good reasons why I think you should, beginning with this, that I don't like it in there on my own when you're in here, then of course I'll be glad to, but if you don't want any of that then just answer yes or no, will you?

After that, until he left, Ruth and Morgan slept together. At first they made love like the starving, they sucked the breath out of one another's lungs, they respired it back in, mixed. Then, recovering their know-how of one another, they slowed and by a sort of thinking – that of the parts that feel – they devised what would be best, each for the other's pleasure. So they came back into their own with a vengeance. At least in Ruth it rather felt like vengeance, a sweet punishing proof. Did I not tell you? See what you made us do without. Here it is now, again, forsake it if you dare, forget it if you can.

They talked less than they might have because, for a while, making love was a more urgent need, and they couldn't do both because on no account in the working week must Ruth oversleep. He always got up before she did, made the breakfast, saw her off to work, then laid in the fires, did the shopping, dug the garden, planted things, mended the guttering, made the tea, for all the world like the man of the house. Their neighbour on the left, Mrs Harrison, a widow, when she saw him pegging out the washing, shouted, You're back then, over the fence, and added, She'll be glad. It's nice to have a man around. And whenever he went into the garden Morgan noticed himself observed by the old lady high up in the gable end of the nursing home, that had once been a girls' penitentiary. Hers seemed the only room occupied in that wall. She's still there, I see, he said to Ruth. Yes, said Ruth. I sometimes think she's one of the fallen girls and they forgot her when the others left.

In the evenings they sat in the big room whose windows looked north. Ruth wrote her reports, Morgan watched her and could tell, whether she chose to tell him or not, how good or bad the day had been. Now and then she glanced his way, saw him trying to read and not quite being able to, saw him absently picking at the skin around his nails. Two or three times every evening he left the room like a man ashamed he must go out for a cigarette but it was only to put on his boots and walk the length of the garden and stand by the bank, smelling the dug soil and the damp elder tree, till a train had gone by on the far side, far and high beyond the faintly audible river. Ruth felt the draught. She finished her work as soon as she could. When she had stopped and packed her things away the tiredness came over her. By stopping work she signalled it was allowed to come. It was a sweet permission, the tiredness coming so infused with desire they were, to all intents, the same. Sleep and sleep with. She sought his face, to know was his tiredness made like hers.

One night – a Friday, no work in the morning – instead of making love – they could defer it, it was certain, till birdsong – she told him stories from her caseload, not the happiest nor the unhappiest, but those that had clarified and travelled now through the heavens of her consciousness like constellations.

She told him about Jack whom she had helped move from sheltered housing, where he could not manage, into a home, where he sat against the wall with the others and looked out in bewilderment on the little world. In the fifty years before this endgame he had passed on and on through casual wards and reception centres, the Church Army, Simon, the Sally Ann, hospitals, jails and any number of desperate skips in sheds, graveyards, railway trucks and buildings awaiting demolition. But in his story, which he told her whenever she visited and began again as soon as he had finished it, he was a free spirit, the rolling stone, the wanderer, the gentleman of the roads who came and went as he pleased and everywhere everyone liked him, Good to see you, Jacky, they cried, come in, have a beer, they sat him down, he was one of the family, the children loved him, he made them spinning tops and whistles, wherever he turned up the kindly people of the North East couldn't get enough of him, he was a joy to have around, he gave and gave, he was the pal, the confidant, the singer of songs, teller of tales, indispensable handyman fixing this and that, he was father, grandfather and favourite uncle, what would the bairns do without him if he left? But no, after a night or two, he'd have his boots back on, Very sorry, he'd say, I'm a travelling man, got to hit the road, can't stop, God bless now, and off he went with a wave and behind him the family shouting, God bless you, Jacky, thank you for everything, come again soon, there'll always be a place for you at our table. In fact, said Ruth, lying in Morgan's embrace, he was only fourteen when his stepfather told him, Fuck off out of here and get yourself a job you idle little bastard and hardly once in the next half century did he sit at a family table or by a family hearth again.

Morgan said never a word. Never asked a question, never commented. But Ruth knew he listened. Indeed he tensed, he became hard and so focused he trembled with it, as when she began her practices of love on him. Then she was pleased with herself and told him another story out of her stock.

Mr Ferens, she said, is almost a neighbour. He lives with his wife in one of the new houses just below here. They always wanted a house like that and they worked hard for it. They've got two boys, both at university. Neither he nor his wife had much schooling. So they've done very well. And do you know what? Six months ago he comes home from the office in tears. Nothing had happened. Nobody had been unkind. But he suddenly couldn't bear it any more and he walked home through the streets in tears. Several people saw him and said, Whatever's wrong, Mr Ferens? So the doctor signed him off work until he got over it. But he hasn't got over it. Every working day he rises at 5.30, shaves, dresses in a suit and tie, eats his breakfast and sets off to walk to Chester-le-Street. He does that five days a week. Throughout last winter, in every weather, in the fewer and fewer hours of daylight, that is what he did. When he gets to Chester-le-Street he turns round and walks home again. He comes in, eats his tea and falls asleep. After a while Mrs Ferens wakes him and gets him to bed. I have all this from her. Why Chester-le-Street? I ask. Search me, she replies. When she pleaded with him, he agreed to wear a luminous yellow jacket over his coat on the way back, but otherwise he won't be ruled at all. Once she went there herself on the bus. She thought she might catch sight of him but the bus called in at the villages off the road and she must have missed him. However, she was there in the market place when he arrived. She couldn't even speak to him she was so upset. He came into the market place walking quite quickly. It upset her to see how tired and staring he was. He walked twice round the war memorial and set off home again. She had a cup of tea to steady her nerves and then she caught the bus. Again she looked out for him and this time she was lucky – or very unlucky – and saw him walking along the road, facing the traffic at least and wearing his yellow jacket. She was on the righthand side of the bus, sitting downstairs, and she saw him very clearly from behind and then, just for a second, in profile and nothing has ever upset her like that in all her life, she says.

Morgan's mood is high. He invests all common activities with a passion that exceeds them and looks up wonderingly at the excess. Where shall it go, what will answer it? Ruth watches. At times she is quite persuaded: an armful of logs really is such a joyous thing, the look on his face is no more than it deserves. At other times she mocks him: the love-feast of the fish and chips, the sacrament of the bread and Wensleydale, the communion of the washing-up and more epiphanies a day than most kids on her books get proper breakfasts in a year. Morgan answers her that Jakob Boehme saw God immanent in sunlight reflecting off a pewter dish. You don't believe in God, she says. Makes no difference, he answers.

He tells her why he loves walking and of course cannot sit down to do so but must pace to and fro in her room like a creature caged while she sits under the lamp with a file or her notebook in her lap regarding him. His talk is rapid and almost in an undertone, she misses a good deal but that hardly matters, the sense of it is obvious in his being unable to keep still. I like being slant on to habitual lives, he says, I like walking through a town when people are going to work, I like walking on their busy streets, and out. That pace of change is right, no faster than a man can walk, then truly the eyes and the mind and the heart will take things in. Why should you hurry even through ugliness? You should come among beauties very gradually. That is why I like climbing rivers at their vilest, to see where they began. And being alone is good, the trance the feet induce, the constant repetitions of the stride, fatigue, so that at times it's like sleepwalking, some days and nights I pass among people and their trades like a somnambule. How do they view him? Ruth wonders – vagrant, miscreant, angel? In that big coat he perhaps looks like a demobbed soldier trying to find the place where he used to live. People talk to me, says Morgan, women especially, they invite me in, they tell me their life stories, they look at me as though I might know what they should do next. Of course I don't and they only tell me things because I'm passing through, they'll never see me again, nothing they say to me, however intimate, is binding. I leave, they stay, for miles and miles I think about the story until it thins and dissipates like cloud. And the fears in the evening when you need somewhere to sleep and the elation in the mornings when you wake unharmed, that is a solitary addiction. And a man's, says Ruth. A woman can't do anything like that. She'd end up in a bin bag by the M25. And suppose she does decide her life is falling short and some gypsy rover turns up at her front door and says, I am your chance, come away, she's got three kids by then and a job in publishing and the very thought of the necessary arrangements makes her faint. But carry on, Morgan, I do like listening to you.

Morgan kept house and paid for anything necessary – the food, cleaning things, anything for the garden or repairs – from a wad of £20 notes in an inside pocket of his shoulder bag. One evening he fetched the bag and offered Ruth all the money in it, towards the mortgage, council tax, electric, but she shook her head in a way he took to mean he should watch his step. He blushed and mumbled he was sorry. He left the bag lying and she heard him in the hall putting on his boots and leaving by the back door. He was gone an hour. When he came in she tried to make light of it. Where did you go? she asked. Just to the river, he answered. Down through the hawthorn field, through the new estate, to the river and along to the weir. There's all sorts of stuff lodged on the weir. A whole tree, for one thing, tall as a house, prone in the water with its dead branches sticking up, on the edge of going over and grass and plastic and God knows what else backing up behind it. You shouldn't go looking at the weir in the dark, she said. You should come to bed. And never think money is anything between you and me. It isn't. Oh you're right, he said, at once too exalted, so that she flinched. It's from that awful house, there's a lot of it, I want to be rid of it. You buy things for this house, she answered. This house is lovely when I come home. There are things in the garden that wouldn't be there but for your money.

That night he told her in a rush that he had kept nothing from his mother's house, nothing of her life with and without his father, and nothing of his own life that she had hoarded since his birth in scores of boxes, but had paid to have it all cleared out and then had sold the empty shell and would live off the money while it lasted. Then he fell asleep, as though even the telling exhausted him, and she lay in the dark and wondered.

He wakes, the spirit in him has curled up small as a foetus whose only wish is not to be born. He sits naked on the bed, leaning forward, leaden, it is not a coffin-lid, it is a cowl and cope of lead over his head and shoulders and under this weight he must start the day. April, the birdsong, he is not fit to live. Ruth wakes, she sees him palely in the dawn-light bowing forward. You OK? With her left hand she touches his bare spine. Her fingers are like the birdsong, a further proof that he is not fit to live. How lovely her white arm, the warmth of sleep between her breasts, between her legs, oh the scope and intricacy, the skills and goodness of her body, all comes over him, facing away, bowing his head into his hands, she and his love for her come over him as an abundance he is only fit to lose. He is weakening. So in a first deployment of the will against annihilation he answers, Yes, in a voice not from the mouth and lips but from a sepulchre somewhere low in him. Stands up, stoops for his clothes, she watches. To her in the brightening daylight he looks intact and beautiful and lost.

Leaving for work, Ruth says, I'll bring something in for tea. No, no, he says, I'll see to it. I must, I have to do things. He will not look her in the face. He is not fit to, nor to be looked at, least of all by her. She touches his face, feels the stubble. Weakened again, he seizes her hand, presses it to his mouth, kisses the fingers. You'll be back? Of course I'll be back, usual time, earlier if I can. Ashamed, he turns away indoors.

That day and the days following he does everything by rote, he is meticulous, he leaves nothing undone that he would normally do, savagely he does what he always does but now without love, only in a savage satisfaction that these things he believed to be loving acts, for her house, can be done just as well without love, without joy, without the soul's participation, by the shell and semblance of a man, by his unliving twin. Everything is clean and tidy when she comes home, the meal preparing, the fire in the black range lit, and calling out for him and getting no answer, all things wearing a benign appearance, truly she feels she might go through into the garden and see him there in his shirtsleeves digging the vegetable patch or still working at the steps by the elder tree and he will turn and she will witness a further heightening of the happiness in his face when he sees her. Instead, she calls, he turns, and she sees that whatever it may look like to her, to him all his doing is a simulacrum that may passably resemble life but isn't life.

In the evenings he can't sit with her. She writes her reports. She has driven out to Finchale, to the caravan site the

Council uses for its most difficult people, and leaving one man who has shown her a letter from his daughter (Fuck off back to the asylum, Dad), she watches the farmer towing away what's left of the caravan in which last week another burned to death. The blackened thing passes through the ruins of St Godric's priory towards the filthy yard and the company of other wrecks. Morgan has been gone for half an hour. He must know how it worries her. If it's that long she knows he has gone down to the weir. She can smell it on him when he comes in, his voice sounds battered to death by the weight of water, the river's slanted breadth, the unspeakable amount of toppling-over water and always more and more to come from the sodden hills and the countless streams to the west of Crook. And what has he got to say to her anyway in his submerged voice? Nothing, unless it's another word about the clogged-up skeleton of a tree that cannot even make it into extinction but must lie there in the stink and din night after night, cadavers of all kinds backing up against it. I'm going to bed, she says. Are you coming? I'll lock up, he says. In bed he turns aside. She presses her nakedness against his. Sleep, she says. Better in the morning. But it won't be.

See this, Ruth said, coming in from work. I've bought you a present. It is a long jacket, or a short coat, slim at the waist then widening below, of dark green corduroy, soft and rather worn. Try it on. He turns, his arms feel backwards for the sleeves, he turns again. Fits! she cried. I knew it would. He is watching her face, the delight. He thinks, this time when I come out of it the start will have been her delighted face. Do up the buttons, she says. The many buttons are cloth-covered and do up high to a soft broad collar. There are two deep pockets on the hips. You look the part, she says. I saw it in Hetton-le-Hole, it was in the window, everything else was jumble sale. I asked the woman where on earth she got it. She couldn't remember, thought it might be theatricals. What's this? Morgan asks. His hands are in the pockets, from the right he takes out a mobile phone. Oh yes, says Ruth, that's the other part of your present. Both or neither. It is, as you see, a mobile phone. You may have noticed that lots of people have them nowadays. I've put my number on it and this evening I'm going to teach you how to send a text to me, in case you're away and you want to ask how I am, and also how to dial 999, in case some bad thing happens. I see, he says. And now what's for tea? Ruth asks. But heavens you look beautiful in that coat!

The next few days are bad. She watches him swing this way and that, north seems to move around under the earth just as it pleases and he is pulled violently after it, halts for a moment trembling, then swings away again. He can speak to her only if he weakens and abandons himself like something that has clung on the brink by force of the will and now lets go and acquiesces in its own dissolution. Only then, abject, weeping, given up, can he speak to her. He despises himself for this indulgence, but what does she care? At least he speaks. She asks how he manages every day in the shops and meeting people on the streets who know him by now and must surely stop him for a chat. Very well, he says, I do very well. And that frightens me, they don't even notice I'm as distant as a smiler on the moon. A semblance of me is perfectly adequate. Not for me, it isn't, she says. I've had you close, they haven't, I can't survive on the ghost of you. The weakness is sweet, he can surely be allowed to bide there a while? But no, back comes the imperative to stand up straight and walk. It's OK now, he says. She shakes her head. He cajoles himself along with the thought that after a decent interval it will be all right to collapse again.

Morgan wakes before first light and hears a voice that must be Ruth's say, 'And twenty minutes, more or less,/ I felt, so great my happiness,/ That I was blessèd and could bless', those lines. He has no doubt that she, asleep beside him, has said them aloud as she did once before, and the lines preceding them, in a café on the quay in Newcastle, closing the book then and looking him in the eyes to see what he made of it. She is sleeping, he kisses her hair, slips from the bed and dresses. Downstairs he sees that his preparations are already made. He finds an apple, bread and chocolate, £300 in cash and his mobile phone on the kitchen table. Waterproof, scarf, cap, wash things and the light sack to sleep in, if it comes to sleeping out, are piled on top of his coat on a chair. Quickly he tips cereal and milk into the bowl set ready in his usual place. He forces himself to make some coffee and drink it. But he can't sit still. He stands at the window with the hot mug in his hands, watches the coming of daylight, hears the birds. Then it is time, the bag is packed, he puts on the coat, goes into the hall and sits on the bottom stair to fasten his boots. He is absorbed and in a hurry and does not hear Ruth till she sits naked on the stair above him, enclosing him between her legs and bending over him. Did you say them? he asks, speaking down towards his boots. Say what? The last lines of that poem you read me on the quay in Newcastle – about being blessed? I suppose I must have if you heard me. Have you got your phone? He nods. Then you can go. He begins a sentence the first words of which are 'I'll be' but already she has closed his mouth with her two hands and raised his head against her breasts. Don't promise, she says. I don't want you bound to me by a promise. It's not a promise that binds me to you. With her legs and arms she holds him tight. That's how I'm bound to you, I should think your spine can feel it. Now go.

He leaves, the cold draught of the April morning enters along the hall. Ruth goes back to her bedroom and stands at the slightly opened window. He strides down the garden without a backward glance and disappears down the steps he has made in the bank by the elder. The sky is white, against it she can see the other tree, on the far side, where the lane goes up and over. The birds, they make a whistling and a clear fluting. At her lighted window in the home the old woman is already in place. Ruth thinks, She will have seen him go and now perhaps she can see me faintly at my window. How sad for her to be in that room and watching.

Now in the evenings, not wanting to light a fire in the marble hearth, Ruth works upstairs at a window facing north in the room adjoining hers, it had been a child's when Ruth bought the house and there she has her books. Some evenings, having written her reports, she combats sleep by taking up her notebook and continuing in that, as though the stuff of the things she must compose is much the same. So, for example, she writes: Morgan, only child; father, a merchant seaman, died when he was nine; mother left poorly off, her whole life in the child. He is bright, she works very hard and stints herself for his education. For years he is completely docile, he advances, she is proud of him. Then he revolts. Quite suddenly, between school and university, he withdraws, he barely speaks. It is that he can't admit how much there would be to say. Everything that might have been said gets converted after a time into drastic acts. In the final year of his university course he walks out of a class being given by a man he adulates, speaks to no one, and vanishes. In two years his mother receives four postcards from him, telling her nothing more than that he is alive. His teacher receives fifty pages of old computer paper, as one long sheet, handwritten and effectively one sentence, explaining why he walked out of the class. After that he wanders, but never abroad. For much of the time you might have found him within fifty miles of where he was born and where his mother waits. (Did he ever go back? Was he there when she died? Find out.) He meets people, they think him engagingly strange, they invite him to stay. Then he leaves. How many households in the north of England have something of his, a coat, a book, a pair of socks or trousers, that he might come back for one of these days? How many of the wives and mothers got him to sleep with them?

Next, leaving a space, Ruth writes: Two poets, both mad, the beloved woman in each case dead. One incarcerated in a madhouse in a forest takes advice from gypsies on how best to abscond. In four days he walks home, up the main highway north. He trespasses into a barn for a place to sleep, he lies down in there on bales of clover and dreams the woman is taken from his left side. He lies with his head pointing north so as to be sure which way to set off when he wakes. He sleeps in a porch, he can hear the people indoors turning over in their beds. He eats grass, he can scarcely walk for the pain in his feet. A carter throws him a penny, he buys a half-pint of beer. Nearing home, a man and a wife, once neighbours of his, throw him fivepence from their cart, he buys beer and bread and cheese. Then at home he is told the woman died long ago. He does not believe it, he has heard this lie before. Soon he is taken to another asylum in a town but he never ceases to believe that she is alive. The second poet lodges in a tower overlooking a river. He is cared for by a carpenter and his family. But before he came to them he had been in a harsh clinic. He has a mother but she wants nothing to do with him. In the tower his foster family are kind, they give him the freedom of their riverside garden in which there are apple trees. But he cannot rest, he is agitated, he paces to and fro, muttering and plucking at leaves and grasses. He always has something in his hands to pluck at and tear. Then one day he announces that he intends to leave their custody and walk to the city in which his beloved lives, to be with her again. It is only a matter of following the river, he says, and then the river which this river flows into, and then a few miles up another river that comes in. He thinks it will take him perhaps a fortnight, he will leave at once, it is April, a good time of year to set out on foot. They reason with him: the woman he loves is dead, she died before he was carried off to the clinic. He smiles, he will not be reasoned with. Finally they confiscate his boots. He walks barefoot up and down in their garden, up and down, all the hours of daylight. Not until the autumn does the fit subside and not until the last months of his life, after thirty-five years in the tower, can he keep still.

Below that Ruth wrote: Journeys end in lovers meeting. One thing in my favour is I am alive.

The hawthorn was out. Some evenings, coming in from work, Ruth went straight through the house, stood by the elder tree and looked down at the bank of blossom. The steps Morgan had made would have led her into it, into the scent. But she turned away and set her mind on the longer evenings.

Ruth was pegging out the washing. Still on our own, are we? said Mrs Harrison at the fence. Not for long, said Ruth. She had her back to Mrs Harrison and said this over her right shoulder. She was more conscious of the old lady in the home, in the topmost room, who seemed to be watching her with particular attention. Well that's good, said Mrs Harrison. Once they've made themselves useful it's hard to do without. And I daresay you'll be wanting to start a family and you won't want to leave it too late. How old might you be, not that it's any of my business? Rising thirty, said Ruth. And Mister? Have a guess, said Ruth. Excuse me, that's my phone.

That evening – it was a month since Morgan had left – Ruth decided the time had come to start leaving the curtains open and a light on when she went to bed. And next morning at work she arranged her annual leave. She had worked through Christmas and New Year, not wanting to be in the empty house. Now without much arguing she got three clear weeks, around the middle of June. Come back in time, Morgan, she said aloud. This is important. I will leave the light on for you when I finish writing my notes and go to bed.

So she did. She sat at the window and read aloud from her notebook odd lines she had copied out over the years. She went to and fro among the pages and read without connection whatever caught her eye. She raised the book to the old lady watching her from the former penitentiary and read, for example, Because I am mad about women, I am mad about the hills, But she is in her grave and Oh the difference to me! Western wind, when wilt thou blow The small rain down can rain, Christ if my love were in my arms and I in my bed again! And so on. She made a chant out of some of them and stood up to deliver it: Cold in the earth and the deep snow piled upon me, I loosen my fragrant bodice, by degrees, Far, far removed, cold in the dreary grave! My rich attire creeps rustling to my knees. Then she went through into her bedroom, closing the door on the light at the window. She lay in bed, listened for trains, the river, owls, shooting stars.

A week or so later, 31 May, a Friday, Ruth had to attend a case-conference on one family, the Robsons of New Brancepeth. About thirty experts had been summoned, from various agencies, services, charities and institutions, and they had been warned it would last all day. The chairman said it never ceased to amaze him how much trouble one family could cause. Doesn't amaze me, said Mrs Simmons, nearing retirement. We met for a whole weekend once on the subject of a man called Jimmy Smith. Just him. Bottomless pit. Thank you, said the Chairman. Now will you please turn off your mobile phones.

At coffee, lunch and tea, of course, there was a bedlam of them. At 4.15 Ruth stood in a bay window and consulted hers. She had five text messages the last of which was, Please leave the light on in that room tonight. M.

She waited up till midnight, first in her workroom then, leaving that light on and the curtains open, at her bedroom window. To her watcher in the home she chanted, But one man loved the pilgrim soul in me at magic casements opening on the foam of perilous seas in fairy lands forlorn. Poor lady, she thought, never sleeping must be terrible.

Ruth sleeps at once and only wakes when he, a man, tall, thin, and in the fading darkness appearing pale with markings of shadow, arrives through the open door and stands in silence shivering by her bed. Evicted, by waking, from your sleep and dreams it can be hard to get a bearing on who and where you are. This man, this creature, his pallor, silence, trembling and smell, seem strangely to continue where she was. She apprehends his silence and his whiteness as having entered the roar and darkness of her dream. Or perhaps that is where he has come from and it still clings to him. Perhaps she was sanely and quietly asleep in her own safe house and he came in from the back of beyond through night and noise. She turns back the cover for him and he slides in and not beside her but between her legs. She has never known him cold in bed before. She is the one who shivers, he warms her. But now he shakes and chatters like clattering ice. He is a stranger. Ah, she thinks, he is the river, that is the smell he has, the smell of underwater mud, and that is why he can't keep still, rivers never can, and he thinks I'm the riverbed, where he's come from it seems to him quite reasonable that if he's the river I must be the riverbed. He is the river but he also smells of hawthorn, he smells of mud and hawthorn. How can that be? And so cold. Sinking deeper back into sleep and dreaming, perhaps already as deep as he is, it occurs to her that if she fails to warm him he will freeze her. That's a thought, she thinks, it is a matter of life and death, it is up to me to warm him or he'll freeze us both.

She does warm him. Both sleep. Some while later – 1 June is already well under way – she goes down in her dressing gown, leaving him. There are muddy footprints on the stairs and along the hall to the back door. One great beauty of that house is the opening of its back door on to a space so sudden, clear and vast the soul cries out at the sight of it. Where the garden ends the ground drops away but that is like a launch pad for the vision which lifts and continues out across the valley and beyond and above into the clear and infinite northern sky.

Mrs H. is leaning her broad arms on the fence and the old lady in the former penitentiary has gone so far as to open her window and is peering down. Their eyebeams meet on a pile in the middle of the lawn. He's back then, says Mrs H.

Yes, says Ruth, I told you he wouldn't be long. And she goes out barefoot in her dressing gown to look more closely at the heap. It is made of Morgan's belongings, not the bag, but all the rest, sodden and filthy, smeared with weed and with a sprinkling of white hawthorn. The three women contemplate the evidence. Funny things, men, says Mrs H. Yes, says Ruth. She is thinking of her dream, or of the two of them together dreaming, of river and riverbed, of her undulations of warmth which combated and overcame his helpless hurry and his shuddering with cold. The boots and clothing look like something cast off by an animal in its passage from one form of being to another. Better take him his tea, she says.

She sets the mugs down and pulls the cover off him. His feet and legs are muddy. Yes, he says, suddenly wide-open-eyed, so you got my text, you did as I asked and left the light on, I thought perhaps I'd be able to see your light from that tree and indeed I could and from there, keeping your light in view, I was in a great hurry and when I came to the river I felt there was no time to go all the way up beyond the weir to the bridge and I seemed to remember there used to be a ford somewhere near, in medieval times, but in the dark I must have missed it, the water was quite deep and fast and I had to hold my bag up high. But here I am after all. I came up the bank, your little path. It was a sacred grove. My coat will be OK, I think, and don't worry, I'll wash these sheets. Ruth doesn't want her tea and doesn't care whether he wants his either. The smell of the river and of their mixing is still on him and her. She takes off her dressing gown and climbs on to the bed and sits astride him. I like it when your eyes widen, she says. I like it when I see what it does to you when you look at me like this. Tell me, eel, salmon, otter, seal come up from the sea, or creature still evolving and not in the text books yet, tell me, muddy incubus with hawthorn in your hair, did you hear any bits of poems on the breezes in my voice as you walked along and when you slept and when you woke? I know you did. Deny it, if you dare. And now, poor you, poor naked thing, no rest for the wicked, next week we're going for a walk, you and I, down one river and into another until a third comes in and we go some miles up that. Not in these parts, the three rivers in question are abroad. Yes, abroad! I have decided you need to be more eccentric. And I've had an idea that will interest you, there's this vacancy, a sort of gap, a space, at the end of the walk we're going, you and I, the river walk abroad, there's something waiting where it finishes that very much desires to be brought to life and I can't do it and you can't do it alone.